Choice

BLACK ROSE

Choice
Copyright © 2024 by Black Rose

All rights reserved. No part of this publication may be reproduced, distributed, or transmitted in any form or by any means, including photocopying, recording, or other electronic or mechanical methods, without the prior written permission of the author, except in the case of brief quotations embodied in critical reviews and certain other non-commercial uses permitted by copyright law.

Library of Congress Control Number: 2024920402

ISBN
978-1-964982-38-0 (Paperback)
978-1-964982-39-7 (eBook)

TABLE OF CONTENTS

Acknowledgments ix

Introduction xi

Chapter 1 1

Chapter 2 8

Chapter 3 15

Chapter 4 19

Chapter 5 21

Chapter 6 24

Chapter 7 28

Chapter 8 33

Chapter 9 36

Chapter 10 38

Chapter 11 40

Chapter 12 42

Chapter 13 47

Chapter 14 49

Chapter 15 51

Chapter 16 55

Chapter 17 57

Chapter 18 59

Chapter 19 62

Chapter 20 68

Chapter 21 80

Chapter 22 95

Chapter 23 97

Chapter 24 99

Chapter 25 111

Chapter 26 125

Chapter 27 128

Chapter 28 131

Chapter 29 136

Chapter 30 137

Chapter 31 146

Chapter 32 149

Chapter 33 151

Chapter 34 155

Chapter 35 158

Chapter 36 161

Chapter 37 168

Chapter 38 170

Chapter 39 172

Chapter 40 174

Chapter 41 176

Chapter 42 179

Chapter 43 181

Chapter 44 182

Chapter 45 183

Chapter 46 187

Chapter 47 189

Chapter 48 195

Chapter 49 200

Chapter 50 203

Chapter 51 209

Chapter 52 212

Chapter 53 216

Chapter 54 218

Chapter 55 222

Chapter 56 225

Chapter 57 228

About the Author 232

ACKNOWLEDGMENTS

I want to say thank you to my wife for standing by my side through the tough times and for believing in me to always do and be my very best.

From the time you open your eyes in the morning until the time you close them at night, every unique individual, whether it's good or bad, has a choice.

—Terence Ramone Gills

INTRODUCTION

This is a fictional story about a young man who has the choice to take part in some of life's greater opportunities, but he chooses some of life's greatest mishaps, which ultimately *strip* him of some of life's more prominent opportunities.

CHAPTER 1

One brisk October morning in 1972, Clara, a young single mother, gives birth to a handsome baby boy in Muscogee County, Georgia. Clara, who only has her family to lean on during this time of happiness, is afraid of what lies ahead for her and the delicate life that has developed inside her for the past nine months. Her mind travels at a thousand miles an hour as she lies in a hospital bed trying to bear the pains of childbirth, both physically and mentally.

She ponders over the idea of staying in Muscogee with her newborn son, Trevor, but the reality of an unfamiliar place quickly sets in, and she returns to the quiet, peaceful small town of Bo County, Alabama, where she is surrounded by family and friends. She is determined to succeed in life and doesn't allow anyone to slander her name because she's a single mother living in a small country town where everyone knows your name and some might even say it's a shame to have a baby out of wedlock.

Clara and her loving mother, Letha, join together to raise this bundle of joy who has entered their lives with great values, spiritually and physically, with hopes of seeing him sprout up as a respectable young man whom society will tolerate. Clara takes a job as a seamstress in a sewing factory that makes clothes for children, and Letha stays at home with her grandson, making quilts and feeding him the spirituals of the Bible, while he lies in a crib, gurgling bubbles, trying to figure out this new world that surrounds him. The day has come to an end, and Trevor's mother has come home to enjoy the best part of her day.

The two meet, and there is an explosion of happiness as she wraps him in her loving arms, showering him with the kind of love that can only be shared between a mother and her baby.

Time grows wings, and suddenly, the infant that can only jibber jabber is now standing before them waiting to be taken to the bus stop so he can go to school. He loves his kindergarten schoolteacher and all his new friends, but there is one thing he especially likes, and that is being Mr. Popular, aka the class clown. He's bored with the activities that his kindergarten teacher asks him to do because his mother and grandmother has already taught him how to do all these things before he started school. He finishes all his classwork and spends the rest of his time trying to impress the rest of his classmates with jokes and silly games. The one thing he cannot get off his mind are the beautiful kindergarten girls whom he adores so much. His teacher would often tell his mother at PTA meetings that he does very well in his classwork, but he just can't stay away from the girls in class no matter what. He always finds himself next to the girls at nap time. He's the center of attention in his kindergarten class because he can run faster than any kid in his class and all his friends think he's the coolest kid to be around.

The days turn into weeks, weeks turn into months, and months turn into years. Trevor finds himself very sad because his mother finds herself a husband, and Trevor doesn't want to share his mother's love with anyone because he's afraid he will lose her. He comes home from school one day to discover that he's going to move to Tuscaloosa, Alabama, with his mother and new stepfather. He's devastated because he's very comfortable living with his grandmother, and he loves his fourth-grade teacher Mrs. Green, along with all the friends he has been with ever since kindergarten.

The school year has come to an end, and his heart is heavy with sadness as the hours race away. He knows this will be the last time he will get the chance to embrace his pals in his class because he's about to enter a new life in a new place. The bell rings out a shout of happiness to all the students as they pour out of the building like wild beasts on the open African plains, but he sits in his chair motionless and quiet, trying to prepare himself for the departure from the known into the unknown.

Mrs. Green kneels down beside him. "It's been a pleasure having you in my class, and I know you will do very well at your new school."

He slowly gathers his books with tears of sadness in his eyes. "Thank you, Mrs. Green, for being such a good teacher. I will never forget all the fun and excitement I had in your class."

The school bus turns into a slumber party with laughter and joy that he once indulged in, but today is different because he knows this is the end of the good life as he knew it, and his life in the unknown will never be the same. The school bus pulls up to his stop. He slowly drags himself out of his seat, walking sluggishly down the aisle. He passes his friends as they all say goodbye. The school bus pulls off as he waves goodbye to his friends until he can only see a faint yellow blur traveling off in the distance. The short walk from the bus stop feels like the longest and most painful task he would ever have to complete in his life. Letha is standing at the bottom of the steps awaiting the arrival of her beloved grandson. When the two meet, she gently wraps her arms around him, hugging him very tightly for several minutes.

"I'm not going to be that far away from you. Maybe I can come visit you in your new home, and you can show me around the place," says Letha. He is very happy to hear his grandmother say she will come to see him, but that still doesn't take away the pain that he's feeling inside about leaving his grandmother.

The newlyweds pull up in the yard after spending several hours at the courthouse, signing all the paperwork and performing the ceremony in front of the judge. Clara gets out of the car, and Letha abruptly runs up the steps, slamming the door behind her. She looks saddened by her mother's actions.

"Trevor, I want you to meet your new father, James, and James, I want you to meet your new son, Trevor," says Clara. She proceeds to go up the steps into the house. Trevor can hear yelling and screaming from within the house as he races up the steps, crashing through the door, finding his mother and grandmother both in tears.

"I'm not going!" he yells. Running to his bedroom, he slams the door and starts to cry uncontrollably.

Clara comes into the room. "Get your things and let's go."

"I'm not going anywhere with you or that man!" he yells.

Letha enters the room. "Clara, leave the room now. I'll take care of this situation!" She sits down on the bed. "You have to go with your mother and new father because that's what makes your mother happy, and eventually, you will be happy too."

"That's not my father, and I'm not going to leave you. I'm staying with you, and they can go away by themselves," he says.

She picks him up, sitting him on her lap. "You have been Grandma's little champion all these years. Don't let something like this get in your way. Be strong, and you'll get through this just fine."

"This isn't fair. I shouldn't have to leave you and my friends just to move to a place that I don't know anything about. It's not fair," he replies.

"Trevor, someday you'll see that life isn't always fair. At times, it may seem as though you are the only person that's being affected by what's going on, but believe me, you're never alone, because there is always somebody out there who's in a tougher situation than you," she says.

He gently hugs his grandmother and slides down out of her lap to gather his things so he can begin the new phase of his life. Clara and James are waiting outside for him as he and his grandmother slowly appear, walking down each step as if he were going to the death chamber to be executed. He gets into the car, buckles himself in, and waves goodbye to his grandmother as they zoom down the hill, leaving a trail of dust following closely behind.

The drive to this mysterious place leaves him with mixed emotions. He's anxious to see what his new life is going to bring, but on the other hand, he's still very sad about leaving his old life behind. On the way to Tuscaloosa, James says, "Son, you're going to love your new house, and I know you're going to make lots of new friends because you're a good boy. Oh yeah, I forgot to tell you. You have a friend that's ready to meet you as soon as we get to the house."

Trevor is very confused and becomes a little excited now because there's someone awaiting his arrival, and he has no idea who knows him in this new and unfamiliar place. He sits in the back seat, restless, thinking it might be one of his friends from his class. "Are we there yet?" he asks.

"No, not yet honey, but we will be very soon," replies Clara. James looks at Trevor through the rearview mirror and begins to laugh at all the tension and excitement that fills his eyes. He continues to scramble his brain trying to figure out who this mysterious person is.

Then the moment arrives.

"We're here!" yells Clara.

He looks around energetically through the windows in the car, trying to find his mysterious friend.

"Come on, Trevor, there's someone I want you to meet," says James.

They walk toward the backyard following the sound of a whimpering puppy. Trevor runs to the gate as a beautiful brown puppy comes running up to the fence, wagging its tail vigorously, with its tongue hanging out of its mouth. He quickly turns to James. "Is this my puppy?" he asks.

"Yes, but you have to promise me that you will take care of him and you will help me build him a doghouse," replies James.

"I promise, I promise! Now can I go play with him?" he asks.

James looks at him, smiling. "Sure, have a good time, but don't play too rough because he's just a little puppy."

Trevor rushes through the gate to play with his new pal as his parents unload the car. Clara is excited to see that he's happy with his new friend. She turns to her new husband. "I'm happy we decided to get married and move away from that small town. I was getting so tired of that place, and I wanted to get out of my mother's house."

"I didn't know things were so bad between your mother and you," replies James.

"Things between my mother and me aren't bad at all, but I was ready to get out on my own and start a new life for my son and me," says Clara.

"Well, I'm proud to be the man that's going to make your dreams come true," James says excitedly.

Trevor continues to play with his new friend until the sun begins to pull the blankets over its face and the moon begins to appear brighter and brighter with every minute that passes by.

"Trevor, it's time for you and your friend to come in!" yells Clara.

"His name is Rusty, not friend, Mom."

"Why did you name him Rusty?" asks James.

"I named him Rusty because of his color. It kind of reminds me of a rusty nail," he says.

"I like that, but there's one more surprise that I kind of forgot to tell you about. It's in your room," says James.

Trevor runs to his room full speed ahead, flips the light on, and the jungle comes to life. He's so excited to see his room. He stands in the middle of it, spinning in circles, amazed to see how his parents transformed his room. The bright lights shine like the sun, creating a bit of a glare, ricocheting off the glossy green leaves that cover his walls. There is a giant painted tree in the corner of his room with real steps that lead up to a beautifully painted tree house covered lightly by branches. The thing that catches his eye the most is painted around the head of his bed. It's a cave surrounded by panthers, with one panther crouched down on top of the cave as if he were posing for a picture.

"This is so cool. I love it!" he yells. He hugs both of his parents. "This is the coolest thing that any kid could ever have." That night, he lies in the jungle thinking of how cool his room is and about the new friends he will get to meet. Rusty sleeps peacefully in his soft, cozy little bed that's made out of a cardboard box and raggedy old blankets.

The next day, Trevor and Rusty are playing in the front yard when they're bombarded by several kids who live in the neighborhood. They introduce themselves one by one, excited to see a new playmate move into the neighborhood. That night, he's so exhausted from playing with his new friends he could barely take a bath to get ready for bed. His parents quietly peek in, finding them comfortably asleep in their beds.

"I'm so happy he's adapting to this new neighborhood, and he's having so much fun," says Clara.

"I told you he would be fine, and we would have nothing to worry about," replies James.

Trevor and his family got to meet all their neighbors during the summer, forming a great relationship with one another. The summer is winding down, and it's almost time for school to start back.

"Clara, I think it's about time for you to give your mother a call and invite her up to see her grandson and the house. I also think it's time for you to resolve your differences. Life is too short, and you should never take tomorrow for granted," says James.

"I agree. I'll give her a call right now," says Clara as she picks up the phone and dials her mother's number. "Hello, Mom, how are you? It's been a long time since we've talked to each other. James and I would like for you to come up to visit us this weekend. Trevor will be very happy to see you."

"I'm very happy we've decided to drop the differences between us. I've been thinking a lot about you and Trevor and wonder if you're still happy with your marriage," says Letha.

"Mom, I'm very happy, and so is Trevor. He's made a lot of new friends, and he's adapting very well to this new neighborhood. Mom, I know you didn't want me to get married so soon, but I promise you, it was the best thing for us, and it's still going strong," says Clara.

"I love you so much, and I only want what's best for you and Trevor," replies Letha.

"I know, Mom. I promise you that James is a good man who loves Trevor and me very much. He works very hard to try to provide us with the things that we need, and Trevor gets along with him very well," replies Clara.

"I think it would be a great idea for me to come up to visit this weekend so I can spend some time with my lovely family," says Letha.

Clara is very excited about her mother coming up to visit this weekend. She can't wait to tell Trevor the good news. That afternoon, he comes in from a hard day of playing.

"Trevor, your grandmother is coming up this weekend to see us."

"That's great! I haven't seen my grandmother in months. I'm going to tell her all about my new room, my new friends, and Rusty!" he says excitedly.

CHAPTER 2

The time has come for him to start school, and he's a little nervous about being the new kid. He remembers how some of the kids would pick on the new kid at his old school. The first day of school is intimidating because he feels like he's the smallest fifth grader in the whole school. Some of the guys and girls tease him about being so skinny. He feels out of place in this castle they call a school. The hallways seem to be miles and miles long, and there are several kids who tower over him, making him feel insecure. He's in shock to see how many pretty girls swarm around the halls, and he has several crushes on various girls who are in his classes.

The day finally comes to an end, and he tells his mother and father everything he could possibly tell them about his first day in school.

"How many new girlfriends have you found?" asks James.

"I think I'm going to have a problem with finding a girlfriend because they're all so pretty and tall. They all tease me about being so skinny," he replies.

"In time, son, you will have so many little girlfriends you won't know what to do with all of them," replies James.

"You don't have time for those bad little girls because you're going to be busy with your schoolwork!" yells Clara from the kitchen.

James and Trevor look at each other with sneaky little smirks on their faces. He enjoys his new school but hates being teased about his weight by the kids in school. He tries to get involved in different sports, but he's always told he's too skinny. It's disastrous. He tries really hard to find something that's interesting to him that he can excel at.

One day, at the park, a song that he really likes is playing, and he begins to dance very gracefully. In fact, he draws a crowd of kids who begin to join him, and he enjoys being the center of attention again. His parents get a thrill out of seeing their little baby boy dancing around, having a good time at the playground.

"Wow, Trevor, I didn't know you could dance like that!" James says excitedly.

"I don't know how I do it. It just comes natural to me," he replies.

There's a talent show being held at the local theater, and he asks his parents if he could be in it. Clara and James are enthused about their son wanting to be a part of this talent show, and they give him all the support they can.

The night of the talent show is a frightening experience for him because he didn't expect to see that many people show up. His parents give him words of encouragement.

"I want you to get up there and do your best, and we'll be proud of you even if you don't win," says Clara.

He finds great comfort in his parents' support. It gives him a strong sense of pride and confidence. He imitates the moves of several pop and R&B stars. He does well enough to qualify as one of the contestants chosen to move onto the finals. He is overly excited about this, and he chooses to break-dance as his second act. The judges make their final decision, and he wins first place in the dance division of the talent show. He can't believe what just happened to him. He's so happy about his first-place prize he takes his trophy to the restaurant with him to stare at as he eats. His parents, along with several other people in the restaurant, congratulate him on such a great performance.

He's bombarded by his friends at the bus stop and all day at school. He feels as if he were back at his old school with all the popularity that he receives from his new classmates. The best thing of all is the attention he gets from several of the girls at school, and he never has to ask for a date when there's a school dance. He finds himself teaching his friends how to dance in his neighborhood and at school. He finally finds something that he can do very well. He feels very good about his newfound success, but there's still something missing from his image that he couldn't place his hands on.

Monday afternoon comes with a great surprise. He's approached by Crystal, one of the prettiest girls in the school. She invites him to her birthday party.

"Sure, I'll come. What time do you want me to be there?" he asks.

"I want you to be there at one o'clock," replies Crystal.

That night, he gives his parents the invitation, asking if he would be able to go. Clara calls Crystal's mother and talks to her about the party and agrees to be there with Trevor at one o'clock.

The next day, Crystal and Trevor sit together at lunch.

"Trevor, do you have a girlfriend?" she asks curiously.

"No, do you have a boyfriend?" he asks nervously.

"No, I don't," she replies.

They continue to enjoy each other's company until the bell rings, interrupting their conversation. He can't even concentrate in class because all he could see is Crystal in his mind and all he could hear is the sound of her sweet voice ringing in his ear. The bell rings, and he's so excited because he will have the chance to gaze into the prettiest eyes God ever created.

The bus ride home is a memory that he would never forget. Crystal sits very close to him on the bus.

"Have you ever kissed a girl before?" she asks. Stunned by her question, he's at a loss for words and doesn't know exactly what to say. She leans over and kisses him on his lips. He's surprised because this is the first girl he has ever kissed. "That wasn't bad for your first kiss," she says.

He looks at her with excitement in his eyes. "No, that wasn't bad at all. In fact, it was great!" he replies excitedly.

The bus pulls up to her house, and they wave goodbye to each other. He's in heaven for the rest of the bus ride home.

He dashes off the bus, runs in the house, throws his books down, slams the door to his room, and begins to scream at the top of his lungs. James and Clara look at each other with concerned faces. James gets up off the couch and goes into his room. "Trevor, what's wrong with you?" he asks.

"If you promise not to tell Mom, I'll tell you what's wrong with me," he says.

James closes the door. "Okay, I promise this will be between you and me," says James. He tells James what happened to him on the bus on the way home. James looks at him. "I think it's time for you and me to have a talk about the facts of life."

He looks at James with a confused face. "What's the facts of life?"

"Let's take a trip down to the lake, and I'll tell you all about it," says James. Clara looks at the two of them with a blank face as they walk out the door.

There's a cool breeze blowing off the lake as the rays of the sun dance on the ripples. The day is calm, and the birds and squirrels are dancing happily around the big oak trees. James begins to explain to him what the facts of life are, and Trevor listens to him very closely.

"My teacher talks to the class about sex education, but I never raise my hand to ask questions because I don't want to look stupid," says Trevor.

"The only stupid questions are the ones that aren't asked," replies James.

"The kids in class always make fun of the other kids for asking questions, and I guess that's why I never ask any questions," he replies.

"Trevor, I don't ever want you to let anybody make you feel stupid for asking questions. That's the only way you're going to learn, and it will let the teacher know you're listening to what she is trying to teach you," replies James.

That night, after he's in bed, Clara asks, "James, why was he so excited this afternoon?"

"Our son just got his first kiss from Crystal, a little girl that's in his class," he replies.

"What? That's it, I'm going to call her mother right now because this is unacceptable behavior, and I won't tolerate it!" she says in an angry voice.

"Calm down, calm down. I've already talked to him about it. I also talked to him about the facts of life, and he understands more than what

I expected him to. The school curriculum requires the teachers to teach sex education," he replies.

"Trevor is just a baby, and I think you're taking this situation too lightly. I don't want anybody teaching my son about sex when they should be educating him about what's really important, like math and science," she replies.

"Clara, listen to yourself and think about what you're saying. He's not a baby anymore, and I like the fact that they're being educated about sex in class. I believe they're doing us a favor. Have you taken a close look at who's carrying the babies now? Times have changed. Kids are experimenting with their bodies, and they don't even fully understand what they're getting into because they're not educated about the risks and responsibilities that could take place if they're careless. Trevor will be in junior high school next year, and I don't think you want to jeopardize his freedom or his education because he was not taught about safe sex until after he has gotten some girl pregnant," he replies.

"You're right. I don't want our son to get anybody pregnant, but it frightens me to know that our son has grown up so fast when it seems like he was just a baby in his crib, crying to be fed," she replies.

"Kids don't stay kids very long anymore. That's why we have to make sure he's fully educated about sexuality and the devastating consequences that can happen to him if he isn't careful," he says.

"I'm going to give Crystal's mother a call because I think this is something she should know," says Clara.

The next day, Clara and Crystal's mother, Jennifer, meet each other at a local coffee shop, and they sit in the corner by the window. Jennifer is wearing a short midthigh body skirt with high heels and a cigarette in her left hand. The men in the coffee shop gaze at her as she crosses her long, sculptured legs that match very well with her surgically altered breasts, which overflow the boundaries of her dress. Clara feels embarrassed by Jennifer's appearance and wants to leave, but there's an area of concern she feels is important enough to talk to Jennifer about. She begins to explain what happened between Trevor and Crystal on the bus, and Jennifer looks at her with a bland, unconcerned look on her face.

"They're just kids being kids. I don't think there's anything to be concerned about," says Jennifer.

"I agree that it was probably just a little harmless kiss, but I think you should talk to Crystal and explain to her this type of behavior can lead to something much more. My husband has already had a talk with Trevor, and he understands the consequences of his actions," replies Clara.

"You make it sound as if he laid her down in the back seat and fucked the hell out of her! I don't believe the situation is that critical, and I think you should lighten up on your son before you turn him in the opposite direction. I don't need to talk to Crystal about sex because her teachers take care of that for me," says Jennifer sarcastically.

Clara's anger is now in the red, but she continues to conduct herself in a professional manner, saying, "Thank you for your time. Trevor won't be attending the birthday party."

"That's fine with me. I'm not the one that's going to be disappointed," replies Jennifer.

Clara gets up from the table, leaving Jennifer sitting there, puffing her life away. On the way home, Clara tries to forget the conversation she just had with Jennifer, but she can't. She gets angrier and angrier the more she thinks about it until she lets out a screeching scream that hurts her ears and throat, and then she became calm.

That afternoon, Clara tells James all about the conversation that took place at the coffee shop. They both agree that Trevor should not go to Crystal's birthday party.

At the dinner table, James says, "Trevor, we changed our minds about letting you go to Crystal's birthday party."

"You told me that I would be able to go, and now all of a sudden, I can't go!" he yells.

"I think you better lower your voice when you are addressing adults, and furthermore, this is a decision that your mother and I have agreed upon. I don't appreciate you questioning our decisions," says James.

"Sorry, can I be excused now?" he asks. He's so mad at his parents he cries himself to sleep.

The next day, he spends the day in his room playing video games, thinking of how much fun he's missing at Crystal's birthday party. He imagines her party is a blast and she is getting all types of pretty dolls, clothes, and money for her birthday. He thinks about how disappointed she may be because he didn't show up when he told her he was coming.

CHAPTER 3

"Mom, why didn't Trevor come to my birthday party? I invited him, and he told me he was going to come," asks Crystal.

"I'm sorry, honey. Trevor's mother told me yesterday that he would not be able to make it," replies Jennifer.

She runs in the house to her room, jumps on the bed, and begins to cry. There's a knock on her door. Her mother's friend enters her room.

"Crystal, why are you crying?" he asks.

"My boyfriend didn't come to my birthday party," she replies.

The tall man sits on her bed, saying, "I'll be your boyfriend. Come here and sit on my lap so I can tell you a little secret." She walks slowly over to the man with her head down. He gently lifts her head. "You're a pretty little girl, and if you promise not to tell, I'll show you something that makes little girls into big girls," he says.

"I promise I won't tell," she replies.

The tall man begins to unzip his pants just as Jennifer stumbles into the room, smelling like she fell into a bottle of whisky. "Thomas, what are you two doing? Come and take me to bed, and let me ride you like a racehorse," she says in a drunken voice. He zips his pants up and winks at Crystal as he walks out of the room. She watches her mother and Thomas have sex through a crack in the door until both of their sweaty bodies lie limp across the bed.

The next day at school, Crystal bumps into Trevor at his locker. "I wish some people wouldn't make promises to people and then break them just as fast as they made them!" she says angrily.

He turns to her with a sad look on his face. "My parents wouldn't let me come to your birthday party even after they gave me permission to come. I don't know why they wouldn't let me go. I was so mad I cried myself to sleep."

Crystal looks at him with joy in her eyes. "Awww, you cried for me. That's so sweet." She kisses him on his cheek, and he turns as red as a beet and is excited to know that his girl is no longer upset with him.

That night at the dinner table, he asks, "Why wouldn't you let me go to Crystal's party?"

"We didn't let you go because we didn't feel that it was an appropriate place for you to be," says James.

"I don't understand what you mean by that. Mom told me that I could go, and then all of a sudden, I couldn't go. Did I do something wrong?" he asks.

"No, honey, you didn't do anything wrong, and someday, when you're older, I will tell you why we made the decision that we made," says Clara.

Suddenly, the phone rings, and Clara answers it. The voice of an angel says, "May I please speak to Trevor?"

"May I ask whose calling?" asks Clara.

The angel speaks again, "Crystal."

"Does your mother know you're calling little boys on the phone?"

"Yes," says Crystal.

"Trevor doesn't receive phone calls from little girls right now, and I would appreciate it if you would not call here again," replies Clara.

Trevor's furious at his mother. He runs into the kitchen. "Mom, that's not fair! I'm in the fifth grade, and I can't even receive phone calls from girls yet?" he screams.

"Girls are not your priority. School is. And if I say you can't talk to anybody on the phone, that's what I mean!" scolds Clara.

"She's my girlfriend. I love her, and you can't keep us apart!"

James enters the kitchen. "Son, you will not disrespect your mother like that. If she says you can't receive phone calls, you will respect her decision, and you will never raise your voice to your mother again or I will bust your hide. Do you understand?" James asks with an angry voice.

"Yes, sir."

"Good! Now clean the table off and go to bed!"

The phone rings again. Clara answers it only to hear Crystal's mother yelling at the top of her voice.

"What the fuck is wrong with you making my little girl cry like that? I didn't see anything wrong with my little girl calling your son. What? You think your son is too good for my little girl or something, or are you trying to make him out to be a little fag?"

"I beg your pardon? Don't you ever call my house and disrespect me like that again. I have rules in my house. Trevor isn't an adult yet, and he will listen to whatever instruction I give him as long as he lives under this roof. Maybe you should try to be an example to your daughter before she grows up to be street trash like her mother!" Clara retorts. She hangs up the phone before Jennifer has a chance to reply.

The next day at school, Trevor sees the love of his life. He quickly runs up to her, apologizing for last night.

Crystal looks at him with sad, puffy red eyes. "This is my last day of school. I tried to call you last night to tell you the bad news, but your mother wouldn't let me talk to you," she says in a raspy voice.

"What do you mean this is your last day of school? I know you're not going to drop out of school in the fifth grade, are you?" asks Trevor.

"No, I'm not dropping out of school, but my mother told me last night that we're going to move to another state where she'll find a better job and maybe a good husband," replies Crystal.

He just stands there looking deep into her eyes, trying to hold back the tears and pain that's building up inside of him. He gently hugs and kisses her on the cheek. "I will never forget you." He slowly picks up his book bag and walks to his class. The whole day is devastating because all he can think about is losing the only girl he ever cared about.

That night at the dinner table, he sits very quietly, barely eating his favorite meal of hamburgers and french fries. His mother and father are concerned about his behavior.

"Son, is there something bothering you tonight?" ask James.

He can no longer hold back his emotions as tears begin to flow from his eyes like the Niagara Falls. "She's going away, Dad, and I will never see her again in my entire life!" he utters in broken English.

"Who's going away?" asks James as he wipes the tears from Trevor's eyes.

"Crystal is moving away with her mother to another state, and I know I'll never see her again."

Clara sits at the table, sad to see her little boy in such disappointment. She wishes she had let him talk to Crystal on the phone the previous night.

James leans over to him. "Let's take a walk down to the lake and talk for a moment." They both get up from the table and walk to the lake. "Trevor, you will see Crystal again someday. People have to do what's best for them and their families. You will someday meet the girl of your dreams, get married, and have kids. You will have to make tough decisions for your family, and you will look back on these times and laugh about it with your wife."

Later on that night, after they return from the lake, Clara says, "James, I feel so bad for not letting Trevor talk to Crystal on the phone."

"Everything is okay. I feel you made the right decision." He chuckles. "Puppy love is still holding on strong to its roots."

CHAPTER 4

The months blew in and out like a cool breeze, and Trevor hopes and dreams that he will receive a letter from Crystal telling him how well she's doing, but it never happens. The months turn into years, and he realizes that he may never see Crystal's blue eyes ever again.

Trevor is now a young adult at the tender age of fourteen and an honor student at Randall High School. Time has allowed him to grow to a height of five feet, nine and a half inches, along with a shoe size two years less than his age. There's one thing that time has not taken away, and that's his slender frame, which has haunted him all his life. He often sits around the house trying to figure out what he can do to make himself bigger and more attractive to the ladies. One day, he's watching TV and sees a commercial that says, "Are you tired of being overweight? Are you looking for a great way to get in shape so you can have more confidence about yourself and a lot more sex appeal? Well, why don't you join Body Rock Fitness Center, where our professionally trained staff will help you get the results you've been looking for? We have a special enrollment fee of one dollar to join and seventeen dollars a month if you sign up before the month of October ends."

He jumps off the sofa, startling Rusty, who's sleeping peacefully on the floor next to him. He runs screaming out of the house, "Dad, I want to join Body Rock Fitness! I want to join Body Rock Fitness!"

"Okay, okay! Get your Mom, and we'll go check it out," says James.

He's so excited about joining the fitness center he could hardly sit still on the way over. His first glance of Body Rock Fitness is mind-blowing.

He's impressed by all the people in the gym and all the equipment that he'll use to build himself a new and improved Trevor.

Zoe, the owner of the gym, is very nice as he explains to Clara and James about his facility's safe workout environment. He also comforts them by letting them know he'll personally train Trevor on all the things he needs to know about weight training. Zoe turns to Trevor, saying, "How would you like to take a tour of the facility with me and Tyson?" The young men gladly accept the invitation as they introduce themselves to each other.

Tyson asks, "Where do you live, and what grade are you in?"

"I live in Stone Hinge, and I'm a freshman at Randall High School."

"You mean Stone Hinge as in Stone Hinge Golf Resort?" asks Tyson.

"Yes, that's it. Do you know where it is?" asks Trevor.

"Do I know where it is? I live there too. I live in the white house a block away from the clubhouse, and I'm a freshman at Randall too," replies Tyson. He's very excited to hear this, and it's the beginning of a new friendship that will last a lifetime.

Tyson thinks of Trevor as the brother whom he never had, and in many regards, Trevor feels the same. They are alike in their height and skinny frames, and both have similar facial structures with their high cheekbones, slightly slanted eyes, and pecan-colored skin. Tyson admires the fact that Trevor is a mix of two races just as he is. Tyson is Asian from his mother's side and African American from his father's side, and Trevor is African American and Cherokee Indian from both of his parents. The ladies often admire their facial features but often tease them about their skinny little frames with big feet. They are called nerds because they excel in their studies. Most of the guys think they're gay because they're always together and neither of them has a girlfriend. Despite what people say about them, they continue to push through life like a runaway train.

CHAPTER 5

A year has passed, and they've evolved into Greek gods under the supervision of Zoe, their longtime friend. They both become Mr. Popular among their peers, and no one seems to remember the two little misfits a year before. The ladies often compete for their affection, and their mothers begin to get very agitated over the number of phone calls they receive on a daily basis. The senior prom is next week, and all the seniors are excited about it because this marks a night of getting wild and drunk and graduating from high school into a whole new life.

The halls are full with a mixture of chanting seniors and juniors when Candice, captain of the cheerleading squad, and Vanessa, captain of the dance team, walk down the hall in short miniskirts, like they're supermodels on the runway. There is complete silence in the hall as the guys totally concentrate on the two hottest babes in school. The other ladies in the hall simply snarl their noses up at them. Trevor and Tyson are standing at their lockers, chatting with some of their classmates, totally unaware of the babes who are coming toward them. Candice and Vanessa both stop directly in front of them, pressing them against their lockers. The aroma of their bodies mixed with their long, beautiful hair; beautiful, soft lips; and Coke bottle-shaped bodies are like a mountain of fresh, intoxicating air. There's a brief silence, and then Candice asks Trevor in a soft, sensual voice, "Do you guys have your drivers' licenses yet?"

"Yes, we do. We got them about three months ago," Trevor replies in a calm, resonant voice.

"Good, because we would love for you to come to my house to pick us up and take us to the prom," Candice replies.

Trevor replies in a calm, cool tone, "Very well. I guess we will see the both of you at seven thirty on Friday night."

The two ladies release them from bondage and begin to walk away. Vanessa quickly turns around, slams Tyson up against the locker, and begins to kiss him very deeply and passionately as Trevor stands there looking like a scald dog. Candice says to Trevor as she raises her miniskirt from behind, exposing her Vickie's that fit very nicely between two of the roundest, smoothest cheeks he has ever seen, "Don't worry, baby. I'll take you on a tour of my body Friday night."

When the escapade finally ends, there's a low chant at the other end of the hall, saying, "T-n-T." The chant spreads like an airborne virus and gets louder and louder as Trevor and Tyson are hoisted into the air by members of the football team as if they made the scoring touchdown that won the game.

The principal enters the hall, yelling, "All right, all right, ladies and gentlemen, get back to your classes!" The mob disperses, and they sit across from each other with a look of utter satisfaction on their faces.

On the way home after school, they stop by the mall to look at some tuxedos just to get an idea of what they like. As they enter the store, they're amazed to see all the distinct styles of tuxes that are on display. There are so many to choose from they can't make up their minds. They call their parents, telling them to meet them at the tuxedo shop in the mall. When their parents arrive, they ask, "Why are you shopping for tuxedos?"

"We need them for the prom on Friday," replies Tyson.

Their parents are shocked because they had no idea they were going to the prom. They happily explain to their parents they were invited to the senior prom by Candice and Vanessa. Their fathers are busy in the corner plotting something, while their mothers gossip and complain about what tux looks good on their sons.

James calls them over, and the two sneaky fathers ask, "Do you have any condoms for Friday night?" They laugh out loud as their wives poke their heads up from the safari of tuxedos as if they detect danger is near.

The ladies ask, "What's going on over there?"

The men reply, "Nothing."

The two mothers finally decide what tuxedos they like and call their sons over to get their approval. The two young men fall in love with their mothers' selections and eagerly rush to the counter to check out. They step out of the dressing room looking like they're ready to exchange vows with that special someone. Their mothers are very impressed with the way they look, and they purchase the tuxes for them. They run into Candice, Vanessa, and their parents as they are leaving the mall. The parents introduce themselves as Trevor and Tyson pull the two lovely ladies to the side. They immediately show off their tuxedos as the ladies show off their dresses, which match perfectly.

CHAPTER 6

Trevor and Tyson spend every hour of the day thinking and talking about what they're going to do Friday night at the prom with the hottest chicks in school. They feel privileged because they're sophomores going to the senior prom, and everybody knew about it at school. The young men spend extra hours in the gym trying to make sure they're in top shape, in case the ladies want to continue the party in private. They try to avoid asking each other the obvious, but Trevor finally breaks the silence, "Tyson, when the time comes for us to be alone with—"

Tyson interrupts him, "Just go with the flow and pretend you know what's going on."

"That's easier said than done, my friend. They're going to know that we're 100 percent virgins," replies Trevor.

"Hey, hey! You can't say that word that loud. Somebody might hear you. Our reputation will fall like a rock if anybody ever finds out about this," replies Tyson.

"Tyson, do you realize that we're going to the prom with two porn stars? They're the most sexually experienced women in school. I believe they're more experienced than their parents," says Trevor.

"I know, I know! We're up a shit creek without a paddle, and there's nothing we can do about it except take a fucking beating. And I do literally mean take a fucking beating," replies Tyson. They both laugh as they return to their class.

The big day finally arrives, and they check out of school at noon in order to prepare for the night's activities. James and Trevor take a ride to the Ford dealership where he rents him a beautiful black convertible Mustang GT. The dealer meets the two gentlemen in the showroom and hands the keys to Trevor. He immediately rushes through the almost invisible plate glass doors, jumps in the car, and reclines the seat. He begins to flail around as if he were a fish flopping around on the ground.

James asks, "Well, are you going to sit there all day, or are you going to take us for a spin?" Trevor quickly cranks the car up, pressing the gas pedal repeatedly just to hear the powerful voice of the V8 engine roar like a tiger in the jungle. They take off down the road with the top down, feeling the hot summer winds rush over them as they cruise down the highway. James turns the music down and asks, "Son, do you have any condoms?"

He looks at him with a surprising face. "No."

"I went to the prom a long time ago myself, and I know what goes on after everybody leaves the prom," says James.

"I was afraid to ask you to get me some, and I was embarrassed to go buy some," replies Trevor.

"Son, you should never be afraid to ask me or your mother to buy you something that could save your life. There's nothing embarrassing about wanting to protect yourself."

"I know, but I didn't want you or Mom to get upset with me."

"I understand, maybe more than your mother does, that you're no longer a little kid anymore. You're going to start to experience things in life just as I did when I was your age. The only thing that's going to upset me or your mother is to know that you're having unprotected sex." He looks at his father with a sigh of relief on his face as they drive to the drugstore to purchase condoms. He drives his father back to the dealership, thanking him for being so understanding.

He drives by Tyson's house to show off his prom ride. There's a beautiful red Corvette sitting in the driveway. Tyson barrels out of the house, screaming, "What's up, T? Check out my hot ride!"

"That's really nice, but this is the best." He jumps out of the car and gives his friend a big hug. "Man, we're going to have the hottest rides at the prom, and the ladies are going to flip when they see us tonight," says Trevor.

Tyson waves goodbye as Trevor races home to prepare for a great night. Clara is standing on the porch when he pulls up in the driveway. "How do you like your new chariot?"

"Mom, this is great! I appreciate you and Dad for getting it for me."

"Hurry up and get dressed so I can take some pictures of you in your tuxedo," she says.

A half an hour later, he hears Tyson pull up in the driveway.

Clara yells, "Ohhhhh my gosh, look at you! You're so handsome! Trevor, hurry up and get out here so you and your brother can take some pictures." They stand side by side for a quick shot. Then the two young men run out of the house, wave goodbye to Clara and James, and race to Candice's house to pick up their beautiful prom dates. They arrive at the house where they're met by two beautiful young ladies who scream with excitement when they see what they'll be going to the prom in. Candice and Vanessa's parents gather them all together for a group picture as they nervously place the corsages on their wrists.

On their way to the prom, they pass several of their classmates, yelling and screaming from limousines. The excitement of the night can be seen and heard in every direction on this calm, clear summer night. When they arrive at the prom, they feel like they're attending a royal wedding. Everybody is so dazzling in their prom gowns and tuxedos. They're overwhelmed by a mob of friends who gather around as they exit their chariots of fire, screaming, "Trevor! You and Candice have been nominated as the prom king and queen!"

He looks at Candice with a surprised look on his face. "Did you know anything about this?"

She replies in a soft, sexual tone, "Baby, that's not the only surprise you're going to receive tonight."

The two couples are full of smiles as they enter the prom, amazed to see how the school's gym is transformed into a beautiful ballroom filled with the fragrances of a scented candle shop. They get in line to take pictures as the principal steps up to the microphone.

"I'd like to thank everybody for coming out tonight. I'd also like to thank our faculty and staff for doing such a tremendous job decorating. I feel all of you seniors deserve a pat on the back for accomplishing the first of several phases that you will have to endure during your lives. I, along with my staff, wish you a wonderful graduation and life as you are preparing to enter a new world. Now let's get this party started!"

The gym explodes with screams of joy as the principal exits the stage. They walk onto the dance floor and begin to slow dance as Candice whispers in his ear, "After we're crowned king and queen, I think we need to go somewhere a little more private." He nods as they continue to embrace each other like they are deeply in love.

The senior class president interrupts the mood. "My fellow seniors, may I have your attention please. The votes are in, and I'm proud to announce our prom's king and queen, but before I do, I would like to say a few words about our king. I've had the pleasure of watching this young man grow from an ugly duckling to a beautiful swan, and I'm proud to say that over the years, we have formed a great friendship. I wish him the very best of luck, which he really doesn't need because he's one of the luckiest guys here tonight. Ladies and gentlemen, I'm pleased to have the honor to present to you Trevor O'Riely and Candice Stone as our prom king and queen."

The couple is showered with glitter and screams as they approach the stage to be crowned. The crowd yells out, "Speech, speech!"

Trevor takes the microphone. "I'm very happy to be here tonight. It's an honor to have been chosen as your king. I wish all of you the very best in your future lives, and I hope that you keep me in mind when you see me on campus two years from now as fresh meat at some university." He passes the microphone to Candice.

"This has been an exciting year for all of us. I hope to see at least a few of you in college. Thank you for voting me as your queen, and I definitely thank you for such a fine king."

As they walk off stage, someone in the crowd yells out, "I hope you brought a bag full of condoms!"

Tyson and Vanessa congratulate them as Trevor pulls Tyson close to him. "Candice and I are going to sneak out of here. I'll see you tomorrow."

Tyson looks at him with a big grin on his face. "Just go with the flow."

CHAPTER 7

Candice looks at him with lustful eyes, saying, "Let the top down and drive around back by the old smokestack."

He nervously drives around to the smokestack and parks the beautiful midnight-colored car between the smokestack and the side of the building. She leans over, gently kissing him with her full, soft, perfectly shaped lips, intensifying the passion between them. He tries to keep himself under control, but his emotions begin to spill out to a point of no return as she unbuttons his shirt, caressing his well-built upper torso.

"Lay your seat back," she whispers.

The thud of his heart begins to get heavier and heavier in his ears as he raises his head, watching her slither down to his belt. He lays his head back on the seat as she pulls his pants halfway down, exposing his briefs. His heart is now pounding like the beat of a drum as her soft, warm hand slides inside his underwear, caressing his hard dick. She's stunned to find that he's well equipped for tonight's occasion. She continues to slither down to the point where he could feel her warm breath and soft lips glide across the head of his dick. He clinches up as his dick disappears inside her warm, wet mouth. He hears her moan softly as her tongue massages his dick like it's the best-tasting lollipop she's ever had. His body begins to tremble as the sensation seems to take control of his mind. This feeling, like no other, starts to build up in him, and then she stops and lifts her head, saying, "I just wanted to give you a taste of what's to come as soon as we get to Capital Inn and Suites, where our cozy king-size bed awaits us. He lies there in a relaxed state of mind, trying to recapture the outstanding experience he just endured.

She looks at him, saying, "If you don't hurry up and get us to the motel, I'm going to jump on top of that horse dick of yours and ride you like a wild cowgirl."

"I'm trying to relax so my blood flow will return to the rest of my body," he replies. When things return to normal, he fixes his clothes back to their original position and drives very aggressively to the motel.

When they get to Capital Inn and Suites, they encounter several of their classmates. The suite is romantic with dim lighting, a sweet fragrance, a bottle of sparkling grape juice on ice, and a bubbling Jacuzzi on a private balcony. This night is perfect, and he's about to step out of the arms of innocence and into the world of manhood.

"Why don't you relax while I go freshen up?" says Candice.

He undresses himself down to his briefs, pours them a chilled glass of sparkling grape juice, and steps outside to enjoy the silence of the warm summer night, running his fingers through the warm, bubbling Jacuzzi. The smell of an unusually sweet fragrance captures his attention. He turns to see her beautifully sculptured body standing in the doorway. He admires the very sexy selection of lingerie she is wearing. He passes her a glass of sparkling grape juice as they stand together by the Jacuzzi. "You look so beautiful tonight," he says. She smiles running her fingers through the warm water. He says in a romantic tone, "Why don't we test out the water skin to skin?" She looks into his eyes and begins to unsnap her bra. He quickly stops her. "Please allow me the honor of undressing one of God's greatest creations." She stands still as he slowly undresses her. His wondering eyes critique every curve as if he were an artist putting the final touches on a masterpiece. He steps out of his briefs, and the couple enjoy the warm, bubbling Jacuzzi as it massages their bodies under a moonlit sky. They enjoy the whole bottle of sparkling grape juice as well as each other as he looks into her eyes. "I want you to know that I have never—" She stops him by passionately kissing him before he could finish his sentence. He realizes she's aware he is a virgin, and it makes him feel a bit more at ease. In fact, he feels that she thinks this is an honor and not something to be ashamed of.

They return to the comforts of their suite as their bodies are more relaxed because of the pleasures of the Jacuzzi. They lie down on the bed as he caresses her beautiful body, kissing her all over ever so passionately. She rests his hands at a comfortable position at his sides as she begins to slither her way down his body once again. His mind begins to flash back to the smokestack as she gets closer and closer to his dick. Once again, his heart begins to pound as he feels her warm breath, soft lips, and warm, wet tongue greet him even better than before. He feels his body tense up, and his dick, which is so crammed with blood, begins to throb. She slowly sits up on top of him, saying, "Lie back and enjoy the ultimate ride of your lifetime." She gently maneuvers herself into position to receive the greater pleasures of the night when there's a loud thunder-like sound at their door. They're both startled, like two cats thrown in water, and the pitch of her voice is sharp enough to break glass.

He quickly scurries out of bed with a towel wrapped around his waist. "Who is it?"

A voice on the other end sounds frantic. "Tyson and Vanessa have been in an accident. They're at the police station!"

His heart falls to the bottom of his feet, fearing the worst has happened to his brother. They get dressed as fast as possible and hurry down to the police station. They arrive at the police station surprised to see Tyson and Vanessa standing next to the Corvette. He wonders to himself if Tyson was drinking and driving, but he knows Tyson doesn't drink. They get out of the car, and he looks at Tyson with a confused expression on his face.

Tyson says, "I will tell you the whole story if you promise not to laugh." Vanessa and Candice go inside to wait for her parents as Tyson begins to tell Trevor about the wild and crazy night after they left the prom. "Things started out perfect. The night was calm and quiet as we began our journey to our cozy little love shack. Vanessa got extremely hot under the collar. She began to kiss on my neck, and she started to unbutton my shirt. I told her to hold on, that we will be at the motel in a few seconds, but that didn't work very well. She pulls her gown up to show me that she didn't have on any panties. I got excited and began to drive a little faster, but that isn't why we're here. We're here because she unzipped my pants and began to stroke my dick until it was rock-hard.

She leaned over and started to suck my dick while I'm driving down the damn road! I mean, it was like she unlocked her jaws like an anaconda and swallowed my entire dick.

"To make the long story short, I blew my smokestack, and it felt sooooo gooood. I swerved into another lane as it seemed like my whole body locked up like a vice grip. Out of the shadows of darkness, this police officer with bright, flashing red and blue lights and screaming sirens disrupted my peaceful night and my entertainment. The officer comes up to my window asking if I've been drinking. I said no, and then he asked us to step out of the car. The officer stepped a little closer to me to see if he could smell alcohol, and then he stepped closer to Vanessa and then even closer as if she were an alien or something. He buried his face in his hands and staggered back to his squad car laughing so hard I could barely understand him when he said, 'Follow me to the police station.' We were so confused about what was going on. I didn't realize until we got to the police station that she had jizz splattered all over her face, hair, and dress. It looked like she'd been sprayed with a twelve-gauge shotgun. She was so embarrassed when a female officer gave her a towel to clean herself up before her parents arrive."

They both stood there, silent for a moment, and then began to laugh so hard that all the other police officers begin to laugh also. In fact, the whole police station was a comedy zone until their parents came rushing into the police station with frantic looks on their faces. The police officer who stopped the couple introduces himself to the parents and escorts them into the police station where their children are.

James asks, "Son, are you okay?"

"Yes, I'm okay. I'll tell you about it someday," replies Trevor. Their parents look at them wondering what's going on.

Tyson says, "Mom, Dad, this is all my fault. Vanessa and I were involved…" Trevor begins to laugh as Tyson tries to explain the situation to his parents.

Clara says, "Trevor, go sit in the car."

Tyson explains the whole story to them, and there's a moment of silence before the boys' parents begin to laugh so hard tears run down their faces. They're shocked because they thought their parents would be furious, but their fathers make jokes about the situation, saying, "Wow! That gives a whole new meaning to full speed ahead."

Vanessa's father burst through the doors with the rage of an angry bull. Her mother is so embarrassed she covers their faces as they walk out of the police station to get into their car. Her father drives off as if he were in the Indy 500, leaving tire tracks on the white cement.

Trevor apologizes to Candice for ruining their prom night.

She says, "This was the best night of my life, and I will always remember it until the day I die."

The couple decides this is enough excitement for one night, and he takes her home. Trevor waves goodbye to his parents and whispered to Tyson, "Oh, by the way, thank you for messing up a perfectly good night and thank you for the nice set of blue balls you gave me too."

The drive to Candice's house is full of enjoyment as the two talk and laugh about Tyson and Vanessa's charade. She cuddles up next to him as they cut through the early morning mist only a few hours before the sun turns darkness into light. When they arrive at Candice's house, she gives him a big kiss, saying, "You made me feel very special tonight by being a complete gentleman and by offering me the greatest gift ever. I hope someday we'll get the chance to finish what we started."

"I hope someday we'll meet again, and maybe this time, we won't be disturbed," he replies.

Candice gets out of the car and waves goodbye to him as he disappears into the mist of darkness.

CHAPTER 8

The summer of 1990 starts off with a bang for Tyson. He spends the entire summer at a naval military academy prep school. He's waited for this moment ever since he was a little kid. He has a deep passion for becoming a naval top gun pilot. He spends several hours of his free time in the library, studying about the various types of naval fighter pilots and their phenomenal aircraft. His room resembles the cockpit of an F-14 Tomcat, and he hopes someday he'll join the ranks of the best fighter pilots in the world.

Trevor concentrates deeply in the gym after Tyson has gone. Zoe notices his increase in size and definition and approaches him.

"I was wondering if you would be interested in competing in a local bodybuilding competition."

He's so excited to hear Zoe say this, and he immediately accepts the challenge. Zoe starts right away to prepare him for the Eleventh Annual Bodybuilding Figure and Fitness Championship on July 25 at the Dome Theater. The training is very intense, requiring three grueling hours a day, five days a week, but he never complains to Zoe about the intense pain that he feels. He enjoys the challenge of making himself better and watching himself grow. He feels as if he were a celebrity when they go to the park to run. He entices an enormous crowd of spectators, mostly of the female gender, who clamor around the trail to see him undress himself down to his shorts, exposing his chiseled frame. The crowds of wild women continue to grow to a point where the media gets involved to see what the excitement is all about every Thursday afternoon. He becomes the talk of the town in a very short time, and his parents are very excited about their son and all the attention he's receiving. The local news widely publicizes the upcoming event on the TV, and he becomes the poster child for health and fitness.

The day of the competition is exciting as he and Zoe enter backstage at the theater that morning. Several of the competitors are exchanging their ideas on how they train and what their diets are like in preparation for the event. He's proud to be a part of this contest, and he feels a lot more confident to see that most of the novice competitors aren't in as good shape as he expects them to be.

Zoe looks at him. "I want you to remain focused on what you came here to do, and that's to win overall novice."

"I'll remain focused on what's going on, and I will bring home the gold." He peaks through the curtain, excited to see his parents sitting in the front row among hundreds of bobbing, smiling faces.

The contest host steps up to the microphone. "Thank you for coming to the Eleventh Annual Bodybuilding Figure and Fitness contest. I hope all of you will enjoy the show. We have a number of great competitors backstage waiting to come out here to show off their stuff."

The crowd cheers as the curtains open, displaying all the contestants on stage, ready to go. The curtain closes, and the figure contestants walk out on stage. The men cheer as the lovely ladies strut across the stage, one by one, displaying their beautifully sculptured bodies in their two-piece bikinis. The night progresses with lots of cheers for the figure and fitness contestants. Zoe gives him a thumbs-up as the men's novice competitors walk out on stage in a line to be judged. Trevor is so focused on what poses the judges want them to display he forgets his parents are sitting in the front row. In fact, he doesn't even pay attention to how the crowd is cheering the contestants on as they change from one pose to the next. The judges move them around on stage to compare them to one another and to get a better view. He hopes he's doing everything perfectly.

The judges say, "Thank you. We'll see you tonight."

He doesn't know exactly how well he did until Zoe runs up to him, screaming, "You're the man! You looked great up there. I think it's safe to say you have a good chance of taking home the first-place trophy tonight."

Trevor gets dressed, and they join his parents in the audience. Clara and James are very impressed with how well their son performed on stage. James leans over to him. "Son, I'm proud of you."

"Thank you, Dad. I think I'll go relieve myself of some of the extra pressure I'm feeling right now," he replies. He walks out of the auditorium to the hallway where he's met by several female spectators who think he was outstanding on stage. They inquire about his social status, hoping they would be the lucky one. He replies, "I'm single, but I'm going to attend college in San Diego, California, after I graduate, so I'm really not looking forward to getting involved in a relationship."

"What makes you think we want to get involved in a relationship? Maybe all we want is to have a little summer fun," replies one of the young ladies.

He laughs as Zoe and several of the other competitors from the contest join them. "I see you've drawn a crowd of very beautiful women. Are you being polite?" asks Zoe.

"Yes, I was giving them a brief discussion about my future plans after I graduate from high school," he replies.

"Okay, I'll see you tonight. I have to get back to the gym to take care of a few clients," says Zoe.

CHAPTER 9

Trevor lies silent in his comfortably cozy bed at the motel as the cool air blows across his relaxing body. His heart is full of excitement as he glances at the clock ever so often. Time seems to have taken a lunch break. He imagines how good it will feel to win first place. It will tickle him to death to tell Tyson what he accomplished in his absence.

The moment he's been so anxious to see finally arrives when one of the other competitors knocks on his door, saying, "I hope you've said a good prayer because the time has come for us to be judged."

He rolls out of bed, greeting the gentleman with a smile. "I wish you the best of luck tonight."

They arrive at the auditorium, amazed to see more people at the night show than the morning show. The excitement fills the air as the competitors prepare to show off their stuff once more at the night show. He pays close attention to the sculptured trophies arranged on the table.

Zoe walks up behind him. "They're gorgeous, aren't they? I especially like the first-place trophies on the back row."

"I hope I will be lucky enough to place one or two of those on my entertainment system," replies Trevor.

"I somehow feel you will get your wish tonight," replies Zoe.

The night progresses with lots of spectacular entertainment from all the competitors. Now it's time for the awards ceremony as each class is called out, beginning with the fitness and figure competitors. The tension is high as the judges break the silence, announcing the winners in each class. He feels all the excitement as the first-place fitness and figure competitors return backstage with victory in their eyes and confidence in their hearts as they have proven to be the best. The judges call out the top three in the novice class to present themselves on stage. His body begins to shake with anticipation until he hears his number. He walks out on stage very calm on the outside, but on the inside, his nerves and heart are at their peak. The judges announce, "This year's novice champion goes to number 7, Trevor O'Riely!" The crowd screams his name as he's presented with the first-place trophy. He's so excited he raises one finger in the air, screaming with joy.

Trevor's parents and Zoe take him out to eat at Jack's Steak House. They laugh and talk about the contest as they eat and stare at the bronze statue on the table. The waitress comes by with a dessert menu and offers him anything he wants, compliments of the steak house for a job well done. He selects a succulent double fudge brownie topped with caramel, a scoop of vanilla ice cream, pecans, and a swirl of Hershey's chocolate syrup. He thinks this night can't get any better as he's surrounded by the people he cares for the most, celebrating his hard work, dedication, and determination to be the best.

CHAPTER 10

Trevor is anticipating Tyson to show up any minute. He has so many things in his head to tell him. The phone rings, and to his surprise, it's Tyson on the other end, screaming, "I'm home, honey! Did you miss me?"

"What's up, homey? Hurry up and get over here. We got a lot to talk about!" Trevor says eagerly.

He walks up to Trevor's front door, bursting through, yelling, "Sit back on your heels and strut, soldier! Walk like you have a purpose in life! Get your nasty body in step, son, and make your mama proud—she shit you out!"

Trevor looks at him as they embrace each other with brotherly love, saying, "Dude, I believe you have been seriously brainwashed."

"I'm sorry, but I just had to give you a piece of what I had to endure the entire summer. The first morning I thought we were in a real war. One of the Marine Corps drill instructors threw cherry bombs down the hallway in our barracks at four o'clock in the morning, calling us every name under the sun, and I loved every minute of it!" replies Tyson.

Trevor looks at him with worried eyes. "I think you need some serious psychological help before it's too late."

"No man, this is what I've dreamed about all my life. I'll finally get the chance to live out my dreams of one day becoming one of America's finest pilots and soldiers through strict discipline and training," replies Tyson. Tyson takes a couple of steps back after he takes a few minutes to calm down. "My gosh, what the hell happened to you, man? You look like something out of a magazine."

"I entered a bodybuilding contest after you left, and I won. I was so nervous standing up there on stage with nothing on except tight, shiny black trunks. There were so many babes at the show, and it seemed as if every one of them were screaming my name. In fact, I almost got the chance of a lifetime to get further acquainted with several of them," replies Trevor.

Tyson looks at him with a big grin on his face. "You better be careful. I know you're still a virgin, and I don't think you want that to get around."

"I remember I once had the chance of a lifetime to lose my virginity to one of the hottest chicks I've ever seen, but somebody ruined that perfect moment. What are you talking about? You're still a virgin too," replies Trevor.

"It saddens me to have to say this, but you're correct. I'm still an untouched flower in the garden of Eden," replies Tyson. "I must tell you, brother. I had the pleasure of meeting a babe at the academy."

There's a moment of silence as both of them realize that in a few years, their lives will be split into separate ways, but they refuse to discuss it. They just laugh at each other as they continue to share their stories with each other, strolling through the neighborhood.

CHAPTER 11

The high school years pass, and the two young men stand proudly at the top of the mountain, claiming their titles as seniors. They stroll down the halls with their chests flared like roosters, as if they've conquered the world. Their classmates worship them for being the coolest dudes around, and the faculty adores them for their academic excellence. They receive full four-year academic scholarships to any university in the country. Their parents are very proud of them, as well as the members of their community. Through all the joy and happiness that everyone has for them, they feel a lingering pain that begins to tighten around their hearts as every day flies by with wings.

Every day, as the final bell rings out, Trevor has flashbacks of the sad times when he had to leave his friends and family to move on to another chapter in his life, and now the time has come again for history to repeat itself. To ease their pains, they plan a preprom and pregraduation party and camp out at Webster's Lake for seniors only. The news about the party spreads to several different high schools in less than a week. It is also picked up by the local police who plan to patrol the area in order to keep alcohol out and peace in. This party is the talk of all high school seniors as being the best way to end a great year. It is well-known that anybody who is somebody will be at this party. The big party is only a couple months away, and they're constantly hounded by the underclassmen to let them attend, but they stuck to their rules, only allowing seniors to attend. The ladies gossip about what bikini will look good for this event, and the guys whisper among one another about which babe they want to spend the night with. The young ladies compete fiercely to see who will be the lucky one or ones to spend the night with two of the hottest guys God ever created. The seniors has made a huge calendar and placed it in the hallway so everybody can see it as they mark off the days coming up to this special event. You can feel the excitement in the air as the whole senior class gear up and prepare themselves for a great festival. With only a few weeks to go before the party, they meet every day after school to work out any problems that may occur before the party.

Tyson says, "Man, when I got to class this morning, I had a desk full of letters from different girls asking me if they could be my special friend at the party."

"You too? I have to clean my locker out every day just to have a place for my books," replies Trevor.

James knocks and enters the room. "You guys have a very big weekend in a couple of weeks, don't you?"

"Yes, sir," they reply.

"I have something I want to give you," says James. He empties a whole jug of condoms out on the floor, saying, "I was once a teenager, and I want to make sure you guys have all the protection you need."

"Holy shit!" yells Tyson. He immediately places his hands over his mouth in embarrassment.

"It's okay. Just don't let your mothers know we bought these condoms for you," says James.

"You mean my dad helped you buy all of this?" asks Tyson.

James winks at them as he closes the door behind him.

CHAPTER 12

Monday morning is a blaze of glory as the senior classmen have one more week before the big shebang. Everyone's spirits are up except the poor, underprivileged junior classmen who can only watch the senior classmen scurry around preparing themselves for the biggest event of the season. They try relentlessly to persuade Trevor and Tyson to let them be a part of the festivities, and every time, they receive the same old boring answer. Tyson feels sympathy for the young ones. He devises a little contest for the junior classmen, and Trevor agrees to the terms of the game. The rules are, there will be a car wash fundraiser for the junior classmen composed of six guys and six girls. The team who raises the most money for the party will be allowed to come. The screams from the junior classmen burst through the auditorium doors, filling the halls as they try to complete the rules of the game.

Trevor continues to explain the details of the game after all the commotion subsides, "The winning team will be announced at this Friday's pep rally. The other teams will keep all their money to split up among one another."

The junior classmen quickly form their teams. The excitement energizes the whole junior class to get out there and do their best to win the contest. That afternoon, Trevor and Tyson drive to the lake to make sure everything is okay. They see several juniors screaming "Car wash, car wash!" on this blistering, hot summer day as several motorists line up to get their cars washed.

Tyson looks at Trevor, saying, "Man, we're going to have enough money to feed China after this contest is over."

"That was a brilliant idea to raise extra money for our party. Why didn't I think of that?" asks Trevor.

"I hope this is somewhat of a repayment for me screwing up your prom night with Candice," says Tyson.

"This only covers part of that bill. You still owe me," replies Trevor.

"Don't worry, brother. I have several great opportunities in store for us at this party," replies Tyson.

The final day of the contest has come. The school is as still and quiet as a fallen leaf. The anxiety and tension of the contest results cloud the atmosphere of the school with a dark, dense haze as both the seniors and juniors wait anxiously for the contest results. Trevor and Tyson are in the auditorium arranging the money orders in order by amounts. This is very exciting because most of the money orders are in very high amounts.

The principal startles the audience. "The pep rally will begin in one hour."

The tension grows stronger than ever before as the hands of the clock creep closer and closer. The drum line marks the beginning of the pep rally as the deep thud of the bass drums summons them. The student body files in one by one like convicted inmates awaiting their final sentencing. They approach the stage. You can hear the students gasp for air as they prepare themselves for the results of the contest. Trevor begins by congratulating the junior class for all the hard work and unforgiving, hot summer days that were spent washing cars in order to raise the most money for the contest. He prepares to open the letter to reveal the lucky twelve contestants when Tyson runs out on stage.

"O Romeo, O Romeo! Thoust must not spoil thy great festival!"

"As you wisheth, my sweet Juliet," replies Trevor.

The crowd begins to laugh as the two clowns imitate the worst rendition of Shakespeare's *Romeo and Juliet*. The level of tension begins to drop as the crowd begins to loosen up and enjoy the pep rally, but the tension can still be seen in the smiling faces of the audience as everyone wants to know who the lucky winners are. The festivities are almost at their end when "Romeo and Juliet" approach the stage to announce the lucky contestants. The crowd tenses up as they gaze upon the Roman gladiators coming to announce the victory of a few and the utter disappointment of the others.

Trevor takes out the name of the lucky contestants. He yells, "The lucky winners of our contest are the Crazy Eighty-Eight!"

There is a loud screeching of screams from all the way back in the corner of the auditorium as the Crazy Eighty-Eight explode with joy, hugging one another, jumping around like wild, untamed animals.

Tyson asks, "Would you please come to the stage to be recognized for your hard work and determination." The Crazy Eighty-Eight run up to the stage as the student body stand to cheer for them. Tyson says, "The top contender known as the Crazy Eighty-Eight won the contest by \$1. They raised a total of \$450." Tyson asks, "Why did you choose to call yourselves the Crazy Eighty-Eight?"

The captain replies, "It was our goal to make \$88 in one day, and we did it, so we named ourselves the Crazy Eighty-Eight."

Tyson looks at them, saying, "On behalf of the entire senior class, we would like to invite you to party with us at Webster's Lake on May 11 at 7:00 p.m., and please be prepared to spend the night."

Trevor slowly drifts backstage, leaving Tyson on stage to entertain the crowd, as he walks to his science class where he sees Ms. Sherman, a recent graduate of college and only seven years older. She's preparing the lesson plan for the day as he stands at the door for a moment, watching her graceful body. He enters, startling her. "Good morning, Ms. Sherman. How are you today?"

"I'm doing very well. Thank you for asking." She stops what she's doing, walks around to the front of her desk, and sits on top, crossing her beautiful legs. She asks, "Is it okay if I come to your party Friday night as your guest?" He hesitates to answer her question as if he were afraid. "It's okay. You don't have to be afraid. Everybody is downstairs, and what's said between you and me stays between you and me," she says.

He's amazed to hear her say this. "Sure, I would love to have you as my guest of honor, but how would you explain that to everyone else?"

"I was just teasing. It wouldn't be appropriate for a teacher to party with her students."

He feels a rush of confidence come over him. "Ms. Sherman—"

She interrupts, "Please call me Melissa."

He continues, "I think you're the sexiest science teacher I've ever had, and it's been a pleasure to be in your class."

She looks at him with a smile on her face. "That's so sweet of you to say that. Just between you and me, I wish you were a little older and in college because you're a very handsome, sexy young man."

"I learned a long time ago that age ain't nothing but a number," he replies.

She uncrosses her legs very slowly as he gazes between her soft, firm thighs. She asks in a passionate voice, "Come here and explain to me what that's supposed to mean."

He gets up from his desk, walking slowly toward her. She spreads her soft, succulent legs apart so he can feel the burning passion that's building up inside her. He leans over to her. "I think you know exactly what I mean."

She leans back on her desk, placing her hands behind her for stability. Her skirt creeps up her thighs, exposing her neatly shaven lips. They seem to have a force of their own, drawing him more and more passionately into her zone. "I don't think you're ready for what you're about to get into," she says. He places his hands under her tight, firm ass, lifting her off the desk, kissing her full rose-colored lips repeatedly. The fire inside her begins to burn hotter and hotter as the kisses become more and more passionate. He gently caresses her ass as the feeling of ecstasy begins to control their emotions.

In the distance, they can hear the pep rally slowly coming up the stairs as the laughter, singing, and cheering of the crowd rudely awakens the peaceful halls and their most enjoyable moment. They end their little escapade as she wipes her lipstick from his lips. He turns to walk out the door as she says, "I never wear them. They irritate my skin." He smiles at her as he closes the door, watching the Crazy Eight-Eight run by, screaming, "We're going to the party! We're going to the party!"

Tyson sees him at his locker. "Where have you been? Man, you missed all the excitement!"

Trevor looks at him with a smiling face, saying, "Dude, the excitement was just beginning." Tyson stands there with a confused look on his face. "Never mind. I'll tell you about it later," says Trevor.

CHAPTER 13

That weekend at Tyson's house, Trevor says, "Close the door. I have something to tell you that's going to knock you off your feet."

Tyson closes the door, asking, "Well, what's so important that you just can't wait to tell me?"

"I trust you. That's why you're the only person that I'll tell, and you better not tell anybody else," replies Trevor.

"Dammit, would you stop beating around the bush and spit it out!" says Tyson agitatedly.

"Okay, okay. You remember when we were at the pep rally Friday and how I suddenly disappeared? I went upstairs to Ms. Sherman's classroom, and we started to make out. Dude, she has the hots for me, and I didn't even know it."

Tyson jumps to his feet excitedly. "You better not be lying to me!"

"I'm not, but wait, it gets better. I saw her shaved beaver because she never wears any panties. My left hand is still tingling from rubbing all over her tight round ass," replies Trevor.

"Did you bend her ass over the desk and bang the hell out her?" asks Tyson.

"No, because we were rudely interrupted when we heard you guys coming back upstairs," he replies.

"This wasn't my fault this time. I wanted to stay in the auditorium to continue the party, but the principal insisted that school was not out yet and we should get back upstairs to complete our assignments. You lucky bastard! Now I'll never be able to look at her the same again," says Tyson.

"No, my dear brother, I won't be able to look at her the same again. Every time I see her in class, I'm going to think about her scientific anatomy instead of our scientific environment," replies Trevor.

CHAPTER 14

Monday starts off as a party before the party. The seniors crowd the back parking lot, screaming, dancing, and blaring their music in celebration of the end of another great year. They're celebrating graduation, prom, and of course, the highlight of all—the weekend beach party. Trevor and Tyson drive up in the parking lot, escalating the party to a higher level. They hype the party up by jumping out of their cars, ripping their shirts off like they're strippers. The ladies go wild as they begin to splash water on one another, turning the event into a wet T-shirt and thong contest. The ladies dance around pulling up their skirts or pulling down their pants as the guys stuff dollar bills in their thongs. The tardy bell rings, and everybody scampers off to class hot and wet.

Trevor and Tyson arrive in Ms. Sherman's class, immediately noticing she's dressed exceptionally sexier than before. Her high heels accentuate her calves as she walks. Her tight skirt with a split in the back hugs her ass as if it were made especially for her. Her hair is in beautiful curls down to her mid back. Her makeup seems to have been professionally done, accentuating her beautiful, full lips glistening from the fluorescent lighting. Tyson looks at Trevor with a smile on his face as she prances around the class. The bell rings, and she says in her sweet voice, "Trevor, I would like to speak to you for a moment." Tyson looks back at him with excitement in his eyes as he walks out the door. She closes the door. "I can't seem to get you off my mind for some strange reason, so I would like for you to find a way to sneak away from the party Friday night and call me at this number. I have a little graduation present I want to give you." He gladly accepts the invitation as he walks out the door.

Tyson rushes up to him excitedly. "Is it on? Tell me! Is it on?"

"Nothing will be on if you don't stop talking so loud, and yes, it's on for Friday night, but I need you to cover for me while I'm gone," he replies.

"I will do it under one condition. Let me smell your fingers after you get back."

Trevor laughs, nodding as they go downstairs to the big calendar, marking off a few more days. The seniors and the Crazy Eighty-Eight are huddled around the calendar when they arrive.

"May I have your attention please. My dad has informed me that Police Chief Lillico is aware of our party, and he will shut us down if any alcohol is present or if things get too far out of hand. I'm asking you as your fellow classmate to respect one another, and let's have a wild and crazy, good time!" instructs Trevor.

The next couple of days are agonizing as they seem to have lost the wind in their sails. The hours seem like days as every student eyes the clock every half second, hoping that time will race away as it has before, but there is no such luck, and they have to endure endless torment.

On Friday, the big day, the parking lots are half empty and the halls are quiet as the staff and junior classmen come to realize the senior class has made this day their senior skip day. The staff doesn't seem to mind very much because it gave them a chance to relax and let their minds be at peace without hearing all the chitchat about the party from the senior class.

The principal announces over the intercom, "Let's enjoy our moment of silence as well as the rest of the day." Class will carry on as usual for the rest of the students and staff on this great senior skip day.

CHAPTER 15

The beach is alive with half-naked, screaming seniors as they sunbathe their bodies on the warm sand. The lake is full of Jet Skis and a few skinny-dippers who want to become one with nature. The smell of pine is radiant as the warm summer breezes wisp through, making them dance with every breath. Trevor and Tyson stand alone on top of a small cliff in a semiwooded area where pine straw covers the ground like a soft blanket.

"This is the perfect spot for us to set up our tent today," says Tyson.

Trevor nods as he stares out over the beautiful lake and the wilderness that surrounds it. His mind takes him back several years to a place of peace when he was a kid waking up every morning to the smell of his grandmother's famous chicken and biscuits, surrounded by a mound of delicious gravy and molasses syrup. His body feels as if it has taken flight back to this paradise where he used to roll in the pine straw among hundreds of tall pine trees. The thought of this is so great it brings back many memories of love and happiness. Tears of joy begin to roll down his cheeks as he stands there silent as the gentle breath of God blows all around him. He is awakened from this dream as Tyson repeatedly says, "Trevor, Trevor, hello? Are you still there?"

He turns to him. "I'm sorry, Tyson. My mind has taken me back to a place similar to this where I spent a lot of time as a kid."

"I understand, but can we please put this tent up so we can go down to the beach and party with the babes," asks Tyson. When they finish putting up their tent, Tyson says, "I'll see you on the beach, dude."

Trevor walks down to the beach where he sees Tyson racing across the waves on a Jet Ski, screaming as he splashes water on a few topless sunbathers. He smiles as he watches his classmates run around enjoying themselves without a care or thought of the troubles of the world.

The day begins to dwindle into night as the sun begins to lose its radiance and darkness begins to claim its position. The glaring light from the fires begin to dance in the air and on the ripples of the lake as they feed off the oxygen-rich environment and dry wood. Trevor retires to his tent as he remembers Melissa is anticipating his call. The tent is dimly lit by the fires below as he fumbles around frantically for his phone. The phone rings once then twice as a beautiful voice gently says, "Hello."

He replies in a smooth, relaxed tone, "Hello, how are you? I hope this isn't a bad time to call you. I just want to know if you still want me to come by tonight."

"I'm sorry, but I have womanly problems right now that I wasn't expecting until next weekend. I hope I haven't disappointed you," replies Melissa in a troubled voice.

"No, no, I'm not disappointed at all. I'm sorry that you feel bad. Maybe we can get together some other time," replies Trevor.

"Thank you. You're so sweet. I hear the music in the background. Are you having fun?"

"Yes, I'm having a great time. I wish you could be here to see it."

"I wish there were some way I could have been there. I know I would have had a great time with you," she says.

"I don't want to hold you on the phone too long so I will say good night, and I hope you feel better." He lies down on the floor of his tent with his fingers crossed behind his head, listening to the rustle of the tent from the warm breezes zipping through the campsite.

Tyson stumbles into the tent as if he has fallen into a barrel of rum. "Trevor, are you here?"

"I'm right here, blind ass. What's going on?"

"What are you doing here? I thought you would be at Melissa's house caressing those firm thighs," says Tyson.

"Please don't remind me. My heart aches every time I picture her in my head. Our plans were spoiled because she's on the rag and feels like shit," he replies.

"Not to worry. I have just the right prescription for your pains. Follow me, please," replies Tyson.

They could hear echoes of passion from the shadows of the great pines and dense forestry as they stroll down the hill to the beach where a tent full of beautiful blossoms awaits their arrival." Tyson stops before they enter the tent. "This is my surprise to you. I have gathered six of the hottest babes together in one tent with only one thing on their minds. Prepare yourself for a wild night of hot, uncontrollable, buck-naked sex."

The two gentlemen enter the tent, gazing upon six goddesses. Each of the beautiful ladies introduces themselves as Tyson and Trevor place themselves in the middle of this blossoming rose garden.

"So what's on your minds?" asks Shelly.

There were several smirks from the ladies as Trevor replies, "There are not enough hours in this night for me to explain to you what's on my mind."

Shelly crawls over to him, gently kissing him on his lips, and whispers, "Turn off the lights and let's get this party started."

A sweet voice from the corner interrupts the moment, "Some of us have girly issues that won't allow us to enjoy the festivities of the night."

"Please don't tell me you're on the rag!" says Tyson.

"My dear brother, you have successfully done it again," says Trevor.

"Oh, brother, that's cold. Come on, I had no idea they were—"

Shelly interrupts, "Guys! Guys! Don't get your panties in a bunch! We can still have a great time tonight. You just have to play in the backyard where things may be a little tighter. You'll still get the same great satisfaction, at least that's what my boyfriend tells me."

"You mean you want me to stick it up your... Oh, I don't think so. That's disgusting."

Kim says, "Oh please, don't act like you've never done that before. My brother and the rest of the football team banged your prom date's ass last year so many times you probably couldn't tell the difference between the two. I know you did it because she loved it."

"No, we didn't get that far because somebody decided to ruin the most perfect night of my life," replies Trevor.

"Don't knock it before you try it because you just might like it. It takes a little while to get used to, but I believe the ladies will agree, the feeling is great," says Shelly.

Kim takes a tube of Slick 50 from her purse, saying, "Gentlemen, prepare to lube your tubes."

The ladies begin to laugh as Trevor looks at them like a deer caught between two headlights.

"I don't think it's such a bad idea, and if it's what they want, then it's what they'll get," says Tyson.

"Tyson, I don't think so. You can enjoy all the ass you want, but I'm going back to our tent to clear my head of all this nonsense," replies Trevor. The ladies scream for him to come back as he stumbles out of the tent with a sickening feeling in his stomach.

CHAPTER 16

The rays of the sun pierce through the towering shades, like a light through a prism, bringing life back to the darkness. Trevor is awakened by the sounds of Mother Nature all around him. He steps outside his tent to take a long stretch, filling his lungs with cool, fresh air. He laughs as he watches the squirrels scamper up and down the trees, gathering food for themselves. The fowls of the sky sing sweet songs as the rest of the quiet forest begins to dance to their melodies. He's startled not by the sounds of Mother Nature but of the unpleasant sounds of Tyson, who's moaning like a cow giving birth to her calf.

"What in the hell are you doing sleeping on the ground when our tent is only a few feet away from you, and why are you making those awful sounds disturbing the peace of Mother Nature?" asks Trevor.

Tyson replies in a deep, raspy voice, "Dude, I got so wasted after you left last night I couldn't remember if this was our tent or not. I slept on the cool ground because that gin had me feeling like hell was inside of me."

"Soooo how does it feel to lose your virginity to the grace and delight of a tight asshole? You know what? I'm going to call you Brown Eye for the rest of your life because I can't believe you did something so disgusting," says Trevor.

"Hold on, Father John. I didn't have anal sex with any of those girls. Instead, Kim broke out a bottle of gin that she stole from her dad, and we took turns playing quarters all night."

"You're a maniac with a hangover. Get your sloppy ass up and let's pack this shit up so we can go back to civilization," replies Trevor.

"It's six thirty in the morning. How many of us do you see packing at six thirty in the morning? I tell you what, why don't you go bond with nature for a couple of hours and let me and the rest of us enjoy the peace and silence of the morning?" says Tyson.

Trevor nods as he walks off into the wilderness, admiring the vast forest that surrounds him. He comes upon a beautiful lake surrounded by a legion of beautiful, tall pine trees dancing in unison to the gentle breeze that surrounds them. He sits at the edge of the lake, admiring its beauty as the sunlight bounces off the ripples of waves created by the wind. He stands up with a roaring, deep voice, yelling, "I declare this lake to be known as Crystal Lake in the loving memory of a beautiful woman that I once knew. She had eyes like the blue sky and lips as soft as feathers!" His heart sinks back several years earlier as he gazes out upon the beauty that surrounds him. He remembers that sweet moment in time when he kissed her soft, beautiful lips on his way home from school. That very thought brings happiness and sadness to his heart as a warm tear runs down his cheek into the cool, refreshing waters of the lake. He reminds himself he'll see Crystal again someday, somehow, somewhere. He leans forward on his knees to wash his face. The water feels cool and refreshing to his skin as he wipes the water from his eyes. He gazes upon one of nature's most ferocious yet loving mothers enter the cool, calm lake in search of food for her cubs. He watches in utter silence from across the lake as the beautiful black bear plucks a fish from the water to feed its cubs. Words can't express the grace. He hears a disturbing echo of his name from a distance. He looks back across the lake at the bear with its head raised in curiosity. He calmly eases back into the woods where he finds Tyson and a few other classmates have formed a search party. "Stop screaming, stop screaming! There's a huge black bear on the other side of the lake, and I don't think you want her to come after us," he says frantically.

"Well, let's go, Little Red Riding Hood, before we're eaten. I don't intend to die before I graduate high school, nor do I intend to miss all the parties," says Tyson. They laugh as they run wild through the woods back to the campsite.

CHAPTER 17

The day that every high school student in the world struggles to achieve finally arrives. The senior class of 1992 anxiously lines the corridors of the coliseum, awaiting the final moment to walk out in front of their families and friends to receive one of life's greatest gifts. Principal Green steps up to the microphone to make his announcements as the senior class of 630 students await backstage, ready to greet the hundreds of families and friends who await them in the coliseum. The principal announces, "Ladies and gentlemen, I would like you to meet the graduating class of 1992."

The seniors begin to file out in single-file lines from all four corridors of the coliseum, filling the enormous rows of seats with crimson and cream. Their families begin to cheer as they point out their graduates. The principal steps to the microphone once more to congratulate the seniors on a job well done and how life is now about to begin. He wishes the entire graduating class a lifetime of achievements and further success as they prepare to walk across stage to receive their diplomas. The principal and his staff present every student with a hug and a diploma as they one by one walk across the stage. When every student has received a diploma, the principal rings the bell, yelling, "You are now dismissed from class!" The seniors scream with excitement, tossing their hats as high as they can. They embrace one another with tears in their eyes as families and friends begin to pour onto the floor to congratulate them on a job well done.

Trevor runs up to the stage before everyone leaves. "Seniors, don't forget the after-party at Club Spice tonight. Grads get in free!"

Trevor, Tyson, and their families are all standing around laughing and talking when two hot ladies walk past, saying, "The dance floor is waiting."

James says, "Son, don't let this be another prom night." They all laugh as the memories of that night are so perfectly clear in their minds. Trevor, Tyson, and a convoy of other screaming seniors race away to Club Spice for their last night of fun and excitement with one another before their great departure into the second phase of their lives.

CHAPTER 18

Trevor and Tyson spend very little time around each other in the following months. Trevor and his family are in San Diego, California, touring Mira Mesa University, where he will study business. Tyson and his family are in Annapolis, Maryland, touring the Naval Academy. Although they miss each other, they're happy to see their lives moving forward.

Trevor and his family are excited to be in California to enjoying its beautiful climate, palm trees, and beaches. The cultural differences and the size of the city are very diverse, which worries them a bit, but Trevor seems to be enjoying himself, so they don't mention their insecurities. The privately gated university is impressively decorated with beautiful works of structural design and art. Several uniquely designed fountains are sprawled across the courtyard, with beautiful flower gardens surrounding them.

The tour guide announces, "I will now introduce you to the most decorative buildings on our campus. I will also introduce you to the artists who take pride in shaping all of our students' minds into masterpieces." The parents are excited to meet and greet all the professors who would shape and mold their youngsters into well-educated individuals. They are impressed by the small class size of only students per class.

The tour guide says, "Ladies and gentlemen, I would like to invite you to our scenic cafeteria where the great food from our fine chefs and beautiful view of the ocean will simply take your breath away." The aroma from the cafeteria embraces them as they approach a beautiful Greek-style building with huge columns decorating its entrance. The inside is elaborately decorated as mythical Atlantis with beautiful paintings of Greek gods scouring the ceiling. The view through the elaborately decorated windows gives way to a vast, beautiful blue ocean that looks as peaceful as the blue sky. The food smells delicious as Trevor and his family take a moment to fill their stomachs with the delicacies that have been prepared for them.

The tour guide announces, "It's my honor to introduce you to one of our university's most humble and prestigious men. Ladies and gentlemen, our president, Mr. J. F. Chambers."

He steps to the microphone. "Thank you so much for such a warm invitation. I'm so proud to stand before such a gifted group of individuals. I hope that you have found that our university is what you have expected it to be. As a graduate of this university many, many years ago, I can still vouch for our school's great reputation in educating well-prepared graduates to enter the workforce after completing our curriculum. I promise the parents in this room that your children will be well above standards and ready for today's ever-so-changing workforce. I would sincerely like to thank you for choosing Mira Mesa University as your choice of higher education, and I hope to see all of your young, eager faces this fall."

The tour guide steps back up to the microphone. "Let's give our president a big hand. I know your stomachs are full and your eyes are heavy, and that's why I saved the best for last. If you would kindly drag yourselves from your comfortable seats, I would like to take you to the student residential halls, where every student in this room already has his or her name on their suite."

They all gather in front of the cafeteria where they load three buses by alphabetical order. They arrive in front of six beautiful condominium-like residence halls with a lovely display of mermaids spouting water from their mouths in the courtyard. Trevor is in building 5, along with several other students who are amazed to see the big-screen TVs, pool tables, bars, and a mini snack shop, all conveniently located in the lobby. He looks at a list of names, finding his next to room 530 on the fifth floor. They take the elevator to the fifth floor, where he finds his first name embroidered in gold on the door as they enter the room. He's even more surprised to see his room is elaborately decorated with beautiful furnishings and an enormous amount of space without a roommate. He thinks to himself that things can't get any better than this.

The tour guide announces over the microphone, "Ladies and gentlemen, this concludes our lovely tour of our campus. I hope you've enjoyed the tour of our great university, and I hope to see all of our new students safely back and ready to go this fall. Have a good afternoon."

Trevor looks at his parents, saying, "Well…Mom, Dad, what do you think?"

Clara says, "Honey, I think it's a wonderful school, and your father and I are very proud of you. But it's just so far away from home, and I worry that—"

James interrupts, saying, "Son, we are very proud of you, and if this is where you want to go to school, then it's fine by us. Don't worry about your mother. She'll be just fine."

"Mom, there's nothing to worry about. I'll be fine, I promise!"

"Well, son, I don't know about you, but this has been a very long day. We have a long flight back home tomorrow, and we probably should get some sleep. Oh yeah, here's some cover. Make yourself comfortable on the couch," says James.

"Thanks, Dad! I hope you and Mom rest very comfortably in my bed!" he says sarcastically. He closes the door to his bedroom and lets out a silent scream as he takes a running dive onto his couch.

CHAPTER 19

Thousands of miles away, Tyson and his family are preparing to take a tour of the Naval Academy. He tosses and turns all night long in their motel room in anticipation of tomorrow's tour. He dreams of marching in a battalion, being on the drill teams, wearing his uniform, getting screamed at by the young drill cadets, and most of all, getting the chance to someday become a top gun pilot in the United States Navy. He springs from couch to couch like a jack-in-the-box. He paces back and forth with extreme excitement, checking the time on the clock every half second.

His dad awakes to all the rustling in the room. "Son, its two o'clock in the morning! What are you doing?"

"I'm sorry if I woke you and Mom, but I'm so excited about tomorrow! I can't sleep!"

"Keep your voice down. You're going to wake the whole motel. You know how your mother is when she doesn't get her sleep," replies Ramone.

"I'm sorry, Dad. I'm so excited I don't know what to do," he replies.

"I tell you what you can do. You can lay down right here…just like that…and I'll pull the cover over you, and then you can go to sleep," replies Ramone.

Tyson continues to toss and turn all night in anticipation of tomorrow's events. He finally gives up and sits up on the couch. Ramone gets up at 6:30 a.m., finding his son propped up by the door, fully dressed, and asleep with his head hanging between his knees.

Ramone finds this amusing. He summons Teresa to look at their son. She walks into the room, whispering, "Awww, he's looks so cute. Don't bother him. Let him sleep until it's almost time to go." He peacefully sleeps by the door until seven thirty when he feels a gentle tap on his shoulder and his mother saying in a gentle tone, "Wake up, honey. It's almost time to go."

He springs up like a startled cat, yelling, "Are we there? Are we there yet?"

"Hold on, Gomer Pyle. We're still at the motel," says Ramone.

He quickly runs to the bathroom, washes his face, and brushes his teeth.

"Come on, son, the bus is waiting on us!" yells Ramone.

At the Naval Academy, a huge band is playing the national anthem. Tyson is breathless seeing the young cadets all dressed in their uniforms. A very attractive young female cadet approaches the group, saying, "Good morning, everybody, my name is Cadet Maria Alvarado. I'm going to be your tour guide for the day." Tyson is stunned by her beauty and the way she looks in her uniform. She gives them a brief history about the academy before she leads them to the auditorium to meet and greet the academy's chief of command, Admiral Paul Armstrong.

He steps to the microphone with a clean, clear voice. "Welcome, parents and soon-to-be young cadets. It's a pleasure and an honor to stand before so many motivated individuals who have chosen this great historical academy as a place to further their education, discipline, and become future leaders of our country. I hope to see all of you back here in a few days ready to set sail on an exciting, new adventure in life."

Tyson is more motivated to go now than ever as Cadet Alvarado gathers the group together. She says, "The big white building in front of you is called the cadet building for all new cadets. This building and its staff of ten drill instructors will prepare each cadet for military-style living emotionally and physically for twelve weeks."

One of the parents asks, "What do you mean when you say the building and the instructors will prepare them emotionally and physically?"

She smiles and replies, "You see that obstacle course to the far left? That is where hours of physical fitness training will be conducted, and the gleaming white building in front of you is where all the cleaning, classes, and our Navy's core values of honor, courage, and commitment will be in instilled in every new cadet that ever attends this academy. Our mission at this academy is to take an ordinary individual and train them to become a well-educated, well-disciplined, proud member of an organization with a proud history. That training begins in this building and will continue throughout life."

She takes them on a tour through the barracks, and they're all impressed to see rows of neatly made beds with forty-five-degree corners and floors so shiny you can see yourself on them. "Some of you will make it through the tough twelve weeks that are ahead of you, and some of you will not. For the ones that do make it through this phase of training, life after this will seem like a piece of cake. If you would kindly follow me, I will show you what I mean." She takes them across campus to another set of barracks called the seamen's barracks. "All students who complete the twelve-week program will move and be classified as cadets with only two other roommates instead of eighty in the seamen's barracks. Every student gets more and more privileges as he or she advances until they reach junior or senior status where they're allowed to have a car, no roommates, and no curfew unless they violate a rule."

Teresa raises her hand, asking, "Will underclassmen be allowed to go off campus to tour the town, and if so, how will they get around?"

"Good question, ma'am. Yes, they can go off campus to anywhere they want to by our transit buses that will take them wherever they want to go, but they have to be careful not to stay out too late and miss curfew, which is 2100 hours or 9:00 p.m. for all students until you reach junior status," replies Cadet Alvarado.

They complete the tour by touring the parade deck, which looks like the size of seven football fields, where all drills will be done, morning muster, and graduation ceremonies. Cadet Alvarado says, "Oh yeah, I forgot to mention there's an air show tomorrow starting at 1300 hours or 1:00 p.m. I encourage you to purchase your tickets in advance. Lunch is provided for you free today."

Before Tyson can get the words out of his mouth, his dad pulls out three air show tickets as they walk to the dining hall. In the dining hall,

Tyson sees Cadet Alvarado and her friends seated at a table across from them. He quickly excuses himself from his parents and walks across to where they're seated.

"Excuse me, Cadet Alvarado, is this seat taken?"

"Please call me Maria until you become a student if you can handle the pressure…and no, this seat is not taken."

"I promise you I will finish the twelve-week training as well as the four-year training that will someday prepare me to become a great naval pilot and soldier if you promise me we will go on a date when I move into the cadet dorm," he replies.

"Okay, Mr. Navy Pilot, I promise you I will go out with you after you finish your twelve grueling weeks," she replies.

"Ladies, have a nice day. I'll see you in a few days," he replies.

Cadet Smith says, "Oh my gosh, Maria, he's such a babe. Why can't I ever get a guy like that?"

Ramone says, "Like father like son, you don't waste any time getting to know the ladies."

Teresa looks at both of them, rolling her eyes, laughing, and shaking her head.

The next day at the air show, Tyson is tremendously excited as he watches the pilots gracefully maneuver their aircraft through the vast blue sky, slicing the wind in half as they push themselves and their aircraft to the limit. In fact, he's so tuned in to the show he doesn't even recognize Maria sitting comfortably beside him. She gently taps him on his shoulder.

"Hello, stranger. Are you enjoying the show?"

He puts his arm around her. "I love this. I hope someday I'll get a chance to grace the heavens just as they are now."

"Something tells me you'll get there someday, and you're going to be 100 percent better. Come with me. I have a surprise for you," she replies. He follows her to a sky-blue tent where all the Blue Angel pilots are. They're signing and giving out posters of the squadron in formation.

The lead pilot asks, "Son, would you like to take a picture with the Blue Angels?"

He's so excited he couldn't even get the words out of his mouth. They walk to a little less noisy, less crowded spot where he hugs her tightly for such a great gift. She feels so secure in his arms. She gently kisses him and gives him her phone number as she walks back to the van where the Blue Angels are waiting to be taken to their jets.

"Thank you, I will call you when I get home." She waves goodbye as she gets into the van. Tyson returns to where his parents are sitting.

The announcer says, "Ladies and gentlemen, the moment you have been waiting for, the Blue Angels!" They flew by in formation with streams of blue, white, yellow, red, and orange smoke trailing behind them. Tyson is so excited he stands up for the entire event. He imagines himself being one of the pilots flying fearlessly through the heavens, turning, twisting, flipping, and diving toward Mother Earth with a heart of steel. The evening ends with a beautiful display of fireworks.

On the way back to the motel, Ramone leans over, asking, "Did you enjoy yourself today?"

"I have dreamed of this moment all my life, Dad. I couldn't imagine anything better than this."

"I'm so very happy that you enjoyed yourself today, and we're proud you chose a career to serve your country. You also found a beautiful young lady to help you along the way," says Ramone.

"Thanks, Dad. I'm really happy you and Mom are just as excited about me joining the military. This is a dream come true. I can't wait to get home to tell Trevor about it."

"According to James, I bet Trevor can't wait to tell you about his biiiiiiiiiiig adventure either," replies Ramone.

He looks at his mom and dad strangely as they sort of laugh at one another in a sneaky way. Maria occupies his mind to such capacity that he doesn't even bother to ask them what they mean about Trevor's *big* surprise.

As soon as they arrive at the motel, he dashes off the bus, running to the room with one hand in his pocket, frantically searching for her number. He pulls the piece of paper all wadded from his pocket, takes a deep breath, and begins to dial the numbers nervously. A beautiful voice on the other end answers, "Hello, this is Maria."

"This is Tyson. I thought I would call you to say thanks again for such a great day."

"You're welcome, and thank you for being such a gentleman. I hope I will see you again."

"You don't have to worry about seeing me again. I'll be back in a few days to let the journey begin."

"Great, then I'll be waiting for you on Sunday," she replies.

Ramone walks into the room as he's hanging up the telephone. "You sure don't waste any time, do you?"

"Dad, you got to get it when it's good, if you know what I mean."

Ramone looks at him with a smile. "Son, I was once a teenager, and I know exactly what you mean. I want you to take things slow. You have your whole life ahead of you. Don't make adult decisions with your head. Make decisions with your head, if you know what I mean." The two of them laugh at each other as Teresa walks into the room.

"What's so funny?"

"Just having a man-to-man talk with my old man," replies Tyson.

"I get the feeling this is something I don't want to know about. Anyway, you two need to start packing. We have a long trip back home tomorrow and a lot of visiting to do before you return on Sunday," replies Teresa.

CHAPTER 20

Trevor is just returning home from the gym feeling pumped and full of energy. His parents are in the kitchen talking about something as he walks in.

James says, "Son, what are doing this afternoon?"

"I'm going to drop by Tyson's house for a minute if he's back."

"Why don't you hang out with me for a few minutes after you get cleaned up? There's a few things I want to discuss with you," replies James.

He looks at his mom for some clarity, but she simply smiles and continues to wash the dishes. He racks his brain in the shower trying to figure out what his dad wants to talk to him about. He quickly gets himself dressed, goes into the kitchen, sits down at the table, and asks, "Mom, Dad, what's going on?"

"Well, son, let's take a ride. I'm not sure how well you're going to take this situation," replies James.

"Okay, okay! What's going on here? What are you two up to?" he asks.

"Let's take a ride, and I'll tell you all about it." James whispers to Clara, "I've been waiting for this day for twelve years."

"Time surely flies when you're having fun," replies Clara.

"That's it, I can't take any more of this. I'm going to get in the car now!" yells Trevor.

They wave goodbye as they take off down the road. James says, "Son, your mother and I are very proud of you for being the great son that you are, for being as smart as you are, and best of all, for saving us $40,000 per semester for college."

He looks at his father with tears in his eyes. "Thanks, Dad. It means so much to me to hear you say that. I try so hard to make you and Mom proud of me."

"Get that water out of your eyes before I get some in my eye. It's hard enough knowing we're going to lose you in a few weeks."

"Dad, you'll never lose me. I'll always be in your heart, and I'll try to come see you and Mom every chance I get."

"Your mother has elevated herself all the way to the top by opening her own fashion design shop, and I'm vice chairman of the board for Langston & Langston Industries. We decided that you have been very successful also, so we want to give you this."

"Dad, we're parked in front of a bank."

"So good of you to notice. Now get out and let's go in for a moment."

They walk in, and the receptionist says, "Hello, may I help you?"

"Yes, ma'am, we're here to see Mr. Oliver, please."

"May I have your name?"

"Mr. O'Riely."

She walks to his office. "Sir, there's a Mr. O'Riely here to speak with you."

"Yes, yes, please send them in," he replies.

She reports back to them, "Mr. Oliver will see you now."

James and Trevor walk in.

Mr. Oliver says, "It's a pleasure to finally meet you, Trevor. We've been waiting for your arrival for a very long time. Please have a seat. I'll be right back." He walks out of the office.

Trevor looks at his dad, asking, "What are you up to?"

"Something I have been waiting to do for a long time," replies James.

Mr. Oliver walks back into the office. "Trevor, here's a pen. Please read and sign all the highlighted areas."

He takes the pen realizing it's his own personal bank account. After he signs all the documents, Mr. Oliver takes the papers back to one of the tellers, returning with a receipt in his hands. He congratulates him for opening a new account at Federal Bank of America as he gives him the receipt. He looks at his dad and then Mr. Oliver. He glances at the piece of paper, screaming, "Oh yeah, baby, that's what I'm talking about! I'm rich! I'm rich!"

The people jump up from their seats startled by all the commotion as the security guards rush into the office. Mr. Oliver steps outside the door. "Ladies and gentlemen, it's okay. Everything's all right. We just have a very happy, lucky young man here with us today."

Trevor hugs his dad very tightly. "Thanks, Dad!"

"No, son, don't thank me or your mother. Thank yourself for doing such a fantastic job in school and in your social life. There's more to come, so don't tire yourself out because Santa Claus has a bigger gift to give you," says James.

"You mean there's more? Oh my gosh, I don't know if I can take any more excitement today!" replies Trevor.

"I believe you'll gladly accept this next surprise with ease," replies James. As they're leaving the bank, James stresses, "Son, this money is to be spent very wisely for what you need during your four years of school at Mira Mesa. Your mother started saving this money for you way before I came into your lives, and I assisted her when we started dating. I felt this was a very smart thing to do. That's why I married your mother because she's a great woman, wife, and mother. Spend your money wisely, and don't just buy things just because you have a little money."

"Dad, you and Mom can rest assured that I will not blow money just for the sake of blowing it. I believe you already know I won't do that, or you and Mom would've never given me this much all at once."

"You're right, son. We trust you because you're very mature for your age. That's why we decided to get you this also."

They pull up in the driveway. He rolls out of the car like a man on fire, screaming and kicking, as he stares at a beautiful black Ford Mustang GT with a big red bow around it. Clara and James are standing together hand in hand with tears of joy running down their faces as they watch their son dance around in total bliss. He looks at his parents, screaming, "I have the best parents in the whole wide world!" He runs to them, hugging both of them, saying, "You won't be disappointed in me. I promise you that!"

Clara asks, "Are you going to dance around your new car all day, or are you going to take it for a spin?"

"I'm too excited to drive right now. I need to savor this moment for a minute, and then I'll be okay." He carefully takes the big red bow off the car, opens the door, and sits there, admiring the smell of his new car.

"We chose this car for you because you looked so sad when we had to take the other Mustang we rented for you on your prom night back to the dealership," says James.

"I think you made a wise decision, and I must say you two have great taste," replies Trevor. He starts the car, and the sound of its powerful V8 engine mesmerizes his mind, body, and soul. "I'm going to name her Possessed because the sound of her voice has me possessed," says Trevor. He waves goodbye to his parents as he takes off down the road, yelling, "I'm going to see Tyson!"

"Be careful, honey, and don't drive too fast!" yells Clara. He raises his thumb out of the window as he disappears around the corner.

He pulls into a local gas station for refreshments when he sees someone outside admiring his new car. He quickly recognizes it's Tyson and his parents. "What's up, dude, you like my new ride?"

"What's up, brother, let's go for a ride!" Tyson says excitedly. They jump in the car, excited to see each other. Tyson begins to tell him about Maria, one of the cadets he met at the academy. They both stop talking simultaneously as Tyson says, "Hey, isn't that Candice and Vanessa?"

"It sure looks like them, but what happened to Vanessa? She's so skinny," replies Trevor.

"Circle around and stop," says Tyson. They pull into a parking spot at the park as the two young ladies approach them. Tyson says, "Candice, Vanessa."

The two ladies look at them, screaming. Vanessa says, "Oh my gosh, it has been so long since the last time we met. The both of you are still so fine."

"How is college life?" asks Trevor.

"It's great. I love it because no one looks over your shoulder anymore, and the parties are awesome. And our football team is kicking ass," says Candice.

"That isn't the only ass they're kicking. Cool ride! Take me to the store so I can get something to drink to take my medication with," says Vanessa.

"Are you sick, Vanessa?" asks Tyson.

"The doctors are still running tests on me. They told me my immune system is not functioning like it's supposed to, and that may be the reason why I have lost so much weight. I don't understand all that shit. I wish they would get it together," replies Vanessa.

"How long are you ladies going to be in town?" asks Trevor.

"We're going back to school early because Vanessa's dad is being a real asshole. I think he's still embarrassed about our adventurous prom night. Isn't that right, Tyson?" replies Candice.

They laugh as Tyson says, "I'm really sorry about that night."

"Oh, don't apologize for that. It happened, and that's that, end of story. Take me back to our motel. I'm not feeling too good," replies Vanessa.

Trevor takes the young ladies back to their motel. Candice whispers in his ear, "You're still the perfect gentleman, aren't you?" She kisses him on his cheek. "I have our prom pictures all over my dorm wall. It reminds me of how sweet and kind you were to me on our prom night. You will always be the man I wish I could have but never will get."

"I think of you often. Maybe we'll meet again someday, and things will be different," replies Trevor. They wave goodbye to the ladies as they race off down the road.

Trevor says, "So you were telling me you have found yourself a hottie."

"Man, this is the girl I can spend the rest of my life with. She's so intelligent, beautiful, funny, and sexy. I can't stop thinking about her," replies Tyson.

"Dude, this chick really has you sprung. Maybe you can bring her home during spring break and introduce her," he replies.

"That reminds me. I'm leaving early Sunday morning, and I was wondering if you would take me to the airport?" asked Tyson. There was a brief silence as the two gentlemen come to terms that their lives are about to take two separate pathways and that life would never be the same as they knew it growing up as kids. Tyson breaks the silence, saying, "Enough about me. How did you enjoy your adventure in sunny California where all the finest babes are?"

"Mira Mesa University is great. It's like living in paradise. I have my own private room fully furnished with my name embroidered on the door."

"You're lucky! Your parents bought you this badass ride. I can't even have a car until my junior year according to school policy," says Tyson.

He looks at Tyson with a big smile on his face. "Just between you and me, this car isn't the only thing my parents gave me." He pulls the receipt from his pocket, passing it to Tyson.

His eyes light up like fireworks. "Tell me my eyes aren't playing tricks on me right now, $200,000? Dude, what the hell are you going to do with this kind of money? You don't have to pay tuition because we both have full four-year scholarships," says Tyson.

"This is spending money during my four-year stay at Mira Mesa. My parents have been saving this money for me ever since kindergarten," he replies.

"You have got to be the luckiest person in the world right now. I know you're going to party, party, party, and then party some more," says Tyson.

"No, my dad and I have already had a man-to-man talk about this money, and I promised him I would not waste all this money. I will probably invest it in real estate or something that's going to make me more than what I already have," replies Trevor.

"I knew you wouldn't be stupid and blow all that money. You're way too smart for something like that. Hey, drop me off at home. I've got a lot of packing to do and family to visit before Sunday," says Tyson.

The two of them laugh and chat away about their future lives as they pull into a crowded yard of Tyson's family and friends who've come to say goodbye and wish him the best of luck at the academy.

Ramone says, "Everybody, I would like to introduce you to two young men that I'm so very proud of, my son Tyson and his best friend, Trevor. They'll soon head off into their own worlds to further their education, marry beautiful women, and bring home lots of grandbabies for us to love." The crowd quickly engulfs the two young men with hugs and kisses as they fight their way toward a pleasant smell coming from inside Tyson's house. Teresa invites Trevor to have dinner and celebrate with them, but he turns the invitation down, waving goodbye to everyone.

Tyson runs out of the house. "Pick me up Sunday morning at about 6:00 a.m."

Trevor replies by nodding as he drives off.

On his way home, he enjoys the great sound system and the thrill of owning his very own Mustang. The DJ interrupts the music to announce the arrival of Lana, a rising, new porn star who will make a guest appearance at Drew's Gentlemen's Club Saturday night. He entertains the idea of going to see Lana, but that quickly dissipates from his memory as soon as the DJ returns to the Hot Mix at Six. He arrives at home to find his old pal Rusty sprawled out on the front lawn, enjoying the day, playfully chewing on what's left of his rag doll. He enters the house to find his grandmother patiently awaiting the arrival of her favorite grandson. He embraces her with love, saying, "Grandma, I was hoping I would get the chance to see you before I left for school. How are you doing?"

"My dear grandson, I'm doing just fine. I'm so proud to know that my grandbaby is going off to college to better himself. You have done so well for yourself. Your parents and I are very proud of you."

"Thank you, Grandma. How long are you going to stay with us?" he asks.

"Permanently," says James.

"I would love to stay in this beautiful house permanently, but I have to go back home Saturday so I can tend to my garden, finish making my quilts, and go to church on Sunday. I brought you a little gift to add to your other big gifts," replies Letha. She turns around and gives him a beautiful big quilt that she made by hand.

He hugs her tightly, saying, "Thank you very much, Grandma, but this is no little gift. You made it for me with your own two hands, and I will cherish this quilt forever. Mom, Dad, and Grandma, thank you for all the wonderful gifts that I have received today. If you will excuse me, I think I'm going to bed a little early tonight. All this excitement has worn me out."

Clara, James, and Letha sit at the table enjoying a fresh cup of coffee. Clara says, "Mama, do you think we're doing the right thing by letting our son go so far away from home to go to school? I mean, California is such a big place, and Trevor isn't used to that fast-paced life."

"Look around you, Clara. This is the type of life I wanted for you, and now you have it, but if you would've listened to me and let this fine young gentleman get away from you, your life would probably still be at a standstill, working yourself to death for a little bit of money. I'm simply saying don't be afraid for him to experience life. If he makes a few mistakes along the way, so what? We're all guilty of that," replies Letha.

"I agree. Trevor is not a baby anymore. He has to get out and experience the trials and tribulations in life, or he'll never grow up to stand on his own two feet. I trust our son will do the right thing, and if he gets a little sidetracked, then hopefully he'll learn from it and move on," says James.

"I still feel a little uneasy about the whole thing, but I suppose you're right. Our son has earned our respect and trust, and I shouldn't be so protective of him," replies Clara.

"Clara, Trevor is going to be just fine. Now enjoy your coffee before it gets cold," says Letha.

"I think time has taken its toll on me tonight. I'm going to bed," says Clara.

"I thought coffee was supposed to wake you up, not put you to sleep," says James.

The next morning, Trevor awakens to a familiar smell. He leaps out of bed, running to the kitchen to find his grandmother preparing her signature breakfast. Letha says, "I thought the smell of my biscuits would usher you out of bed."

"You're bringing back too many memories, Grandma."

"Well, I thought I would get up this morning and fix breakfast for the family. It has been a while since you've tasted Grandma's famous breakfast."

James comes running out of the bedroom. "Oh my gosh, I thought I was dreaming! Letha, that smells so good I might have to eat with my feet and hands."

Clara walks in. "Mama, you sure know how to get the day started off on the right foot."

Letha says, "Go wash up. Breakfast will be served in a few minutes."

After breakfast was over, Trevor slumps back in his chair. "I believe I have biscuit poisoning. My eyelids are overpowering me."

"I believe I feel like you, son," says James.

Clara says, "You lazy bums! Go to bed. Mom and I will clean the kitchen."

"Clara, I really enjoyed myself here this week. I'm so proud and happy that you found a great companion to share the rest of your life with," says Letha.

"Thank you, Mom. It really means a lot to me to hear you say that. James is a great husband and father. He's an outstanding role model for our son, and I love him with all my heart," replies Clara.

"I'm really excited about my grandson going off to college. Tell me, have you or James sat down with Trevor to talk to him about protecting himself against AIDS? This disease is spreading very rapidly in the United States, and I'm very concerned about his awareness of this disease."

"Mom, I don't think we have to be very concerned about our son. James and I both know our son is still a virgin. He is curious, but he's more focused on his career than girls right now."

"He's going off to college in another state where he will meet all kinds of women, and his curiosity is going to lead him to experimenting with his sexuality without fully understanding the consequences," replies Letha.

"Mom, James and I have talked with Trevor about the consequences of unprotected sex, and we also purchased him a pickle jar full of condoms that is under his bed collecting dust. Please don't worry about Trevor. He's a smart kid. We know he'll use protection when he decides to become sexually active."

"I hope you're right about this," replies Letha.

"Please don't worry about Trevor. Our son is very smart, and I'm sure he will make the right decisions when the time comes."

"For my peace of mind, please talk to him about AIDS," replies Letha.

"Okay, okay! James and I will talk to him about this before he leaves for college."

"Speaking of leaving, I need to get back home before it gets dark," says Letha.

"Okay, I will take you home as soon as I get dressed," replies Clara.

Trevor gets out of bed just in time to say goodbye to his grandmother. Letha says, "I'm so very proud of you. Take care of yourself and study hard in school."

"Grandma, you have my word that I will study hard, and I'm very happy I got the chance to see you. Thanks for the quilt."

"Tell your father I'll be back soon. I'm going to take Mom home."

He gets dressed, passes the message from his mother to his father, and takes a ride to his favorite spot for a little one-on-one quiet time.

There's a hazy overcast as he pulls up to Webster's Lake. In his mind, he can still hear and see all the laughter and excitement from the screaming seniors as they ran across the beach. He walks up the hill, deep into the arms of wilderness, until he once again comes upon the secluded lake. It is still so tranquil as he walks to the edge, disturbing its calm waters. His mind unlocks past memories as he stares out into the vast wilderness that cradles him. He often smiles as he reflects on several memorable occasions and wonders at the same time how time truly flies. His heart pounds like a drum as the memories of Crystal flood his mind. He envisions her gracefully dancing across the cool waters of the lake with the wind in her hair and her eyes as blue as the sky. His silence is broken by a low rumble in the distance as the clouds roll in like a blanket shadowing the forest. The rumble deepens its voice as rain begins to puncture the water's surface. He turns to run back to his car as the rain comes down in layers as if it were chasing him. He jumps into his car as the heavy drops of rain pound the roof like a heavy bass drum. He reclines his seat all the way back as the beat of the rain has a tranquilizing effect on his mind. The feeling doesn't last long as the sun sneakily peeks its way through the clouds, creating a steam bath as its rays wrap the forest in a blanket of heat.

He drives back home with a feeling of peace. James says, "Tyson called and said don't forget to pick him up at five thirty in the morning for his flight."

The phone rings again. It's Tyson, screaming, "Where the hell have you been, Geronimo? I've been calling all day."

"I took a journey to the hidden lake to visit the white buffalo, young one," Trevor says sarcastically.

"I just wanted to remind you about my flight tomorrow and how early we have to be there," says Tyson.

"I remember. Don't worry, I'll be there on time."

"Dude, I'm so tired of visiting family members I don't know what to do. I didn't realize I had so many cousins. Well, I'll see you in the morning. I'm going to bed," says Tyson.

Time ran the forty-yard dash as Trevor's alarm clock startles him out of bed. He drunkenly drags himself out of bed as the phone rings.

Tyson says, "Good morning, America! I just wanted to know if you were awake yet."

He replies in a scruffy voice, "I'm awake. I'll be there in a minute."

He arrives at Tyson's house finding him standing in the front yard with his bags and smiling like he's won a million dollars. They put the luggage in the car as his mother dries tears from her eyes.

Ramone says, "Son, give us a call as soon as you can and take care of yourself." Teresa hugs her son and runs back into the house with her face buried in her hands. Ramone says, "Don't worry, son. She'll be okay. You boys drive carefully and don't forget to call."

"Goodbye, Dad. I'll see you on Turkey Day," says Tyson. They drive off into the early morning darkness as Tyson says, "I can't wait to get to the academy to see Maria and let the journey begin."

"The time has finally arrived for us to grow up and become real men," says Trevor.

"Man, I'm so excited I don't know what to do. Hey, I picked up the perfect gift for you and me when I was at the mall, but don't open it until I'm on the plane in the sky. It would not be pretty to see two grown buff men crying," says Tyson. They pull up to the drop-off area at the airport. Tyson hands the attendant his tickets as she stamps his luggage. The two gentlemen hug each other like brothers and wish each other the best of luck in their adventures. As he walks through the doors to board the plane, he turns and yells, "I'll always be your brother!"

Trevor walks back to his car happy and sad as Tyson's plane illuminates the dark sky with flashing blue and white lights. He opens the gift Tyson gave him. It's a gold bracelet engraved with "Am I my brother's keeper?" on the top and "Yes, I am" on the bottom. He reclines his seat back as his heart pounds with a happy/sad feeling. He puts the bracelet on and turns back the hands of time to when they first met each other. A tear of sorrow warms his slightly cold cheek as he says, "Farewell, brother, farewell."

CHAPTER 21

Trevor spends the following weeks visiting friends and family until there's only days left before he's off to school. His beloved Possessed left a week ago by airfreight headed for San Diego. He spends the rest of his remaining days around his mother and father.

One night after dinner, Clara asks, "Trevor, how much do you know about AIDS?"

"I've heard that's a gay man's or crackhead's disease. Why are you asking me about AIDS? I'll never have to worry about that," he says.

"I know, son, but I just want to talk to you about it because your grandmother and I thought it might be an area of concern for your own safety and welfare."

"Mom, I'm not gay nor do I use drugs, so I don't think this conversation really applies to me."

"I know you're neither of those things, but it would make me feel a little bit more comfortable if you take some time to educate yourself about this dreadful virus."

"I'll look into it when I get to school," replies Trevor.

James says, "Enough talk about AIDS. I want to spend this last night with our son in peace. Now with that being said, let's fire up the old camera and have a few more laughs on our son's account."

The whole family, including Rusty, all pile up in the great room to watch several videos of Trevor and Rusty growing up through the years. Time quickly ticks away as they indulge themselves in family history. Video after video brings back years of memories and laughter until the last roll of tape plays out. They sit there for a moment looking at the bright white screen as their brains digest all the past memories of happiness, hoping that more will appear. James slowly moves from the couch to turn the video camera off as they look at one another with full hearts and teary eyes.

"Thank you, Mom and Dad. I really needed a good laugh tonight." He walks over to his parents, hugging them as if it were the last time they were going to see one another. Walking slowly down the corridor to his room, he turns watching his parents embrace each other in sadness. The sight of this is too much for him to bear. His eyes begin to flood with tears, and his heart beats with pain. He wants to turn and embrace them, but instead, he walks silently to his room where he lies motionless in a bed of anguish.

The 5:30 a.m. alarm jolts him from a pleasant dream. The house is motionless as Rusty looks up at him with a whimper and quietly lays his head back down on the plush carpet. Breakfast is once served with laughter and conversation, but this particular morning, breakfast is served bland as the four members of the house sit eating quietly. James says in a somber voice, "Son, do you have all of your things packed and ready to go? Your plane leaves in half an hour."

"Yes, sir."

Clara tries to uplift her spirit along with the rest of her family by telling silly little jokes as they drive to the airport. They all pretend to be happy on the outside, but on the inside, their hearts are slowly being torn apart. Just before they arrive at the airport, the weatherman issues a severe thunderstorm warning for the area. The warm wind begins to pick up as they unload his luggage. The sky is still so dark they can't see the thick, dark clouds that have formed around them.

The clerk at the desk checks him in and announces to all the passengers, "There will be a slight delay due to an immense storm that is currently in our area." A weather alert appears on the TV screen as they watch the weatherman issue tornado warnings along with heavy rain and golf ball-sized hail. He walks to the large airport windows in awe over the display of lightning that flashes across the dark sky, giving light for an instance to the darkness. The storm slowly creeps closer and closer as the winds begin to howl with force as they come in contact with the building. Hail begins to pound the roof and windows as if someone were hurling thousands of rocks at the same time. There's a loud roar of thunder that startles the people and shakes the building. A spectacular display of lightning continues to dance all around them. There's a brief silence, and then the rain falls from the heavens, pounding the roof like a stampede of wild horses. He returns to his seat next to his parents as they give him instructions to call them as soon as he gets to San Diego.

The airport announcer says, "The storm will move out of our area soon, and we'll begin to board the plane shortly."

A rush of excitement fills his heart. He hugs his parents, saying, "Mom, Dad, this is not a sad occasion. It's a joyous one. I'm about to begin a new chapter of my life, and that's exciting and scary to me, but I'll do my best to make the very best of my new life.

The announcer says, "We have clearance to start boarding the planes. All passengers, please have your tickets and a valid ID available before you board the plane."

They give each other a group hug as he gathers his luggage and begins to walk toward the entrance. He turns just before entering the ramp. "Thank you, Mom and Dad, for being the world's greatest parents. I love you with all my heart."

A beautiful stewardess checks his tickets and leads him to business-class seating where there are only five seats available. He thanks his parents for spending the extra money for such a comfortable, spacious flight to California. He sits down on the plush black leather that's as soft as a pillow. He puts his feet inside a cushiony footrest, reclining his seat back in style. The stewardess comes by with her beautiful, long legs and long, curly brunette hair, saying, "Excuse me, ladies and gentlemen, I would like to thank you on behalf of our pilots and Western Air for choosing us as your carrier to sunny San Diego, California. I would like to direct your attention to the movie screen where we'll show several movies for your entertainment pleasure. I would also like to call your attention to your seats that have several features that will make your flight even more enjoyable. The remote control that's in the tray holder in front of you allows you to recline your seat back to a soothing body massage. You have a heating pad to control the temperature if you get cold, a port for your headphones, and a satellite radio for your choice of music. Once again, I would like to thank you for flying Western Air. We'll be taking off shortly."

Trevor lays his head back, reveling in the luxury that surrounds him. The pilot announces over the intercom, "Good morning, ladies and gentlemen. We have clearance for takeoff. Please fasten your seat belts and let your seats all the way up in the upright position as our lovely stewardess instructs you on our safety features. This is a nonstop flight to San Diego, California, where the temperature is expected to be ninety-five degrees with clear skies and lots of sunshine. We would like to thank you for choosing Western Air. Please enjoy your flight."

His heart fills with a rush of excitement as the thrust of the jets pin him to his seat as they lift off into the dimly lit sky. He looks out the window waving at the small city he calls home. The bright lights from below get smaller and dimmer as they climb higher and higher through the patchy, cloudy sky. He reclines his seat back once more as the movie begins to play. He listens to a smooth alternative selection of R&B and jazz. The soulful music sets his mind on a wondrous voyage through time as he imagines what life will be like at Mira Mesa. He often smiles as he thinks of all the fun places he'll get a chance to visit—bigger malls, beaches, girls, girls, girls, and more girls. The thought sends shock waves of excitement through his body as the stewardess gently taps him on the shoulder.

"I see you're really enjoying yourself. Would you like for me to get you anything?"

"I'm sorry. I hope I'm not disturbing anybody," he says.

"Oh no, no, you're doing just fine. I was just teasing with you."

"Thank you. I would like a Sprite in the can, please."

The smooth grooves of the music and the comforts of the chair lure him into a quiet, motionless sleep as the four-hundred-passenger 747 glides through the sky. He awakens to a ringing, flashing, bright-red light displaying a seat belt. He removes the headphones from his ears as the pilot announces, "Good morning. We'll be landing shortly at International Airport in San Diego. Please return your seats back to the upright position, stow your trays, and thank you for flying Western Air."

Trevor steps off the plane, filling his lungs with the fresh smell of ocean air as he stares at the beautiful yachts in the marina across the street. He walks inside the airport, unconsciously staring at the massive number of people of all nationalities who surrounds him. He walks to the front desk. "Would you please tell me where airfreight pickup is located."

The attendant kindly replies, "Go to the end of the hall to the freight pickup window, and someone will assist you."

He walks to the counter, gives the pickup receipt to the cashier, and takes the keys to his beloved Possessed. He stops to stare for a moment at its beauty and grace as it sits there in its own little spot, patiently awaiting his arrival. He puts his luggage in the trunk, puts the key in the ignition, and shivers as its powerful V8 engine comes alive once again.

The guard at the front gate stops him. "May I help you?" He pulls out his student ID, and the guard says, "Go up the hill and take your first left. The freshman dorms are located at the bottom of the hill."

The campus is full of colorful banners that read, "Welcome, freshman students, to opportunity and success at Mira Mesa University." He's very excited to be here but sort of feels a little insecure parking his car among several exotic sports cars. He takes his luggage to his room, flopping himself across his bed, indulging in this real-life fantasy. He picks up the phone to call his parents.

James answers, "Hello, how is everything?"

"Dad, how did you know it was me?"

"I'm a psychic. How do you like California for the second time?"

"Dad, it's beautiful out here. I'm in my room right now trying to figure out if this is a dream or not."

"No, son, it's not a dream. It's what you and Tyson have dreamed about for so many years. Now it's time to enjoy the fruits of your labor, but don't get out of hand. You still have a long, winding road ahead of you."

"I won't forget, Dad. Tell Mom I said don't worry about me. I'm doing just fine." He hangs up the phone and walks back downstairs to finish unpacking his car. He's dazzled by the beautiful blue Dodge Viper with chrome rims.

A young man pokes his head up from beside the car, asking, "You like it?"

"Man, that is one badass ride," says Trevor.

"My dad bought it for me as a way to make up for all the time we never spent together. He thinks if he buys me enough expensive things, I will forgive him for the more important business trips he always had to take and all the whoring around he's done behind my mother's back," says the young man. Trevor looks at him, speechless, as the young man says, "My bad. I didn't mean to trouble you with this nonsense. My name is Chris."

"I'm Trevor. It's a pleasure to meet you."

"Hey, me and some friends of mine are going to Spice's tonight to see Lana, the anal porn star. You can drive my car if you want," says Chris.

"I'm really tired. I've had a long day, and I'm probably going to unpack my stuff and just chill out tonight. Catch me some other time, and we'll hang out," he replies.

"Cool, dude. I'll tell you what you missed tomorrow," says Chris.

He returns to his room dragging several cumbersome pieces of luggage behind him. He looks around trying to get an idea of where he wants to place things. A warm ocean breeze rattles his blinds. He steps to the window, pulling the blinds all the way up. The rays of the sun quickly fill every corner of his dimly lit room. He stands there for a moment, basking in the rays, watching the seagulls gracefully glide around the open sky on a hot summer breeze. He turns looking at his cluttered floor as he walks out the door to the beach to enjoy the day in peace.

The hot sand is soft to his feet as he walks along the quiet, secluded beach. Small waves gently roll into shore, crashing on the beach, leaving small schools of fish behind playing in the puddles. He looks out over the blue ocean, admiring the beautiful yachts anchored to the ocean's floor. He sits on the warm sand as the cool ocean water bathes his feet. His mind travels back to several memorable accounts that brought joy to his life. He smiles as a few happy tears roll down his pecan-colored cheeks, leaving a salty trail. He looks over his shoulder at the beautiful university and wonders how one man can be so lucky to have all these luxuries. He looks up as he hears the sound of a Jet Ski approaching the shore. He stands to his feet as a beautiful blonde says, "Hello, my name is Tara. My friends and I saw you sitting here all alone and wondered if you would like to hang out with us for a while."

"I'm Trevor, and I would love to."

"Hop on and hold on tight. Come on, don't be modest. I know you want to get closer than that. I won't bite you, I promise." He slides up closer to her until they fit snuggly against each other. "Yeah, baby! That's how Mama likes it." They race off toward the beautiful white yacht sitting so calmly in front of them. He steps aboard the boat anxiously as several ladies are lying out on the deck, bathing their beautiful, naked bodies in the hot California sun. "Ladies, I would like you to meet Trevor, a fine young gentleman I found on the beach," says Tara.

They all say, "Hello, Trevor. How are you?"

"Fine now," he says.

One of the ladies asks, "Why were you sitting on the beach all by yourself?"

"I'm a freshman at Mira Mesa University, and I really didn't feel like unpacking my luggage, so I decided to enjoy the day on the beach."

"Well, isn't this your lucky day to be surrounded by beautiful porn stars." She walks slowly toward him, taking her bikini top off. "Tell me, Trevor. Are they too small, too big, or just right?"

He crosses his hands in front of him so the other ladies won't recognize the lump that's rising in his pants. "I would have to say they're perfect."

Tara steps between the two of them with her soft perfectly round ass pressing against him. "Ladies, ladies, please control your hormones. He's our guest." She takes his hand. "Let me show you around my boat before these vampires try to suck you dry." They go below where several beautiful young ladies are gathered around a beautiful tint glass table, taking turns sniffing cocaine up their noses. This makes him feel very uncomfortable because he's never seen anybody use drugs like that in real life. "Do you want to try it? It sometimes helps the ladies calm down and relax before a video shoot," says Tara.

"No, thanks, I'll pass," he replies.

They walk into her bedroom elaborately decorated with beautiful silk curtains that have a very unique design. Her bed is draped in silk, and her carpet is beautiful and plush like mink. She lies down on the cool silk sheets, giving them a more appealing look. She looks at him with her sexy, beautiful eyes and pretty, pouty lips, saying, "Concubine is the name of my production company. I'm an adult film actress, producer, and star of one of the best-selling adult films. I've worked with several very successful adult film stars whom I've helped develop into mega movie stars and moneymakers. My latest star is Lana, who's making huge waves in the adult film industry. I can tell you have a lot of sex appeal that you should use to your advantage. I know Mira Mesa is very expensive, and I can help you pay your tuition with ease."

"The offer is flattering, but I have a full four-year scholarship from Mira Mesa. Besides, my parents would kill me if I did this," he replies.

"Very well, but the offer still stands if you decide to change your mind." She gets up off the bed taking out two huge posters of herself, autographs them, and gives them to him, saying, "Put these on your wall so you'll have something to remember me by."

Jenny, one of the many sexy women aboard the boat, enters the bedroom, saying, "Tara, Jeff called and said they're ready to start filming the new movie as soon as we get there."

Tara turns to him, asking, "Would you like to join us on the set to get an up close view of what it takes to be in the adult film industry?"

"Thanks for the offer, but I better get back to campus. I have a lot of work to do," he replies.

"Okay, maybe some other time. Take my business card. If you ever want to hang out sometime, just give me a call. I'm available to you anytime, anywhere," she replies.

He says goodbye to all the lovely ladies as they get back on the Jet Ski, returning to shore. He waves goodbye as she blows him a kiss. He looks at the posters walking back to his room, thinking what a hell of a day this has been. His fantasy ends as he enters his room of clutter. He sits on his bed after a successful battle of unpacking and placing his room in order. He ponders for a moment, holding Tara's posters in his hands. A commercial appears on TV of a beautiful black panther guarding its piece of plush tropical rain forest as timbermen try to cut down its home. He instantly falls in love with the fierceness of the animal crouching down on a small mound above, displaying its razor-sharp claws and sharp, flesh-eating teeth, daring anyone to violate its habitat. He jumps off the bed, grabs his keys, and runs out of his room.

There are several guys standing in front of the building as he hears one distinctly well-dressed individual say in a ritzy tone, "The janitor should park his cheap putt-putt in the back. It gives us a bad image." He laughs along with the rest of the gentlemen as he zooms out of the parking lot. He drives to a nearby mall where he frantically searches for the one store that will hopefully carry the items he's searching for. He stumbles across Zahra's, where he sees a beautiful full-color poster of a black panther. He enters to find the items he's searching for and walks out of the store with several bags in both hands. He quickly rushes back to campus to arrange his room before he forgets where to place everything. The dorm is quiet as he rushes to the elevator with both arms overflowing with bags. He quickly unlocks his door and immediately begins to decorate his room. Upon completion, he falls tirelessly across his bed where his eyelids defeat him as they close for the night.

The beautiful California sun peeking through a crack in the blinds awakes him. He rolls over rubbing his eyes, looking around his neatly decorated room as if he were a kid on Christmas Day. A hot shower, along with the smell of mountain-fresh shower gel, rejuvenates his body as he plans out his day. Stepping out of the shower, he opens the door, allowing the steam to escape as he clears his mirror. He walks to his neatly arranged closet, choosing his favorite blue jeans and a comfortable shirt. He walks downstairs to the game room, where he sees Chris and some other guys playing pool.

"What's up, Trevor? This is Mike and Joe, a couple of guys that went to Spice's with me last night to see Lana. Dude, we had so much fun last night! Lana is the hottest chick I've ever met in my whole life! I mean, her whole body is like fire! She totally mesmerized me and my wallet. I know I dropped at least two grand on that ass last night! Dude, she bent over in my face, and I thought I was going to have a fucking heart attack looking at that beautiful, heart-shaped ass! Dude, I wish you could've been there because words just can't describe the scene!" says Chris excitedly.

"Yesterday was very exciting and unusual for me also," replies Trevor.

"I don't find unpacking luggage exciting. Maybe unusual, but definitely not exciting," says Chris.

"I didn't unpack immediately. I thought the day was too pretty to be inside, so I went to the beach. I was sitting there alone admiring this beautiful big yacht in the distance. A few minutes later, I noticed a Jet Ski coming toward me. A beautiful, tall blonde asked me if I wanted to join her and some friends on her boat. I accepted the offer and found myself surrounded by some of the hottest babes in California."

Joe says, "Come on, dude, all jokes aside."

"I met Tara and a crew of porn stars yesterday, and I was the only guy aboard," says Trevor. They look at him and one another with an expression of disbelief on their faces. "Gentlemen, if you would kindly follow me, I would like to show you something," he replies.

They enter his room in shock as black lights illuminate it, giving it a cool scene. There's a colorful display of lava lamps on the entertainment center, with a huge poster of a black panther crouching down in attack position, displaying its sharp claws, red eyes, and fangs. A high-powered sound system sits behind a beautiful glass door with two huge subwoofers standing next to it, displaying two beautiful black ceramic panthers on top of each subwoofer. Chris walks into the bedroom in shock, gazing at two posters of Tara hanging on Trevor's wall above his bed, displaying her beautiful body from the front to back. Trevor walks in with the other gentlemen. They begin to drool at the sight of Tara totally nude with a heart-shaped chain hanging from her waist.

"Gentlemen, welcome to the Panther's Den," says Trevor. Chris turns to him, taking his wallet out, offering him $1,000 for both of the posters. He says in a cool voice, "Not for sale," as he smiles at the gentlemen standing before him.

"Dude, you have the coolest room on campus. I think we should designate this room as the official party capital," says Chris.

"So what's on the agenda today?" asks Trevor.

"We're thinking about touring Sunset Beach, where all the hottest babes are in abundance," replies Joe.

"Dude, I think you and your good luck should come with us," says Chris.

"Let me change clothes, and I'll meet you downstairs," replies Trevor.

He walks downstairs with his shirt off as they stare in amazement. He gives them a strange look, asking, "Why are you staring at me?"

"Dude, you look like one of those Greek gods. I mean, I could tell you work out, but I didn't know you were that chiseled. I know we're going to get a lot of babes now. He tosses Trevor the keys. "I would greatly appreciate it if Your Highness would drive my car," says Chris.

The drive to the beach is very exciting and scenic as the young men admire all the beautiful women, tall palm trees, and blue ocean water cruising down the California coast. Trevor leans back in the hot black leather seat, thrilled to see hundreds of beautiful women lying out in the sun, playing volleyball, and swimming in the cool blue ocean. A group of beautiful ladies wearing thong bikinis with high midsection-cut T-shirts on Rollerblades wave as they pass by, leaving the young men speechless and drooling over their perfectly shaped asses as they skate by.

Chris yells "Welcome to paradise!" as they gather their blankets from the cars.

"I think we should set up camp right next to those beautiful blondes straight ahead of us," says Joe.

They quickly proceed to the area where six sexy young ladies are enjoying the rays of the sun. Trevor takes his shirt off immediately, attracting the attention of the young ladies.

One of them says, "Excuse me, what's your name?"

"I'm Trevor, and these are my friends Chris, Joe, and Mike."

"I'm Christy, and these are my friends Casey, Shauna, and Lacey. Would you guys mind rubbing some lotion on our backs?"

"No, not at all," he replies. They look at him as if he were a king as they proceed to lotion down six of the hottest chicks on the beach.

"Trevor, untie my top for me, please," says Christy. He gently unties her bikini top, caressing her back in a circular motion with the sweet smell of coconut-scented tanning lotion. She begins to moan in a soft, sensual tone, saying, "That feels so good."

He looks at his buddies with a huge smile on his face. He leans over, saying, "Your back is complete. Is there anywhere else you would like me to put lotion?"

"Yes, she would like you to rub her ass next," says Shauna.

They laugh as Christy says, "I hope you don't mind." She reaches down by her side, untying her bottom, saying, "Please rub it in good. I don't want any lotion stains on my $500 suit."

He takes her bottom off, exposing her tanned cheeks. He looks at his friends admiring her curvy ass. A rush of passion flows heavily through his body as he massages the lotion deep into her soft, beautifully curved bronze ass. She lies there motionless as the touch of his strong hands seems to soothe her every emotion. Her body magnifies every stroke to the highest degree of sensual pleasure until the passion begins to physically overflow. She begins to move to the motion of his hands. Her heart rate speeds up, and she begins to breathe heavily. She turns over, exposing her D-sized altered breast as her body trembles with excitement. He takes a brief second to glorify the moment and the magnificent woman lying before him. She passionately whispers, "Please don't stop." He pours more lotion in his hands, carefully, gently caressing her beautiful breasts until her soft pink nipples stand erect. She begs, "More, more." Her body seems to convulse as she arches her back slightly off the blanket as he sensually glides his hands down the shapely contour of her hourglass frame.

His passion begins to elevate as he embarrassingly tries to hide his protruding third leg by crouching down lower to her body. The discomforting pain that he feels as his new leg tries to free itself is blocked out as he continues to focus his concentration on this goddess. They are both ready to explode as his hands drop below her belly button. Her thighs begin to separate slowly, awaiting his touch in agonizing anticipation. He gently maneuvers his hands between her soft thighs. She balls her fist full of sand as he continues to excite her with every stroke. The voice of passion can no longer contain itself as she screams out a passionate sigh of relief. Their friends stare at them as she grabs his hand, putting an end to a perfect moment. She puts her suit back on, saying, "I think I need to go for a quick swim to cool off some."

Shauna crawls over to him as he lies on the warm blanket, relishing the moment. She places her lips within inches of his, saying, "Men like you make me curious sometimes."

He looks at her confusingly as Mike says, "If you don't mind me asking, what exactly is that supposed to mean?"

"I'm sorry. We're from Santa Barbara University," she replies.

Joe stands up, yelling, "Oh, hell no! This isn't fair. I can't believe you're…"

"Somebody please tell me what's going on," says Trevor.

"Please forgive my friend. He's not from California. Trevor, Santa Barbara University is no-man's-land, or in simpler terms, they're all lesbians," replies Joe.

He sits there in complete silence for a moment as Christy approaches with beads of fresh saltwater running down her beautiful silhouette. She asks, "Why does everybody have sad faces? I just went for a swim!"

"I just told them our little secret," replies Shauna. Christy looks at Trevor with a shameful face as she gathers her belongings.

"We don't have a problem with that. We're lesbians too," says Trevor. They all laugh as the ladies continue to gather their things. "I'm serious. We're students at Mira Mesa University, and I would love to have each and every one of you visit us anytime you like," says Trevor.

Christy walks up to him. "You turn me on. Maybe I'll stop by sometime to finish what we started."

"Thank you for warming that ass up for me. I'll think of you tonight when we're all in bed together," says Shauna. They wave goodbye as the ladies jump into their jeep and drive off.

Trevor utters under his breath, "Tyson, I hope you're having better luck."

The guys gather around him, yelling, "You're the man!"

Mike asks, "Did that ass feel as good as it looked?"

"I thought I was rubbing a pillow," replies Trevor.

"I don't know what it is about you, man, but you've accomplished something that no other man I've ever known has done before. Everybody knows about the women at Santa Barbara University. They're lesbians, and you almost waxed this chick and her friends too," says Chris.

"Brother, I got to give you props because I don't think we would have gotten a chance to rub all over her friends if it wasn't for you," says Mike.

"Don't thank me. Thank Joe," says Trevor.

The gentlemen continue to stroll down the beach, flirting with several beautiful ladies. The sun accentuates Trevor's complexion, turning his skin color into a dark-bronze color. He receives lots of attention from both males and females as everybody admires his chiseled frame. His friends admire him for directing all the attention in their direction as they pass several sunbathers staring at them.

"Dude, you're the coolest dude I've ever met. Remind me to take you with me whenever we go babe hunting," says Mike. He gloats for a moment as every eye makes him feel like the Big Kahuna of Sunset Beach.

The sun is about to set, and the gentlemen find themselves standing beneath a huge cliff. Several couples are scaling its winding, narrow paths to the top.

"Why is everybody walking to the top of this cliff?" asks Trevor.

"This is the beautiful and famous Sunset Cliffs. It's where several couples come to watch the sun set beneath the ocean," replies Chris.

"I think it's something you should see. With your luck, we'll probably run into some bad chicks that need our love and affection," says Joe.

It's fascinating to see the multitudes of people standing atop this cliff just to see the sun set. A group of young ladies drive up, casually laughing and teasing one another. One of them approaches Trevor and quickly wraps his arms around her. "I hope you don't mind. I just couldn't resist the opportunity," she says.

"No problem. Are you comfortable?" he asks.

"Are you kidding? How could a girl not feel comfortable wrapped in these arms?" she replies.

The sun begins to shift its color from bright yellow to a beautiful reddish-orange luster. The ocean seems so peaceful as the reddish-orange rays cast its beautiful array of light across its body of life. He stands there in total amazement with his arms wrapped snuggly around a stranger, watching this fiery giant disappear beneath the ocean. A gentle breeze blows as the stars and the moon begin to take their positions in the heavens. The sky is clear and peaceful as she turns, saying, "I'm sorry for throwing myself on you, but I just couldn't resist the moment."

"It's okay. I've never held a beautiful woman in my arms and watched the sun set all at the same time. Believe me when I say it's a pleasure," he replies.

"You're not from around here, are you?" she asks.

"No, I'm not. I'm from Alabama. I'm a student at Mira Mesa University. I came out here with my friends today to enjoy the beach," he replies.

"My name is Sonia, and I'm a dancer at Chick's. My friends and I stop here every afternoon before we go to work to enjoy the beautiful sunset. It sort of warms us up for the night. Here are some free passes for you and your friends to come watch us dance tonight if you're not busy."

"I'm sorry, but I won't be able to come tonight. Tomorrow is the first day of class, and I have to get up early," he replies.

"That's okay, maybe some other time. Just call me before you come so I can make the night extra special for you," she replies. She gently lifts herself up on her tiptoes to kiss him as her friends blow the horn, yelling, "Let's go, horny! We're going to be late!"

His friends rush over to him, screaming, "They're strippers! They're strippers!"

Chris bows to him, saying, "You're a king among kings."

CHAPTER 22

The first day of class is exciting to him as he stands at the front entrance of his dorm. The morning is cool with a hovering damp mist that dimly shades the sun. The smell of fresh ocean water fills his nose as he walks past several students laughing and talking as they scamper off to class. He quickly walks to building 112, checking his schedule to see what room his first class is in. The building is magnificently designed with huge pillars and uniquely designed windows. The front entrance of the doorway presents grand writing above, saying, "Enter as a student, leave as a scholar." He enters the building in awe, gazing upon the beautiful decor that surrounds him. The halls are peaceful and quiet as he looks upon huge portraits of professors dating from the early 1800s to the present time.

An aristocratic voice startles him as he turns looking at a well-dressed gentleman approaching him, saying, "Hello, young sir. I'm Professor Black, and the pictures you're admiring are my father, my grandfather on the next one, and my great-grandfather on the next. My picture will hang here among these great educators someday when I retire. I've taught thousands of young minds like yours to become highly trained, aggressive businessmen and women in cruel corporate America, where only the strong survive. Now tell me, sir, are you lost or are you here to become one of America's world-class businessmen?"

He replies in a strong, sturdy voice, "I'm Trevor O'Riely, and I'm here to become one of America's world-class businessmen."

Professor Black takes a look at his class schedule and begins to chuckle. "It's going to be a pleasure having you in my class. I admire your admiration and discipline already. Class doesn't begin for another thirty minutes. Why don't you join me for a cup of hot chocolate in our lovely cafeteria?"

The two gentlemen walk across campus as Professor Black lectures him about what it takes to survive in the business world. While they're enjoying the smell and taste of a hot cup of cocoa, Professor Black lowers his cup, saying, "Look across the bridge at the building that towers over all others. That magnificent building belongs to J. D. Hughes, a student that I had the pleasure of educating thirty years ago. He was sharp as a tack, soaking up every bit of information he could pick from my brain. We have remained friends now for some years. He credits me for his success. For years, I've watched him build that company from a little one-story office building into the eighty-story office building you see now. I've referred many of my top students, over the years, to work for him in several businesses that he owns. You have that same sparkle in your eyes that he still has today. I wish his son were more like him. It would give me great pleasure if you would allow me to refer you to him when the time is right."

"I will do my very best to make that dream become reality," replies Trevor.

Professor Black glances at his watch, saying, "I've enjoyed the conversation so much that time has almost eluded us. I'll see you in class."

CHAPTER 23

Chris is running in the same direction, entering the building and classroom at the same time. They sit next to each other, admiring the lovely ladies that surround them. "Dude, this is heaven. The majority of our class is female," says Chris.

"I love California," says Trevor.

Professor Black enters the room. "Good morning, class. My name is Professor Joe Black. It's going to be a pleasure developing your young minds into powerful business minds for hungry corporate America. As your first assignment, I would like you to write a five-page paper on what you think it takes to become successful in business. Your papers will be due on Friday. Have a nice day." He gathers his things as the students look around at one another, wondering if class is over. On his way out, he looks at the class, yelling, "Get out of here! Class dismissed!"

Chris asks, "Trevor, do you have any more classes today?"

"I have another business class at eleven o'clock. I hope that professor is as cool as Professor Black," replies Trevor.

"I'll see you this afternoon, and we'll go to this hot spot where I used to hang out when I was in high school," says Chris.

"I'll go if girls are going to be there," replies Trevor.

"All you can eat and then some," says Chris.

He has a few hours before his next class begins, so he decides to go back to his room for a while. The phone rings as he enters his room. To his surprise, it's Tyson. He yells, "What up, homey! How's the academy life treating you?"

"I love it. Every day is a new adventure. How are you enjoying sunny San Diego?" asks Tyson.

"I'm having a blast. The campus is awesome, and I've met so many babes. Before you ask, yes, I'm… still…well, you know," he says.

"You remember that chick I told you I met when I came to visit the academy? Well, we're dating now, and I'm happy to inform you that my cherry has been popped and I'm no longer a big V. Oh shit! I got to go. I hear my drill instructor coming. I'll talk to you later. Goodbye," he replies.

Trevor smiles as he hangs up the phone, wondering will the time ever come to retire his virginity. He sets his clock to alarm half an hour before class as he stretches out on his plush leather couch for a peaceful nap.

That afternoon, Trevor meets Chris in the lobby to go to this enchanting place of beautiful women. As they walk toward the doors, three well-dressed gentlemen fling the doors open in their faces. Trevor looks at the gentlemen as they give some sort of a smirk passing by.

"If you don't already know, the guy in the front is Todd Hughes. He thinks he rules the world because of his father, J. D. Hughes, an alumnus of this university with more money than the president of the United States. His contribution to this university allows us to live in a life of luxury for four years," says Chris.

"Professor Black and I were talking about him this morning. He was a student in one of his business classes," replies Trevor.

"Put all that behind you. We have more important things to do," says Chris.

CHAPTER 24

"This place is magnificent. I never would have believed an ice cream store could produce so many beautiful flavors," says Trevor.

"Dude, this isn't your ordinary ice cream store. This is Candy Stripers, where they produce the world's best ice cream and babes all under the same roof. We should sit at the counter so we can get a full view of all the babes that come in," replies Chris.

They sit there admiring every rose who walks in and out of the doors, wondering if life could be any better than this. Trevor's eyes capture the essence of beauty seated in the corner under the bright-neon ice cream sign that seems to point them out. He nudges Chris. "Look back in the corner under the neon ice cream sign. Do you see what I see?"

"Whoa, they're almost as pretty as the posters on your wall," replies Chris.

"I believe they're psychic, or they can hear very well because they're requesting our presence. Remember, first impression, best impression," says Trevor. They walk casually to the back where the young ladies are sitting and introduce themselves.

One of them says, "I'm Lauren, and this is my friend Naomi. You guys look lonely sitting up there by yourselves. We thought you might need a little company. Where are you from?"

"We're students at Mira Mesa," replies Trevor.

"What a coincidence! So are we. You must be freshmen because I don't believe I've ever seen you before," replies Lauren.

"We are," he replies. He glances over at Naomi, instantly trapped by her beautiful blue eyes and charismatic smile.

"Chris, I think Trevor and Naomi need some time alone because he's talking to me but staring at her," says Lauren.

They smile at each other as he says, "I'm sorry, Lauren. I didn't mean to be rude."

"It's okay. I know she's pretty. Chris and I will leave you two alone," she replies.

They sit eating ice cream, gazing into each other's eyes, consuming every word that flows from each other's lips. Time eludes them as they enrapture each other in a chemical bond that will flourish into a beautiful chain reaction. Simultaneously, they take their eyes off each other, discovering light has turned to darkness.

"Time flies when you're having fun. May I offer you a ride back to campus?" he asks.

"That would be nice," she replies.

"I guess Lauren and Chris found their way back to campus," he says.

"If I know Lauren like I think I do, she's probably well…never mind," she replies.

He escorts the lovely lady out to his car where they find a piece of torn paper folded in half that reads, "T., Lauren gave me a lift back to campus. I'll see you in class tomorrow."

She laughs, saying to herself, "You little slut." He parks his car, opens her door, and walks her to the front door of her dorm. She says, "Thank you for eating ice cream with me. I had a great time."

"It's my pleasure. I enjoyed our conversation. Maybe we can do it again sometime when you're not busy," he replies.

"Sure, I would like that. Good night," she says.

He returns to his car feeling like this could be the beginning of something great.

Mike and Joe are standing outside in the parking lot when Trevor arrives.

Joe asks, "Where the hell have you been, and where the hell is Chris?"

"We went to Candy Stripers. He wanted to take me there to get a firsthand look at all its delicious flavors."

"You two are snakes in the grass. How come you didn't come and get us so we could enjoy some ass and tits too?" says Mike.

"Don't blame me. I had no idea what Candy Stripers was until we got there."

"Okay, maybe we can cut you some slack, but Chris has some explaining to do," says Mike.

"Speaking of Chris, is he in his room? I've got something I need to talk to him about," says Trevor.

"What's her name? Dude, don't look at me like that. I know it's a bad chick because you're glowing like a glowworm," says Mike.

"We met two of the hottest babes at Candy Stripers. Her name is Naomi Spencer, and she's a student at this university," he says.

"Did you say Naomi? Dude, she's in my history class. She's the hottest babe on this campus," says Joe.

"Okay, now I'm really mad, Let's go wake this punk up and torture him for leaving us," says Chris. They run upstairs to his room, pounding on his door, but there is no answer. They pound and yell louder, and still there's no answer.

"Hey, guys, maybe we can all go out there this weekend and have a blast. I've got to go so I can start writing my paper for class," says Trevor.

The next day, Chris, looking like a street bum, staggers into class five minutes late. His hair is scattered wildly on his head, eyes red as fire, shirt half in / half out of his pants, and mismatched flip-flops on his feet. He looks at Trevor, whispering, "Dude, you're not going to believe what happened to me last night."

Halfway through the lecture, Professor Black walks down the aisle, dropping several books on the floor, making an unusually loud, thunder-like sound. Chris jumps as if his life were at stake. The class laughs as Professor Black says, "Mr. Gray, in order to do well in my class, you must stay awake."

"I'm sorry, sir," says Chris.

That night, Trevor hears a knock on his door. Chris, Mike, and Joe all poke their heads in, at the same time saying, "What's up, dude!" He laughs, inviting the gentlemen in.

"Dude, your room smells like a scented candle shop. Are you expecting a hot babe tonight?" asks Mike.

"No, I always keep my room like this."

"Dude, you're killing me with these posters of Tara on your wall. I would have a hard-on every night if these posters were in my room," says Mike.

"Mike, step away from my posters," says Trevor.

"Dude, thanks for trying to keep me awake in class this morning. I had a hell of a night with Lauren," says Chris.

"What happened?" asks Trevor.

"After we left you and Naomi, we went back to their room and had a few drinks. The next thing I know, she pops out of the bathroom with this see-through gown on and nothing under it! Dude, she's a sex maniac. We did it four times, and she was still begging for more. I must admit, she wore my ass out, and I still haven't fully recovered yet," says Chris.

Joe says, "Yeah, I forgot to tell you thanks for leaving us."

"My bad, man. It was a spur-of-the-moment kind of deal. We can all go again this weekend," says Chris.

"Well, I'm happy that one of us got lucky," says Trevor.

"You mean you and Naomi didn't do anything?" asks Chris.

"Not a damn thing, but that's okay. I got the chance to get to know her a little bit better. As they say, good things come to those who wait," says Trevor.

"Yeah, whatever, you still went home with blue balls," says Joe.

They all laugh as Trevor says, "Laugh all you want. My day is coming."

That Friday, as class ends, Professor Black says, "Trevor, would you mind sticking around for a moment. I need to speak with you."

"I'll see you tonight, dude," says Chris.

The classroom is clear and quiet as Professor Black says, "I did a little research on you, and I'm very impressed with your educational background. You've already taken most of your entry-level freshman courses when you were in high school. That was very smart thinking, and it places you as a sophomore at the end of this semester. I took the liberty of doing you a favor. I had a talk with one of my most captivating students, and he's thrilled to meet you."

"Thank you, sir," he replies.

"This envelope is the key to all your dreams and success," says Professor Black.

He takes the elaborately designed envelope from the professor as he walks out the door to the foyer. He sits down on a bench and opens the envelope. It's a personal invitation from J. D. Hughes, inviting him to a banquet that he's having at his house on Saturday. He's so excited he begins to dance to an audience of paintings hanging from the walls. He leaves the building in a superhigh spirit as he sees a familiar face walking toward him.

"Hello, Naomi. How are you?" he asks.

"I'm doing fine," she replies.

"May I have your phone number so I can call you sometime?"

"Sure, 701-3645. What are you doing later on this afternoon?" she asks.

"I'm going out tonight with Chris and a few other friends to some bar," he replies.

"Don't get too drunk."

"Oh no, no, I don't drink. I'm the designated driver. Do you want to come with us?"

"No, I don't want to spoil your guys' party. Give me a ring, and maybe we can get together some other time," she replies.

"You said it, and I'm going to hold you to it," he replies. He watches her angelic figure disappear across campus, turning periodically, giving him a picture-perfect smile.

That night at Tango's, the gentlemen drink and make fun of one another's drunkenness as they flail around the bar, further intoxicating the air with their foul breath. Trevor's attention goes toward a very sexy woman seated at the bar. Her tight black skirt accentuates her figure, along with a split on either side that further exposes her shapely legs. He stalks her with his eyes as she gets up to walk to the ladies' room. Her sexy figure locks him in a trance as he watches her walk. He reaches back blindly with his hand, searching for his glass of Sprite. His chest and throat begin to burn like fire as he mistakenly takes a drink of Vodka on the rocks. He clutches his chest, coughing and gagging. He turns around quickly grabbing his glass of Sprite, consuming all of it in one gulp to ease the burning sensation he feels inside. His friends laugh uncontrollably as he tries to recover from his first rendezvous with alcohol.

She appears again. He stops to stare at her grace and beauty as she walks back to her seat. Her skirt inches up further, exposing her beautiful thighs as she crosses her legs. She glances across the bar, admiringly watching his eyes caress her body. She begins to entice him more by puckering her beautiful lips, spreading lip gloss across them. She begins to rub her legs in a sensual way, peering at him through beautiful hazel eyes and perfectly curved eyelashes. She glides the tip of her tongue over her top lip, puckering them in a beautiful, kissable fashion. He begins to walk in her direction with his eyes locked on hers. He feels a brief rush of wind whisk by him. Todd rushes up, hugging her, saying, "Mother, you look fantastic."

He quickly returns to his table, appalled, saying, "Gentlemen, this night has come to an end."

The drive home is nauseating, listening to the horrible songs of three drunken men. A police officer pulls up next to them, laughing at the off-key singing. He gives Trevor a thumbs up as he races away on his motorcycle. The quiet parking lots of the dorm erupt with laughter and more singing as they fall out of the car one by one. He drags his friends to their rooms, placing trash cans next to their beds in case of an emergency. Disappointed by tonight's events, he walks back to his room, where he dives on his plush black couch and dozes off to sleep.

The next morning, he awakens to the refreshing smell of tropical mist air freshener and a gentle knock on his door. He quickly runs to the door thinking it's one of his drunken silly friends. He opens the door to a well-dressed gentleman saying, "Good morning, sir. This is your attire for this evening's banquet at J. D. Hughes's estate. The banquet will start promptly at 7:00 p.m. Have a good day, sir."

He slowly walks back to his bedroom, carefully placing the bag on his bed. He unzips the bag, exposing a beautiful black tuxedo with cuff links, shoes, and a silky black bow tie to match. The excitement begins to radiate through his body as he jumps up and down uncontrollably. He takes a note protruding from the left pocket, reading, "Please be downstairs at 6:30 p.m. The car will be waiting for you." His mind, body, and soul are eager with anticipation as he watches every minute tick slowly off the clock. He tries to relax by watching TV, but all he could hear were silly questions in his head repeating themselves. He paces back and forth in his room, trying to find something to occupy his mind. He walks to his window recognizing the sun has hidden itself behind dark-gray clouds and the eminent rays of sunshine are now threatening flashes of light. In an odd sort of way, this soothes his mind as he watches the essence of flashing light display themselves in an array of art across the gloomy sky. Large drops of water begin to pound the ground and splash against his windows, creating a soothing sound. The heavens roar like a lion in the jungle as the raindrops sing a sweet melody, calming his mind and body as he lay across his bed. The clouds begin to disappear as the rays of the sun slowly creep between the blinds, filling his room with light. He awakens disoriented and alarmed, scuffling to find his clock. His blood pressure goes down when he realizes he has two hours before his ride shows up. He lays his tuxedo out on his bed, piece by piece, as the rush of excitement swells up once again. He rehearses in the shower as the hot water seems to calm and relax his mind and body. He wipes a clear spot in the steam-filled mirror, saying to himself, "Be calm, cool, and collected." He enters his bedroom, dressing himself as every piece seems to fit perfectly. He glances at the clock as he slips his feet into the comforts of his shoes. He takes one last look at himself in the mirror as he walks out the door. Every eye stops and every mouth opens as he walks downstairs to the lobby to await his ride.

One of the ladies says, "Hey, handsome, can I be your date tonight?"

He smiles, replying, "Maybe some other time. I'm going to an invitation-only banquet tonight hosted by Mr. J. D. Hughes."

A young gentleman makes his way through the crowd, saying, "Excuse me, but did I hear you say you're going to the one and only richer than rich J. D. Hughes's banquet?"

"That's correct," he replies.

Someone yells, "Man, that's one smooth limousine!"

The driver enters the lobby, saying, "Your car is waiting, sir." The driver escorts him to the car as an entourage of students stand outside chatting to each other as if he were some big rock star leaving a concert.

His heart flutters as the car pulls up in front of a magnificently designed house. The driver says, "Right this way, sir." He steps out of the car, glimpsing a beautiful familiar figure approaching him. She hugs him tightly as the fragrance and the touch of her body sends his mind into a sexual spiral. She asks in a soft, sweet voice, "Do you like the tuxedo? I personally picked it out for you."

He looks into her beautiful eyes, saying, "Yes, ma'am, thank you for such a fine choice."

She smiles, saying, "Please call me Elizabeth." She takes his hand as they enter the house. He tries to keep his composure as his eyes wander around the most magnificent house he has ever seen. He smiles nervously as she stops him in the middle of the hall, "Do you think I'm pretty?"

His heart seems to have stopped beating for a split second as he replies, "I think you're beautiful."

She smiles as they enter the large ballroom where JD smiles, saying, "Ladies and gentlemen, may I have your attention please. I would like to introduce you to Trevor O'Riely, a fine young gentleman who's my distinguished guest of honor. He attends Mira Mesa University, where many of us are proud alumni. Trevor was brought to my attention by our very own well-respected Professor Joe Black. Joe tells me this young man reminds him so much of me when I was a young student at Mira Mesa. I was honored and humbled at the same time. I invited him here tonight as my guest of honor to offer him an intern position at Hughes Enterprises during his junior year."

The crowd begins to cheer as he is blown away by the announcement. He steps up to the podium with confidence, saying, "Thank you, Mr. Hughes. It's an honor to stand here tonight in the presence of

California's most well-respected business leaders to receive a gift such as this. I accept your offer, Mr. Hughes, and I will continue to strive for success in the classroom and at Hughes Enterprises." He steps away from the podium, asking, "May I use your restroom? All of this excitement has given me a full bladder."

"Sure, son. Go to the top of the stairs, turn left, and go straight down the hall. Hurry back, there's something I want to show you," replies JD.

He walks up the spiraling stairwell, admiring the beauty that surrounds him. He enters an elaborately decorated bathroom that looks like the size of a football field. He admires all the gold finishings on the sinks and towel holders. The floor is completely designed in black marble, with a huge shower and swimming pool-like bathtub in the corner. The walls are designed with beautiful paintings, and the ceilings are painted in a beautiful mythological design of the Greek gods. He hears a beautiful melody coming from one of the rooms. He quietly peeks through the door at Elizabeth standing in the mirror.

She says, "Please come in." She's dressed in black stockings that accentuate her beautiful legs, a black garter belt, with matching bra, and black high heels. He stands there motionless as this beautiful woman begins to approach him. The fragrance of her body mesmerizes him as she whispers in his ear, "Do you still think I'm pretty?"

He replies very quickly, "You're gorgeous, Elizabeth."

She looks passionatcly into his eyes, kissing him with her beautiful ruby-red lips. He stands still, confused, not knowing what to do as she whispers, "Please don't be afraid. My husband doesn't give a damn what I do. Most of the time, he doesn't even know I exist."

He steps back, saying, "I'm sorry, Elizabeth, but I can't do this."

"It's okay, I understand," she replies. She wipes the lipstick from his lips as he returns downstairs where JD is entertaining several of his guests.

He turns as Trevor approaches, saying, "There you are. I thought for a moment I was going to have to send a search party for you. Come with me. I want to share a little secret with you." They walk through the palace to the garage were a fleet of magnificent chariots are on display. JD says, "These are just a few of my toys. I have a very special one that you will truly appreciate in the next garage." JD flips the lights on, but there's nothing there but a gray cement floor. He looks at JD as the floor begins to separate, exposing a beautiful '67 Shelby GT500. He drops to his knees, clasping his hands together in amazement, as beauty and grace display itself. "My daddy slaved in the Kentucky mines for years in order to buy me this car. He was proud of me for choosing school instead of the mines." He throws Trevor the keys, saying, "Let's take her for a spin."

He revels in the grace of this beautiful machine as they slowly leave the garage. "Elizabeth will wonder where we are," says Trevor.

JD smiles. "Elizabeth is a lovely woman who loves to entertain. She probably won't even miss us. Take a left at the top of the hill. There's something I want to show you." They park in front of a beautiful beach house hidden behind palm trees, overlooking the vast blue ocean beneath. "This is my little getaway when I need some time away from the world. You, my son, are privileged because I'm going to give you the keys to this palace and all its luxuries. You may come here anytime you like, but you must promise me you'll take care of it and never share our little secret with anyone except that special someone," says JD. He drops the keys in Trevor's hands as he rushes to the door, entering His Majesty's palace. His heart fills with excitement as he travels through the palace's astonishing layout. "I hardly even know you, and I feel as if you're blood of my blood. In simpler words, I see myself through you twenty years before. Your presence is charged with enthusiasm and ambition just as I was when I was your age. I like that. I wish I could teach my own son how to have the same drive and enthusiasm," says JD.

A startling vibration in JD's coat pocket ends a brief moment of silence as the two gentlemen stand behind huge decorated stained plate glass windows overlooking a quiet, calm ocean. "Excuse me for a moment. I have to take this call," says JD. Trevor stands there, tranquil, trying to digest this afternoon's events. JD reenters the room. "I'm sorry, but I have to leave. There's a matter of business that I must take care of. Would you mind giving me a ride to the office?"

"You have to go to the office at this hour?" asks Trevor.

JD smiles. "Son, you will soon learn that business is a twenty-four-hour job with very few breaks or holidays. I tell you what, take me back home. This could be an all-nighter, and I know you have more important things to do."

The party is still rumbling on as they pull into the garage. Elizabeth meets them in the ballroom with the same captivating smile, saying, "There you are, darling. The guests are having a marvelous time. Oh, look, darling, it's Judy, the mayor's wife. Excuse me, I'm going to say hello."

JD looks at Trevor. "That's my wife, such a lovely entertainer. Well, I hope you've enjoyed tonight's episode. It's a pleasure to finally meet you, and remember, my palace is your palace. Please feel free to visit anytime. I have to go to the office now. Joan will take you back when you're ready."

He stares at Elizabeth in her beautiful ball dress as she entertains a host of guests. He smiles as he takes a glass of wine from the server's tray, walking toward the door. Joan is waiting outside by the car. "Are you ready to leave, sir?"

He looks back through the glass doors at the crowd. "Yes, Joan, I believe I'm partied out." Joan laughs as he quietly closes the door. The campus is quiet as he gets out of the limousine, waving goodbye to Joan. He walks quietly upstairs to his room and quickly dresses for bed.

The next morning, Trevor is rudely awakened by loud laughter and banging on his door. He stumbles to the door where Chris and the crew are pounding him with questions about the party.

"Can I at least take a piss before I'm interrogated?" he asks. The gentlemen wait eagerly as he returns from the restroom, clearing his throat as if he were about to give the inaugural speech. They're enthused and happy to hear detail for detail about last night's events.

Chris says, "That's it, I don't care if today is Sunday and we have to go to class tomorrow. This calls for a celebration, and we're going to Spice's tonight to see Lana."

"Who's this Lana chick you always talk about?" asks Trevor. They look at him like he's an alien.

Chris yells excitedly, "Are you from outer space? She's the hottest porn star in the world! She's three times hotter than Tara, her eyes are the color of heaven, and her ass is rounder than the roundest peach."

"Enough talk about Lana. I'm getting a hard-on. All in favor of seeing Lana tonight, raise your right hand. Well, it looks like you're going to have a wonderful experience tonight, Trevor," says Mike.

"Okay, okay, I'll go if it's going to get you guys off my back. She better be all you guys pump her up to be," he replies.

"I bet you one of Tara's posters she'll blow your mind," says Chris.

"Deal, I'll give you the one of your choice, but if you lose, you're going on a date with Cafeteria Kim," says Trevor. They cringe at the thought and sight of that picture in their minds.

"Deal, that poster is going to look so sweet on my wall," says Chris.

"You're going to feel so sour when Kim engulfs you between her King Kong-sized ass cheeks," replies Trevor. They all laugh leaving his room.

"We'll see you at eight o'clock," says Chris.

CHAPTER 25

The night is calm, and the warm breath of the wind blows gently, carrying the fresh smell of the deep blue ocean. They're all excited to be traveling in style in a brand-new, fully loaded Range Rover that Chris's father bought for him. The parking lot is almost full as several ladies and gentlemen scurry in to see Lana. The bouncer at the door looks like Goliath as he checks them with a metal detector. The club is very elaborate inside with an array of lights that illuminate the eight stages, plush black leather couches that surround each stage, and of course, the most beautiful waitresses and bartenders all dressed in black lingerie. Trevor is so taken by the scenery that Chris has to guide him to their table.

The house turns black as a beautiful voice and the sound of high heels approach the center stage. Dim lights begin to appear, outlining her vivacious silhouette on stage. The house begins to rumble with whistles and yells as the beautiful figure begins to take on more of a shape as the lights begin to get brighter. She says in a soft, sexual voice, "Hello, ladies and gentlemen. Many of you may know me by a selection of adult movies that I've starred in. Here are a few to get your juices flowing: *Bottoms Up*, *Horny Coeds*, *Naughty Housewives*, and my favorite, *Rear Entry*. Now if any one of you fine gentlemen or ladies can tell me who I am, I have a special surprise for you."

A tall gentleman from the back stands up, yelling, "You're Tara!"

The house lights go up as she stands there in a red-and-white Candy Striper outfit, sucking on a candy thermometer. She raises her hand to quiet down the house. "What's your name, stud?"

"Joe!"

"Well, Joe, why don't you bring up a chair because you're about to receive the ultimate lap dance. I hope your girlfriend doesn't get too jealous," says Tara.

"I don't have a girlfriend. I'm here celebrating my divorce from the wicked witch," he yells.

"Well, strap yourself in because this could be a rough one. Oh, I forgot to mention, feel free to feel or lick anything you like," she says.

The house lights go down as the music and cheering goes up. Tara lifts her long legs high above his head, straddling him, ripping her top open, exposing her beautifully enhanced breasts. She grabs the back of his head, forcefully rubbing his face between two soft twin peaks. The crowd goes wild as Tara turns the temperature up with her exotic dancing. When the song ends, she's fully nude sitting in his lap as the crowd chants his name. She stands up, saying, "Let's give another round of applause for Joe." Goliath steps on stage, covering her with a beautiful gown. He lifts Joe off the stage still seated and smiling in his chair. "Wow, that was fun! Now I'd like to introduce to you the main attraction of tonight. She's a gorgeous woman whom I've had the pleasure of working with on several occasions. She's one of my closest friends. I've watched her mold herself into one of the hottest adult film stars ever. Ladies and gentlemen, I'm pleased to introduce Lana!"

The lights are dimmed, and the sound of a thousand lions fill the room with their beastly roar. Smoke fills the room as a beautiful queen appears. She's dressed in a beautiful two-piece bathing suit dazzled with sparkling stones that shine like diamonds, with glass high heels to match. Trevor is so taken with her beauty he steps closer to the stage to get a better look. She turns as her sky-blue eyes lock with his light-brown eyes. He stumbles back gasping for air as if he were having a heart attack. She screams and stumbles back as Goliath quickly steps on stage, trying to figure out what's going on. The lights go all the way up as the crowd looks around in a confused state.

Trevor walks on stage. "Crystal, is that you?"

Goliath turns with fury in his eyes, charging toward him.

She yells, "Wait! He's okay." She walks up to him with tears streaming down her beautiful face, embracing him in her loving arms. He quickly wipes the tears away, kissing her soft lips. His friends and the rest of the audience are going wild as he embraces a goddess. She whispers in his ear, "Please wait for me in my dressing room. I don't want you to see me like this."

He looks deep into her beautiful blue eyes, nodding as he walks backstage to her dressing room. Her room is filled with beautiful roses of all colors, giving it a very pleasant smell and look. He lies down on the couch, listening to the crowd yell and scream as the empty space in his heart is filled once again. The thought of her makes him twitch like a junky as he anticipates her arrival. He could hear nothing but screams and cheers as the door opens and the lady of his life enters. He immediately says, "You're so beautiful."

She places her hands over her face and begins to sob. "I'm so ashamed of what I've become. I hate myself."

"Hold on, hold on. I believe I just gave you a compliment," he says.

"I know. I'm sorry. I truly believe that you're the only man that says that from the heart. I just don't know how much longer I can do this," she replies. She begins to cry uncontrollably as he hugs her tightly in his arms.

"Listen, I know this place we can go that's so beautiful you'll forget all of your problems. Don't ask any questions. Just get dressed and let me be your chauffeur."

The night is still pleasant when he drives her to the place where they'll have peace and solitude from the world.

She says, "Wow, I always knew you would do very well in life."

"This isn't my house. It belongs to a well-known friend of mine," he says.

"And who might this friend be?" she asks.

"J. D. Hughes," he replies.

"You mean super filthy rich J. D. Hughes?" she says.

"The one and only. I was introduced to JD through my professor at Mira Mesa. JD was impressed by my academic efforts and energetic attitude, so he offered me a job as an intern in his corporation at the end of my junior year," he says.

"Now I truly feel like a failure. I mean, I'm a porn star."

He interrupts her, saying, "What do you mean you're a failure? I don't see you that way."

She interrupts him, yelling, "Oh, bullshit, Trevor! Don't be naive. I'm a porn star. I have oral, anal, and any other kind of sex with males and females for money and America's entertainment. Every man that looks at me has one thing on his mind, and believe me, it's not to make me his wife or mother of his children. Trevor, someday you're going to be a role model to millions, and people will love you, but I'll always be known as Lana, the anal porn star. Sometimes I wish I wouldn't wake up in the morning because I know I have to face another day of pretending while some guy or guys whom I don't love or know shove their dicks down my throat and up my ass. Doesn't that sound like a failure to you?"

"Hey, I've had enough of this. I brought you up here so we could have a good time with each other. Don't spoil it with the bad mishaps life has dealt you. Why don't we go inside and enjoy a big cup of ice cream and discover the other pleasures this palace has to offer?" he replies.

"I'm sorry. I didn't mean to carry on like this. I'm so very happy to see you again," she replies.

She falls in love with the master bedroom overlooking the moonlit ocean. It seems so serene as she gazes as far as her eyes could see over this beauty of nature. She feels comfort and peace for a moment and even smiles as she turns watching him neatly roll back the beautiful silk sheets. She imagines how great it would feel to spend the rest of her life with a man who truly loves her unconditionally.

He looks up with the same beautiful smile she remembers as a child, saying, "Hey, beautiful, your ice cream is melting."

She skips over like a naughty little schoolgirl cuddling up next to him. Her body sinks into comfort as he embraces her in his arms. Her mind sets sail far from the troubles of her world as she enjoys the taste of vanilla and chocolate swirl ice cream in the arms of a gentleman she adores.

Several hours later, his arm begins to fall asleep as he looks at her peacefully asleep. He imagines how great life would be if this moment could last a lifetime. His heart fills with joy as he stares at this beautiful creation, so serene and delicate. She mumbles a few words as she positions herself closer to him with a slight smile on her face, drifting peacefully back off to sleep. He quietly places the empty ice cream cups on the table, trying not to disturb her as he repositions himself next to her. His arm feels instant relief as he drifts off to sleep.

The next morning, she awakens in his embrace. She smiles and then begins to cry silently. He awakens to the trembling of her body. He asks, "Crystal, what's wrong? Did I do something?"

She rolls over with red puffy eyes. "No, you haven't done anything wrong. I had a dream about us that was so real I could actually feel it. We were so happy, but then I woke up and realized it was all just a dream."

"It doesn't have to be a dream. Together we can make it a reality. It's what I've been waiting for my whole life," he replies.

She looks at him. "We can never be together. I don't want to ruin your life." He tries to interrupt, but she silences him by placing her finger against his lips. "I'm a porn star, and we'll never have peace in our lives as long as we're together. I love you too much to see you suffer."

He places his hand on her chin, looking straight into her eyes. "I don't care what the world thinks of us. We're back together again. Don't let this rule the rest of our lives."

She kisses him gently on his lips. "I want you to listen to me for a moment. Don't say anything. Just listen. When that tramp moved me away from everything I loved, we ended up in some small, little town right outside of Dallas, Texas. My next-door neighbor drove me and his daughter to school every morning because my mother was always too drunk or drugged up to take me. I became good friends with Amy, but I never really liked her father because he always seemed strange, and Amy always acted strange when he was around. She never told me what was going on or why she seemed to act so strange around her father.

"One night, I was outside emptying the trash, and I could hear her crying. I quietly walked to her bedroom window and saw her father raping her. I was terrified. I didn't know what to do. So I ran back to the house and called the police. I told them my next-door neighbor was hurting his daughter. They laughed at me, saying, 'You badass kids need some discipline in your lives,' then hung up the phone. I tried to tell my mother, but she yelled at me, telling me I was disturbing her party. I ran to my room and locked the door. A few weeks later, my mother was having one of her get-high parties, and she invited Amy's father. I ran to my room and started to play with my dolls. I must have fallen asleep because the next thing I remember was someone pulling my hair, picking me up, and throwing me on my bed. I screamed for my mother, but she never came. He ripped my dress and panties off, saying, 'I'll teach you to call the cops on me, you little bitch.' I thought he was going to kill me. He grabbed the back of my head, forcing me facedown on my pillow, sodomizing me repeatedly. I screamed and tried to fight, but it was useless. I was thirteen years old. I tried to tell my mother, but she was always too high to realize what I was saying. This went on for several years, willingly or unwillingly, by several different men that my mother invited over for her get-high parties. I cried inside for years. I had no one to turn to, no shoulder to cry on, and I felt like life was over for me. I was dead inside.

"Finally, I had had enough, so I went out to an old abandoned house. I invited the animal that took my childhood away from me, and I gave him my body instead of him taking it. He never caught on to what was going on. He thought I had finally accepted him after several years of abuse. When he went to sleep, I pulled out a brand-new, shiny straight razor and cut his throat from ear to ear. I sat up on top of him, laughing as I watched him gurgle and choke on his own blood. The police found him a couple weeks later with two bags of cocaine that I stole from my mother and planted under the bed. They ruled it as a bad drug deal, and I was never a suspect. I ran away from home at sixteen years old. The only person I missed was my friend Amy, whom I loved. I placed red roses on her grave as I left with only the clothes on my back.

"I hooked for money to feed myself and to get as far away from hell as I could. I landed in Los Angeles, California. I worked the streets for a couple of months until I ran into a wealthy gentleman named Gray, who took me off the streets and cared for me for several months. I thought I had finally found that special someone to love for the rest of my life. In the long run, I found I was just another investment. I was introduced to the adult entertainment industry by him. I worked for him for several years, making us a ton of money, until I decided to branch off and open several of my own production companies and adult shops. I thought all the money and fame would bring me happiness. Instead, it brought more pain. I have traveled the world, and I still feel empty inside until now. You've made my life so complete with your presence. In one night, you've released my mind and heart from years of torment. Now I'm free. I'll always love you. Take this necklace and remember me as your Crystal Blue Eyes every time you look at it." He lowers his head in tears. She raises his head, saying, "Shhhhh, don't cry. You've set me free. I'll always remember that."

He looks deep into her beautiful eyes and gently kisses her soft lips. He says with a smile, "I'm sorry, but I had to do that. I've been waiting for years for this moment."

"I wish we could do more, but my body is a ravaged shipyard used only for money and power, not love," she replies.

He hugs her tightly. "Life has its good moments and its bad moments. We're in a good moment now. You'll always be my one true love no matter how horrible our pasts are." Tears roll down her face as he quickly wipes them away with the soft silk sheets, saying, "No more tears. You're with me now, and I only know you, respect you, and love you as Crystal and nothing else. I say we get dressed, go down to the boathouse, and race the dolphins on some superfast Jet Skis."

She acts like an excited little child looking at the beautiful yacht, several Jet Skis, and ski boats. She yells, "Oh my gosh, look at all this stuff!"

He lowers the Jet Skis in the water, and they zoom off, yelling and screaming, zigzagging across the waves. He takes a dive into the warm, salty water, feeling free as his body seems weightless. He surfaces to see Crystal screaming with her knees up to her chest clutched in bloody terror. He jumps back on his Jet Ski, rushing to her rescue. He clearly discovers her problem as an enormous sea turtle has crested underneath her Jet Ski with its huge, long fins extended out as if it were sunbathing. He laughs uncontrollably at her, reaching down into the water to rub its enormous coarse shell. He says, "It's just a sea turtle, nothing to be afraid of. They don't eat people. Why don't you touch him? It's okay."

"No, thank you, I'll pass," she replies.

The turtle splashes its fins and quickly disappears into the deep blue. He says, "All this laughter is burning up too many calories. Why don't we go out for breakfast? I know this nice, quiet little spot." She lowers her head in silence as he says, "Hey, I didn't ask you to go to a hog killing. I asked you out for breakfast."

She looks at him sadly, saying, "You don't realize what you're getting yourself into. Your quiet little spot will become a photo session, and your face will appear on the cover of every sleazy tabloid in the world."

"Once again, I don't care what the world thinks of us," he replies.

They pull up to Anne's, a very elegant country-style breakfast inn. The valet stares at Crystal in amazement, trying to speak. Trevor looks at him laughing as he takes his ticket from the gentleman dressed in old country-style clothing with a straw hat on. The entire restaurant is in a silent stare as they're escorted to their table. Anne comes out of the office to personally meet and greet them. She offers them her finest pancakes, scrambled eggs, and steaks on the house. They recap the memories of their short-lived relationship while listening to soft country music in the background.

A gentleman approaches the table. "Excuse me, sir. Do you mind if I take a picture with Lana? I'm one of her biggest fans."

Trevor looks at her as she says, "Sure."

The gentleman is so excited he almost topples a whole tray of food out of the hands of one of the waitresses. Soon, there's a line of ladies and gentlemen wanting autographs and pictures from this goddess. Anne brings out their food, speaking in a deep country accent, "All right, all right, please return to your seats so this lovely couple can enjoy some of the best country cooking they ever had. I apologize for any inconvenience. We don't get a lot of you celebrity types very often."

"It's okay. I understand how they feel," says Trevor.

"Please enjoy your breakfast and let me know if I can get you anything," says Anne. The food is fantastic. Crystal leaves an autographed $100 bill as they prepare to leave. Anne says, "The front of this place is running over with photographers and media. If you like, I can have George bring your car around back so you won't get mobbed by them."

Crystal looks at Trevor with disappointment as he smiles, saying, "We don't mind. Let's give them something to talk about."

They're swarmed by flashes of light as they walk out the door. One of the reporters asks, "Hey, Lana, I heard you're working on a new film. Is the guy next to you your new lead stud?"

"Yes, I'm working on my final film, and no, he's not in my film."

A reporter from the back of the crowd says, "I just received info that the young man next to you is a student at the prestigious Mira Mesa University. Are you worried your image may tarnish this student and the school's reputation?"

She begins to reply to the question as Trevor steps forward. "I'm not ashamed to be here with this lovely young lady. I actually feel very privileged to be in her company. If the powers that be at Mira Mesa think I've tarnished their image, then I will happily transfer from their university to another one."

Several reporters rush up to his car, yelling and screaming as they drive off. Crystal looks at him, disappointed by his reaction. "I really wish you wouldn't have done that."

"I will never let society dictate who I can or cannot associate with. You're a very special person in my life no matter how society labels you," he replies.

"Someday you're going to make some lucky lady a very good husband," she says.

"If I had it my way, it would be you," he replies.

She angrily says, "Trevor, get this in your head. I'm no good for you. Don't say a word. Just listen. No matter what you say, my life is a wreck, and I will not drag you down with me. End of conversation. Please drop me off at the Palace." He drives her in silence to this exquisite five-star hotel. She grasps his hand tightly, saying, "Thank you for allowing me the opportunity to know what it feels like to enjoy life. These past two days have been the most enjoyable of my life. I wish things were different because I would love to spend the rest of my life with you. Please remember me as we were in the past when we were so innocent and our lives were carefree. Oh yeah, take care of the necklace. It looks good on you. It's the most precious thing I owned." She kisses him gently as she opens the door.

He looks at her with tears in his eyes. "Crystal, you'll always have a spot next to my heart no matter what."

"I'll always be with you," she replies. She closes the door gently as her tears stain the ash-white concrete.

His emotions begin to intertwine as he drives off slowly, peering at her through his rearview mirror. He turns his music up, ripping onto the interstate like a race car driver out of the pit. He accelerates to almost a 120 miles an hour, dodging in and out of traffic. The rush intensifies his emotions as he takes a sharp curve at 80 miles an hour. Tears begin to blur his vision as he continues to test the power and performance of his Mustang GT. His foot becomes heavier as he pushes the speedometer to 130 on a straight stretch along the coast. The road seems to diminish as he demands more power from his supercharged V8 engine. He quickly approaches an overturned tractor trailer in the middle of the road with chickens fluttering everywhere. He quickly shifts his foot from the accelerator to the brakes and clutch, trying to downshift. But he is still too fast, and there's not enough highway in between him and the tractor trailer. The back end of his Mustang zigzags as he pops off the clutch, sending him to the shoulder of the road where he spins uncontrollably in the dirt and gravel. The machine comes to a stop inches away from the rear of the trailer. He jumps out of the car barely able to stand as his legs tremble uncontrollably.

The truck driver approaches him with a jaw full of tobacco and a spit cup, yelling, "Son, are you okay?" He looks at her tarnished brown teeth, foul breath, and dirty overalls. The thought of his life flashing before his eyes and the sight of her sends him to the back of his car, where he begins to puke. She approaches him again, saying, "I probably would have done the same thing in a close call like this." She offers him a dirty handkerchief.

"No, thank you. I'm fine. Just give me a minute to relax," he says.

In the distance, he could see red and blue flashing lights approaching them with sirens blaring. He jumps back in his car and drives off, watching the lady chase chickens all over the road.

The parking lot is an arena of students screaming and yelling as he drives up. Chris crowns him and places a red cape around his shoulders. They yell, "All hail King T.!" The crowd bows to him as he laughs at this spectacle.

A young lady asks, "So how does it feel to sleep with the hottest chick in America?"

The crowd is in complete silence as he says, "It felt wonderful, but I must inform you that we didn't have sex." A great gasp breaks the silence as they look at him with confused faces.

Chris says, "You're full of shit. You just spent the night with Lana, the hottest porn star in the world, and you didn't have sex with her?" He yells to the crowd mockingly, "It was so good he has become delirious."

Trevor steps forward, waving his hand to silence the crowd. "You know her as Lana, but I know her as Crystal. We attended the same elementary school. She was my first girlfriend and the first girl I ever kissed. She moved away several years ago, and I lost contact with her until now. She means everything to me. Life has dealt her a bad hand, but I hope I can change things around, and we can start over."

The ladies in the crowd scream, giving him a round of applause. Chris says, "You're going to have a difficult time explaining this to the world." He steps forward with a tabloid that reads, "LANA'S NEW STUD." "I admire you for trying to help a friend, but you're still the coolest dude I know," says Chris.

A red flashing light illuminates his room as he closes the door behind him. He's not too surprised to see thirty messages on his answering machine. He takes a deep breath as he picks up the phone to call his parents.

Clara answers on the first ring, yelling, "What are you doing gallivanting around town with a porn star? Your father and I never would've imagined you would associate yourself with that type of trash."

He interrupts, saying, "Mom, it's Crystal, the little girl that I liked in elementary school. She's also the one whose birthday party I missed for some reason."

"I remember. She's the little girl whose mother I had the pleasure of talking to in the coffee shop. I see the apple didn't fall far from the tree.

Honey, we don't want you to throw your life away on some tramp. You have so much potential to do so many great things in life."

"Mom, I'm not a kid anymore. I can take care of myself. Crystal is not a bad person, and I love her. Her life may not be picture-perfect, but if you knew what I know now, you wouldn't be so quick to judge. Don't worry. I'll be fine."

James comes home from the office and takes the phone from his distressed wife. "Hello, son. How are you? I guess I don't have to tell you your picture is on the front cover of every magazine and tabloid in the world. I'm not going to waste my time lecturing an adult, but I want you to be careful not to get yourself involved in something that you'll regret for the rest of your life."

"Dad, it's Crystal. I found her after all these years."

"You mean the little girl you kissed on the bus?"

"Yes, Dad. It's her. I'm so happy I can hardly stand it."

"Wow, she's not a little girl anymore. Hey, the guys at the office think you're the luckiest man in the world. As a concerned parent, I think you should consider very carefully what you're getting yourself into."

"Dad, please don't worry about me. I'll be fine. Tell Mom not to worry. I have everything under control."

"Okay, I trust your judgment. You've never let me down before, and I don't expect you to start now. Are you coming home for summer break?"

"Yes, Dad. I'll see you this summer. Good night." He sighs in relief as the phone rings just as he places it on the receiver.

A voice on the opposite end says, "The first day I met you, I knew there was something special about you. That's why I liked you so much."

He yells, "Tyson, is that you?"

"Hell yeah, it's me. How the hell are you?"

"I'm doing just fine. How are you?" asks Trevor.

"I would be doing better if I was standing next to a gorgeous babe like this. How in the hell did you snag Lana? I've watched every movie she made, and now I'll get the chance to meet her in person because she's my brother's girlfriend," says Tyson.

"Tyson, you already know her. Remember the pretty little girl I had a crush on in elementary school named Crystal?"

"You mean pretty little sky-blue-eyed Crystal that every guy in our class had a crush on?" asks Tyson.

"Ding, ding, ding, you're a winner!" replies Trevor. They laugh and talk for hours until the battery in his phone begins to beep and the clock displays 2:00 a.m. He turns the ringer off and climbs into bed for a few hours of sleep.

The thought of having Crystal back in his arms again revives his system as he walks across campus to Professor Black's class.

Professor Black greets him, saying, "The early bird always gets the worm. Your presence was missed in yesterday's lecture. I don't like to pry into other people's affairs, but I was a little disturbed by your friend's occupation and your acquaintance with her. I say that because we live in a very political society, and as you already know, it's not what you know in many cases. It's who you know. She could possibly close several prominent doors if you continue to associate yourself with her."

"Professor, I admire your concern, but I will not allow society to dictate who is or isn't acceptable in my life. I knew her as a child, and I consider her to be one of my personal friends," he replies.

"Very well, Trevor. I will respect your wishes."

The halls begin to come alive with chitchat as he sits quietly, watching Professor Black write out the day's assignments on the board. He daydreams about Crystal as his name burns the ears of several students gossiping in the hallways. The ladies enter the classroom glaring and smiling at him as he sits quietly, enjoying the moment. His friends huddle around him, interrogating him further about Lana.

Professor Black reenters the class, saying, "Good morning, class. I have some very important info to deliver to you this morning. I was tallying up your grades last night because I was bored and I had nothing else to do. To my surprise and yours, the class average is 90 percent. The top scorer among you is Mr. O'Riely, who has an average of 99.9 percent. I want to improve Mr. O'Riely's score as well as the rest of you by giving you a five-point quiz on last week's lecture of supply and demand. Since you have done so well this semester, you are free to go as soon as you finish."

Several students are standing in the hallways, chatting as Trevor leaves the class. They separate, simultaneously pointing and chanting his name.

He stops in the middle of the hall and takes a bow as the students begin to crowd around him, patting him on his back. Several shades of lipstick from the ladies mask his face as he exits the building. He gloats with pride for a moment as he walks quietly, smiling, all the way to his room.

He opens the door to a gentle knock. Naomi is standing there looking like a beauty queen, saying, "I was in the area, so I decided to stop by for a moment to see how the big man on campus is doing."

"I'm doing fine. Thank you for stopping by. Come on in and have a seat."

She walks in, impressed by the layout of his room. "Did you do the decorating yourself?"

He stands tall with pride, saying, "Yes, I did. Do you like it? Welcome to the Panther's Den."

"The Panther's Den, huh? Should I be afraid?" she asks.

He laughs, saying, "No, ma'am, you're perfectly safe within these walls."

She looks at him for a moment with glaring eyes, "Are you and Lana dating now?"

"No, she doesn't think we should be together because of her lifestyle. She thinks she'll ruin my reputation and my career. I'm going to see her this weekend at Players in Los Angeles. I'm so excited I can hardly breathe."

"Well, I guess I better get to class before I'm late. I'll talk to you later," she says.

Every corner of his mind is occupied with Crystal as he gyrates around his room like a kid on Christmas Day. He turns the radio on to listen to the DJ advertise Lana's arrival at Players Saturday night in Los Angeles. He calls Chris, "Tell the guys we have a road trip this weekend to see Lana at Players in Los Angeles Saturday night."

"I'll get right on it. I'm stopping by tomorrow to get my poster of Tara," he says.

"I'll have it rolled up and ready for you when you get here," replies Trevor.

CHAPTER 26

The whole week is perfect as he watches the days go by, anticipating the moment when he gets to hold her in his arms again. The semester is coming to an end, and he imagines bringing Crystal back to the place it all started. The thoughts and ideas in his head leave him tossing and turning in bed all night as he anxiously waits to see her again.

He honks his horn, eagerly waiting for Chris, along with a convoy of out-of-control men behind him, revving their engines, ready to go. Chris dashes out of the dorm like Superman and jumps in the car. They blast their music, weaving in and out of traffic, screaming to the sound of hard rock music barreling their way to Players. The DJ interrupts their entertainment with a breaking news report. He says, "We've just received confirmed information that Lana, top female porn star, has tragically taken her own life this afternoon. She was found by her hairstylist in her car. Police say the cause of death was carbon monoxide poisoning. She ran a hose pipe from her muffler to the inside of her car window. The adult film star was twenty-two years old."

Trevor swerves to the side of the road, jumping out of his car, throwing up uncontrollably. He falls to his knees, screaming in pain as his friends rush to his side, crying and trying to comfort him. Chris and a few of his other friends lift him to his feet, putting him in his car. Chris leads the convoy of distraught men quietly back to campus. The entire campus is standing outside their dorms with flames held high from lighters in honor of Lana. Trevor opens the door in tears as several of his classmates embrace him, giving words of encouragement. Pain runs through his body like poison as the announcement of her death replays in his mind like a broken record. He falls to his knees beside his bed, sobbing uncontrollably, until his eyes could cry no more. Grief finally defeats him as he slumps over beside his bed in a motionless sleep.

He awakens to the chimes of bells as he looks out his window at several smiling faces hurrying across campus to class. He immediately closes his windows, pulls the curtains closed, and lies there in total silence and darkness. He blocks the constant ringing of his phone from his mind as he lies there motionless like a corpse. A persistent knock on his door disturbs him, sending him into an angry rage. He leaps off the bed, violently yelling, "Get the hell away from my door!"

The gentleman says, "Mr. O'Riely, I have very important documents for you. I'm Jack Ross, attorney for the late Ms. Crystal St. Claire, along with her personal accountant, Mr. Tom Dunbar."

He opens the door slowly, shielding the bright light from his eyes, saying, "Please excuse my attitude."

"It's okay. We understand. Mr. Dunbar and I are deeply sorry for your loss. We're here to read you the last will and testament of Ms. St. Claire," says Mr. Ross.

"Please come in and have a seat," replies Trevor.

Mr. Ross opens his briefcase, taking several documents out, spreading them across the table. "Despite your tragic loss, you're one lucky man. Ms. St. Claire named you sole beneficiary in her will, leaving you her vast empire of several businesses and real estate," says Mr. Ross.

"Mr. O'Riely, Ms. St. Claire was a very smart and powerful businesswoman. Her net profit last year was $252 million dollars. I have done some calculations for this year, and it seems you will make a profit of $300 million," says Mr. Dunbar.

He looks at the gentlemen for a moment and says, "I want this matter to be kept strictly confidential. I don't want anyone to know I inherited Crystal's empire. Mr. Ross, Mr. Dunbar, you two have done a fantastic job for Crystal. I extend the invitation to hire you as my lawyer and accountant. I hope you will work just as hard for me." They generously agree to accept the offer by shaking hands in partnership.

"Now that the papers are signed, we need to go to the bank to set up your accounts," says Tom.

"I want my accounts to stay at the same bank Crystal had," he says.

"I will call the president of the bank and arrange a private meeting," says Tom.

"Mr. O'Riely, it's going to be a pleasure working for you. If you don't mind, I would like to get back to the office to finish up some paperwork," says Mr. Ross.

"No problem. In two months, we have a business trip in Alabama. Please put that on your calendar," replies Trevor.

Mr. Toddler, the bank's president thanks him for trusting World International with his assets.

CHAPTER 27

"Tom, I feel like spending a little money. Do you know how to drive a stick shift?" asks Trevor.

"Pardon the expression, but I can shift like a bat out of hell," replies Tom. He parks across the street from High Performance Automotives. Tom is immediately approached by a salesman and offered something to drink in an air-conditioned office as he browses through a selection of sports cars they have for sale. Trevor is outside in the heat, window-shopping for thirty minutes before he's approached by an eager young salesman.

He asks, "Sir, would you like a bottle of water? I just got here from class. Is someone helping you?"

"No, and thank you for the water. Did you say you were a college student?" asks Trevor.

"Yes, I'm Quincy. I attend Escondido Junior College. I hope I will have enough money saved next year so I can transfer to Valley University. They have the best computer science program in the country. I'm not doing so well in sales because all of our high-end clients are referred to the more senior salesmen," he replies.

"This is your lucky day. Why don't you get me the keys to this beautiful machine?" says Trevor.

A tall gentleman comes outside with the keys in his hand, saying, "Sir, we have a policy stating no customer can test-drive any of our cars unless they intend to buy."

"Thank you very much. Please send Quincy back out here with the keys to this vehicle," says Trevor.

Quincy returns, apologizing, "I'm sorry, but I can't let you test-drive this car because I'll get fired."

"Okay, why don't we go inside so you can give me the title to this beautiful Ferrari?"

"Yes, sir. Right this way, sir," replies Quincy.

The manager dashes out of his office, saying, "I'm sorry, but this is not a thousand-dollar dealership. This is a million-dollar dealership, and we don't have time for games. The sales price of this car is $100,000, not $1,000. There's a lemon lot around the corner that sells cars that are in your price range. Have a good day, sir."

He smiles, saying, "Tom, will you call Mr. Toddler and tell him to send me $300,000 in cash by armored truck?"

"Yes, sir."

The owner stands there laughing as he walks to the window with his arms folded, looking for an armored truck. A few minutes later, an armored truck along with two guards pulls up to the dealership with two bags in their hands. One guard says, "I'm looking for a Mr. O'Riely."

He steps forward with picture identification, and they give him the bags with $150,000 in each bag. He turns to the owner of the dealership, saying, "I don't see you laughing anymore. You said this car costs $100,000. I have $300,000 in cash. If my math is correct, I can buy three of these vehicles right now if I want to. I will give you the benefit of introducing myself, and maybe next time a customer walks through your doors, you will not judge him so quickly. My name is Trevor O'Riely. I'm a student at Mira Mesa University majoring in business. I'm a friend of J. D. Hughes, and this gentleman is my personal accountant. Thank you for your business and have a nice day. Quincy, would you clock out and assist me in finding this car across the street?"

Quincy quickly clocks out and races across the street to V-12 Motor Sports, searching through a fine selection of Ferraris. Trevor and Tom whistle as they walk across the street with two armed guards carrying $300,000. The owner of the dealership meets and greets them before they get to the front door. Quincy is standing by a beautiful black Ferrari that

Trevor immediately falls in love with. The owner offers the car to him for $85,000 if he drives it off the lot today. He accepts the offer, and the deal is done. He gives the armored truck drivers a $2,000 tip apiece and instructs them to take Quincy to any bank of his choice to deposit the rest of the money in his account for school. Quincy looks at him with tears in his eyes as Trevor says, "Don't mention it. I already know what's in your heart. I would like you to remember one thing. When you have achieved success in your field of study, please remember this moment and help the next individual in need fulfill his or her desires the best way you can."

Quincy looks at him with gratification in his tearful eyes and hugs him like a brother. Quincy turns once again to Trevor as he's getting into the armored truck. "I'll tell my children and my grandchildren of a kind, generous man who allowed my dreams to come true."

Trevor hopes the performance of this machine is just as good as the sound of it. They leave the dealership, waving at the idiot standing in the car lot with his hands in empty pockets. He's eager to give her a go as Tom pulls up beside him, yelling, "You're not afraid of her, are you?" He smiles, tightening his grip on the steering wheel and the other firmly around the sterling silver gear shift. He punches it to first, second, and third gear, screeching the tires as he takes off like a rocket. He peers at Tom through his rearview mirror as he pops the clutch to fourth and then fifth gear. The speedometer registers 135 as they rip down the coast with no fear. A police officer sitting on the side of the road ahead of them makes them decelerate their engines quickly. The officer stares at them through dark sunglasses as they pass by. The green flag comes out a mile down the road as Tom zooms by him, waving. The tires screech against the black pavement as he shifts rapidly, closing the gap between himself and Tom. The excitement ends as they come upon Mira Mesa Boulevard. The guard at the gate admires his cars as they drive through to the parking lot.

Trevor looks at Tom, asking, "Where did you learn to drive like that?"

Tom laughs, saying, "My father used to race when I was a kid, and I got into it when I was in high school. I paid the majority of my tuition in college by racing rich college brats. Well, I guess I better get home before my wife sends out a search party."

"Thanks for everything today," says Trevor.

CHAPTER 28

He sits quietly on his bed, smiling, thinking of Crystal, as the light from the lamp makes the diamond necklace sparkle like her pretty blue eyes. He imagines for a moment that he sees her standing in front of him, smiling, with her arms extended. Reaching into shadowy space, tears of joy stream down his face as he feels the warmth of her hands against his. He stands to his feet as she comes closer, laughing and smiling. Her eyes are as clear and blue as the heavens. He reaches out to hold her in his arms as she disappears. He denies this was just an illusion as he sits on his bed, anxious for her return. A gentle knock at his door rushes him back to reality as he wipes the tears from his eyes, asking, "Who is it?"

A soft voice from the other side says, "It's me, Naomi. I thought you might need some company and a little something to eat, so I baked some brownies for you. I can leave them at your door if you don't want any company right now."

He opens the door, saying, "No, no, thank you for stopping by. Come on in and make yourself at home. Thank you for making me brownies. They're my favorite, and they smell so good."

"Wow, where did you buy that beautiful diamond necklace?" she asks.

He quickly takes it off, saying, "A very special friend gave it to me."

"You really loved her, didn't you?"

He looks at her emotionally crushed as tears begin to pound his hardwood floor. She hugs him gently, soothing his emotions like a mother would for her child. He steps back, apologizing for his behavior as she silences him with soft kisses on his forehead and cheeks. He softly kisses her lips, looking into her eyes. Gently raising her chin, he kisses her again. Lust begins to subdue their minds as they stand their enveloped in each other's passion. He quickly backs away, saying, "I'm sorry."

"It's okay. I've been waiting for this moment ever since we met at Candy Stripers," she replies.

"I just don't want things to go too fast. I need time to think," he says.

"It's okay. I understand," she replies. They hug each other as she leaves his room with somber feelings.

The phone rings just as he lies across his bed to relax. A voice on the other end says, "Good afternoon, I have some good news and some better news."

He says, "Tom, give me the good news first."

"Well, I just finished adjusting your books, adding an additional $1.5 million from Crystal's new movie. Did I mention it's number 1 since its release a month ago? As a matter of fact, I need your permission to release more because the video stores are selling out. Tara, owner of several production companies, made a very attractive offer to buy Crystal's production studios and her novelty shops. She made me an offer of $255 million dollars. So far, no one else has outbid her."

"Call her and tell her I accept the offer. Contact Jack and have him draw up the papers. Deposit the check in my account and call me when everything is complete."

"Yes, sir, I'll get right on it," replies Tom.

He peacefully reclines back on his bed, enjoying its comforts as he dozes off to sleep.

The next day in class, Professor Black says, "Good morning, class. I know you're all excited that this semester is almost over. You've all done well in my class this semester, and I'm proud of each and every one of you. Every professor in this institution reserves the right to allow its top-performing students to skip his or her final exam if their average is 90 percent or higher. We have one more test before finals. If these five students score 90 percent or higher on this test, they will be exempt from the final exam. The five are Mr. O'Riely with an average of 105 percent, Ms. Richardson with an average of 99.9 percent, Mr. Jackson with an average of 99.9 percent, Mr. King with an average of

98.9 percent, and Ms. Battle with an average of 98 percent. Class, let's give them a round of applause for a job well done."

After class is dismissed, Trevor walks back to his room to have breakfast before his next class starts in an hour. He glances at his phone displaying one voice message. It's Tom confirming everything is clear and the money is in the bank. He dances around the room for a moment, wondering what he's going to do with his newfound fortune.

That afternoon, walking across campus to his dorm, he decides to pay Naomi a visit to thank her for her hospitality. He stands outside her door for a moment, gathering his words in his mind. As he's about to knock on her door, Lauren flings the door open, surprising the both of them. "My, my, what a fine specimen you are. How can I help you?" she asks.

"I'm here to see Naomi. Is she busy?"

Naomi yells, "Lauren, who are you talking to?"

"A fine gentleman requesting your presence."

Naomi gives herself a quick makeover in the mirror as she hurries to the door. "Trevor, hello, how are you?"

"You know this heartthrob?" asks Lauren.

"Remember, we met him and his friend at Candy Stripers about three months ago? They sat and ate ice cream with us, and you disappeared with his friend," replies Naomi.

"Yes, I do remember you now. I hope you have more stamina than your friend has," says Lauren.

Naomi, embarrassed, sends her away, saying, "Please excuse her. She's a little retarded sometimes."

"No problem, I just wanted to stop by to say thank you for the other night and to apologize," he says.

"No apology necessary. I understand. Things have been pretty tough for you lately. Would you like to come in for a moment?" asks Naomi.

"Actually, I was wondering if you would accompany me to a special place for a little while?" he asks.

She smiles, asking, "Where is this special place we're going to?"

"It's not too far away from here. It's very nice, and I'm sure you'll enjoy it," he says.

"Do I need to bring anything with me?" she asks.

"You already have everything you need."

"Okay, give me one minute to get my keys and tell Lauren to lock my door when she leaves."

They smile at each other all the way to his car.

She says, "Wow, this is very nice. I thought you had a black Mustang."

"I do. You're standing next to it… I know, I know, I'll explain it to you later," he replies. He lets the top down, waving goodbye to Lauren and a few other nosy ladies as they zoom out of the gate with their hair blowing in the wind.

He parks by the curb, joining several couples on Sunset Cliff, admiring one of Mother Nature's most spectacular events. Her heart fills with joy as he gently cloaks her in his arms, gazing at this romantic scene. Her mind is carefree as she stands there wrapped in his arms atop this cliff, gazing off into infinity, while a fresh, warm breeze dances around them. The mellow love songs playing on the radio enhance the mood as the couples sway to the music and watch the stars appear in the half moonlit sky.

She trembles as he whispers, "Are you ready? I have one more place I would like to reacquaint you with."

They walk back to the car holding hands with the feeling of butterflies in their stomachs. She reclines her seat, enjoying this romantic moment as they pull into the parking lot of Candy Stripers. She covers her mouth as she screams with excitement. He leans over, saying, "I thought you might like it if we had some ice cream here. I heard it's very good." They sit admiring each other's company, enjoying delicious ice cream. He says, "I wish this night didn't have to end."

She looks into his eyes, saying, "It doesn't." Startled by her response, his face turns as red as a beet.

The trip back to campus is full of anxiety as he tries to figure out how to tell her he's still a virgin. The same thoughts are rushing through her mind. They both sort of smile at each other periodically, not knowing what to expect or say. Walking from the parking lot to his room is the most intimidating of all because neither of them knows exactly what to expect. She nervously rushes to the restroom as he fumbles around his room, trying to figure out a way to put the both of them at ease. He dials the radio station to a soothing selection of soft beats and dims the lights to a more romantic mood. She joins him as he passes her a glass of chilled sparkling apple juice. The environment sets the tone for the two of them as they serenade around the room. He kisses her lips softly as she looks deep into his eyes. Their kisses become more and more passionate as he lifts her off her feet, carrying her to his bedroom. His voice trembles as he says, "Naomi, there's something I want you to know."

"It's okay. It's my first time too," she replies.

They lie coiled in a naked bond, exploring their deepest passion for each other. She trembles as he enters her vagina, grasping his arm tight as the sensation is painful and pleasurable at the same time. Moans of pleasure begin to fill his bedroom as her body begins to become more receptive. He feels an intensifying sensation coming upon him like no other. He begins to perspire heavily as his body endures slight paralysis. He belts out a grunting, growling sound of relief as he collapses between her legs, breathing heavily. They lie there in lust, satisfied as they have stepped out of the arms of innocence and into the arms of deceitful passion.

He asks, "So how do you feel?"

"It hurt at first. It felt like you were sticking a log or something inside of me, but after a while, it started to feel really good, and the pain wasn't as bad. How do you feel?"

"I feel like a million bucks! It was awesome! I wish I would've done this a long time ago. I think we should do it again," he replies.

"Oh no, I can't take any more of that today. I'm a little sore," she says. He folds his hands behind his head, smiling as the feeling of this sexual sensation lingers in his mind. She peacefully sleeps next to him.

CHAPTER 29

Lauren says, "Good morning, slut. Did you have a good time with Mr. Lover-Lover last night? I called you at one this morning, and I talked to the answering machine." She looks at Lauren, blushing and smiling, oblivious to what she's saying. Lauren yells, "You little bitch, you got your cherry popped last night, didn't you?" Her voice echoes throughout the hollow classroom.

"Shhhhh! Don't tell the whole world," says Naomi.

"So tell me, how does it feel to finally become a real woman?" asks Lauren.

"It hurt at first, but after a while, the pain turned into pleasure."

"The more you do it, the better it gets. Hey, if you're not busy fucking your brains out tonight, come with me to see Men of Desire. A friend of mine told me they were hot strippers," says Lauren.

"I'm going to have to take a rain check because I probably will get my brains fucked out tonight," says Naomi.

CHAPTER 30

Several weeks travel by, and their relationship flourishes. Great business decisions, smart investments, and charitable donations incredibly increase his financial gain and respect from Tom and Jack. With all this success, his heart is still uneasy; there's a piece missing from the puzzle in his life. He would often sit alone at night, gazing at the brilliance of the diamond necklace, imagining Crystal is there. A tear of joy would often trickle down his smiling face as the images of her seem so real. He tries to move on with his life by occupying his time with Naomi. She never feels or sees the gap in their pseudo relationship because he shadows his heart with false presumptions when they're together.

Her heart sinks into a bottomless pit as she hugs him tightly before he boards the plane. She tries to hide the pain by repeatedly reminding herself it's only a month. The announcer says, "Flight 603 to Miami, Florida, is now boarding at gate 3."

He says, "Tell your parents I said hello, and I hope you have a wonderful holiday with your family." They wave goodbye to her as she fades into the crowd among hundreds of travelers. Tom gives his handkerchief to him, laughing as they board their flight to Alabama. He says, "Jack, Tom, I really appreciate you for leaving your families to handle this business matter in Alabama. I want to be as prompt as possible about this matter. Jack, there's some property surrounding a lake that I want to purchase. I need you and Tom to find the owners and make them an offer. I also have a great surprise for my parents, but we'll discuss that later. I have a gift I want to present to you now. It's called I raise you $100,000 each, along with a holiday bonus of $50,000."

They yell out like uncivilized kids, disturbing the quietness of the business class. The stewardess rush to their seats, asking in a frantic voice, "Gentlemen, is there something wrong?" They apologize for their behavior, sending the stewardess away at ease. They enjoy the rest of their flight watching movies coddled in luxury.

Clara and James happily greet their son as they walk out of the terminal. Tom and Jack walk past them like they don't even know him just as they had planned.

"Dad, you drive the Mustang home, and I'll drive the other one," says Trevor.

Clara and James look at each other, confused, as he receives two sets of keys from the clerk. "Is something wrong with your car?" asks Clara.

"No, I just decided to buy another one."

"I'm not sure I understand," says James.

"Trust me, Dad. In an hour, you and Mom will walk into a brighter light." He unlocks the doors to the beautiful Ferrari as his parents stand dazed at the sight of this pearly black car. "Dad, congratulations! She's quick as lightning, so be careful."

"Son, are you serious? How did you…?"

He gives his mother a little brown envelope. She curiously opens it, screaming at the top of her lungs with excitement, waving her hands around.

James asks with anticipation, "Clara, what is it? What is it?" She shows him a check from World International Bank for $2.5 million dollars. Jack and Tom sit in their rental car, laughing at the excitement from his parents.

After all the commotion settles a bit, he says, "Mom, Dad, I have a lot of explaining to do, so let's go home and dive into it."

They pull into the driveway, excited to hear how their son has become so wealthy in such a short period. Tom and Jack park in the driveway, greeting his parents.

"Mom, Dad, I would like to introduce some very important gentlemen, Mr. Jack Ross and Mr. Tom Dunbar. They established themselves beside Crystal, helping her become one of the most powerful businesswomen in California."

"Son, what are you talking about?" asks James.

"Dad, remember the little girl I had a crush on when I was a kid who became a porn star?" He hesitates for a moment as the thought of her conjures up heartache. Gathering himself, he continues, "She passed away a few months ago, leaving me sole beneficiary of her estate. These gentlemen have worked diligently by my side, day after day, helping me maintain economic and social efficiency in my businesses. They're here today to find out who owns the land on the other side of Webster's Lake and to introduce themselves as your lawyer and accountant."

They all look at each other surprised as Clara asks, "What do you mean our new lawyer and accountant?"

"Well, I've watched you two work hard for years to achieve the success you have today, and I believe you should be rewarded for your dedication. Mom, I know you have a business of your own, so I'm going to add to your prosperity by making the two of you CEOs of my corporation. Crystal was a real estate tycoon owning several properties spanning from Las Vegas to San Diego, California."

In unison, they say, "Son, you have a deal."

"I will announce my retirement Monday," says James.

"Thank you, Mom and Dad. Now let's have our first official meeting to bring you up to date."

The next morning, his parents are up early, strategizing on how they would continue to build and improve their corporation.

"Good morning. I see you're getting right down to business just as I knew you would," says Trevor.

"We want to make a good impression on our new boss. We've asked Jack and Tom to accompany us on a tour of our businesses after the holidays to introduce ourselves and hopefully make minor adjustments. I think it would be good if you went with us to introduce yourself as the new owner and to meet and greet the employees," says James.

"I would prefer to stay low-key right now. I want to concentrate on school without a lot of hassle," he replies.

"We understand. Don't worry. Enjoy your youth and let us do the rest," says Clara.

"I remember the land across from Webster's Lake used to be owned by the Ledlows," says James.

"Thank you. I'll call Jack," says Trevor.

"It's already being taken care of." He smiles as his father says, "What can I say? You're working with the best."

The phone rings, and on the other end, Jack says, "I'm standing next to the owner of the land you want to purchase. Would you like to speak with him?"

"Good work, Jack. Please put him on the phone," says Trevor.

The young man says in a strong Southern dialect, "Hello, this is David Ledlow."

"Mr. Ledlow, I understand you own the property across from Webster's Lake?"

"Yep, my grandpa left me a thousand acres of worthless farmland and a couple of broken-down tractors in his last will and testament. I work at the paper mill to support me and my grandma. The pay ain't that good, but I guess I can't complain 'cause it puts food on the table. Why are you asking me 'bout that land? It's not worth anything. I tried to sell it when my grandpa passed away, but nobody wanted it."

"Mr. Ledlow, I would like to purchase all one thousand acres from you. How much would you sell it for?"

"I reckon I could sell it to you for $5,000. That would surely help me and my grandma out a lot. We could move into another house and live like common folks then."

"You'll sell me one thousand acres of land for $5,000?"

"All right, all right, I'll take $2,000 for it, and I'll throw in the two old tractors with it. Do we have a deal?"

He hesitates for a moment and then says, "Mr. Ledlow, I accept your offer. Thank you so much. Please give the phone back to Mr. Ross."

"Tom and I have all the papers here ready to sign. You have made a steal of a deal for this property. They're celebrating behind me right now," says Jack.

"Jack, make the check out for $5 million dollars and tell them I said Merry Christmas."

"Crystal would be very proud of you if she could see you now," says Jack.

He smiles as the thought of her captivates his spirit.

A familiar voice says, "My, my, look at how much you have grown."

He quickly embraces his grandmother, lifting her off her feet. "Grandma, it seems like forever since I saw you. How are you doing?"

"I'm doing fair. This old house isn't as springy as it used to be when you were a little boy. My bones are weak, and I just can't get around like I used too."

"Don't kid yourself, Grandma. You're still young and feisty. Why don't you come with me to visit California? It's beautiful with sunsets that will take your breath away."

"That's nice of you to invite me, but I don't believe my weary body will allow me to make such a long trip. I feel my days on this earth are coming to an end and I'm going home to glory."

"Mother, don't talk like that. You'll sadden our spirits," says Clara.

"Well, it's true. I didn't come here to stay, and my time is coming soon," replies Letha.

"Grandma, I still have a lot to learn from you, and we want to enjoy your presence for as long as we can. Dad, can I borrow the car? I'm going to make a quick run to the store and to Tyson's house. I'll be back soon."

"Be careful and don't drive too fast," says Clara.

Tyson's father is outside raking leaves as he pulls up to the curb, yelling, "Hello, is Tyson coming home for the holidays?"

"No, he's in a special naval pilot program. I think he told me he would be home in April for spring break. I'll tell him you stopped by the next time he calls. That's a nice car you're driving," replies Ramone.

"It's my dad's new toy. I'll see you later."

He zooms around the corner onto the highway, enjoying the moment as he drives by his old high school. Memories of the past flood his mind as he smiles, blowing his horn in remembrance. A familiar face catches the corner of his eye as he speeds by. He makes a quick U-turn, parking in the empty parking lot.

A voice says, "Well, well, look who it is." He frowns as he looks at the gentleman, trying to recall who he is. The young man approaches him slowly, limping with a cane. He says, "Trevor, don't look at me as if you don't know me. I know I've gained a few pounds and I walk with a limp, but you should remember me. I'll give you a hint. We won state championship in football my senior year, your sophomore year, right here on this field. They called me Ice Man Jones because I could slide through any hole the defense made for me."

"Darrell Jones, is that you? What are you doing here? I remember you received a full scholarship to play football at any university of your choice."

"I went to play for the Titans at Dice University in Miami. My first year I was starting running back, and we won the national championship. We were on our way to winning our second championship when tragedy struck, and I shattered my knee in the third quarter. We still won that year, but I was on the sidelines, hobbling around on a bum knee. I wasn't too fond of going to class, and when the coaches and doctors told me that my career in football was over, I dropped out of college. The only thing I have now is three championship rings and memories. Coach Titer lets me hang around as his assistant, helping him rebuild a stronger, better program. It looks like you're doing very well."

"Oh, that's my dad's car. I'm here for the holidays. I'm studying business at Mira Mesa University in San Diego, California."

"I wish I would have paid more attention in class. Right now, my life is slightly better than the lady in the park," replies Darrell. He looks at him, confused. "She graduated from this school, and now she lives in the park's sewer system. She used to be one of the hottest babes on campus. She was also the football team's head cheerleader, if you know what I mean. I don't know if it's true or not, but I heard she and her best friend went off to college sleeping with everything that had two legs and a dick. One of them contracted the AIDS virus and died about a year ago. I think their names were Candice and Vanessa," says Darrell.

Trevor stumbles back with a flushed face, saying, "I know them. Tyson and I went to the prom with them. Which one of them lives in the park?"

"I'm not sure, but the park is just around the corner if you can stand the smell of her. I better get back to work. It was nice to see you again. Take care of yourself," replies Darrell.

In the park, he sees a frail, humped-over woman with tattered clothes hanging from her body. He stands silently for a moment, watching her dig through a garbage can, searching for scraps of food. He slowly approaches her, trying not to startle her. He says, "Hello." She simply shrugs her shoulders, making grunting sounds. He steps closer as the stench of her body pushes him backward. He says again, "Hello, miss. My name is Trevor. I don't know if you remember, but I believe we double-dated to prom a few years ago."

She turns slowly with her head tucked inside a torn, dingy sweater. Her hair is dirty and matted together. Her shoes are worn and torn, exposing her dingy, crusty feet. She shivers as tears fall from her dirty face. He takes off his jacket and drapes it around her shoulders as his stomach begins to churn and boil from the foul odor of her body. She lifts her head as he tries to see who's behind the mask of dirt. He takes a handkerchief from his pocket, dipping it into a small water fountain, clearing the rest of the dirt path created by a trail of tears. A face starts to appear as several spectators stand, taking pictures of this event. He recognizes the face beneath the mask. He says in a tearful voice, "Candice, it's me Trevor. Don't you remember me?"

She reaches into her blouse, taking out a dirty torn picture, looking at it and then at the gentleman standing in front of her. Her body begins to tremble as she screams with pain. Tears flood her face as she drops the photo and runs back to her home in the sewer. He picks the torn photo off the ground, crying, as he looks upon the beauty of them together crowned as prom king and queen. He returns to his car feeling heartbroken and useless as another piece of his soul fades into the shadows of darkness. He drives off to the one and only place that allows him the comfort of peace and sanctity.

The lake is still beautiful as he glances at wilderness. His body shivers among clouds of mist as he stands with his hands deep in his pockets. His mind travels into endless space as voices of the past seem so prevalent, ringing in his ear. He smiles looking around vivaciously as if they were standing next to him. He begins to laugh, emitting clouds of vapor into the frigid air. Nature gives no response to his sanity as they're protected by Mother Nature's rapture in this wintry season. He falls to his knees, sticking his hands into the glacial water, disturbing its peace. Out of the ripples, he imagines seeing Crystal smiling and dancing gracefully on a blanket of mist hovering above the lake. He stands to his feet, yelling, "Crystal, I love you!" His arms are stretched out, ready to receive her love and warmth. His voice echoes through this hollow paradise as she fades away, leaving him stranded alone in the wilderness.

Clara notices his solemn attitude when he walks through the door but decides not to pry, thinking it may escalate the situation. Rusty is in his favorite spot at the foot of the bed, whimpering as he acknowledges something is bothering his longtime friend. He gives him the old paw handshake as Trevor lies back on his bed, capturing memories, wishing there is some way he could recover the past. Clara peeks in at him, finding him peacefully asleep.

James asks, "Clara, is there something wrong?"

"I feel that something is bothering our son. He just doesn't seem like himself."

"Stop worrying. He'll be just fine. A lot of changes have occurred in his life recently and the stress of holiday traveling. I think he'll be okay. He just needs to get some rest. I'll talk to him in the morning so you can be at peace," says James.

The next morning, after breakfast, James says, "Trevor, I haven't finished Christmas shopping for your mother and grandmother. Let's play Santa and sneak away in my hot, new sleigh."

"Sure, Dad."

On their way to the mall, James asks, "Is there something bothering you?"

"No, Dad. I'm an eighteen-year-old multimillionaire."

"Son, I know you're smart enough to know money doesn't make you happy."

"I'm okay. Don't worry. I admit things have been a little crazy, but I can handle it."

He eludes his parents during this season of happiness by masking his thoughts and feelings. Inside, he feels like a scrooge, ready for the season to end. Every afternoon, he sneaks away to the seclusion of his peaceful paradise. Standing alone in the wilderness is therapy as he releases his frustrations with tears and a vivid imagination.

CHAPTER 31

Christmas Day this year is unusual. Layers of snowflakes cover the ground as thousands more fall from the heavens, creating a delightful scene. This is the first time in his life he has awakened to a white Christmas. The streets are full of kids and adults throwing snowballs at one another. The entire family, including Rusty, stand in the window admiring this spectacular event. Rusty gallivants back and forth through the house, barking at this unfamiliar scene. Trevor dresses himself warmly and takes Rusty outside to investigate. He whimpers like a baby, lowering his nose to the ground, trying to sniff out this new land. Rusty walks with caution as if he were a sensible human trying not to fall. He stuffs his snout into the cold, powdery snow, startling himself as it clings to him. He zips across the yard full speed ahead, sneezing and slapping himself in the face, trying to rid himself of this unfamiliar content. The entire family laughs at Rusty as he makes a spectacle of himself. Trevor cuffs a ball of snow in his hand and hurls it at Rusty, smacking him right in the face. He laughs uncontrollably as Rusty blindly flops around in the yard like a headless chicken.

Seconds later, he takes cover behind his dad's car as several snowballs are launched at him. Letha gathers a handful of snowballs, throwing them aimlessly at James as Clara sneaks up from behind, filling his trousers full of frosty ice. The entire family is now included in this neighborhood snowball fight as friends across the street begin to attack them. This is a day he will never forget as he watches his parents and grandmother flop around in the snow in their pajamas like they were kids again.

A kind thought enters his mind as he enjoys this Christmas Day with his family. He runs into the house looking like Frosty the Snowman. He gathers a large plate of food, a picture from his scrapbook, a large blanket, and his checkbook. He runs outside with his hands full, saying, "I'll be right back to open presents. I'm going to lift the spirits of an old friend of mine." They wave goodbye as the snowball fight continues with the next-door neighbors.

He pulls into an empty snow-white parking lot, gazing at a figure sitting alone on a park bench drawing in the snow. He says, "Merry Christmas, Candice. I brought you some gifts I think you might enjoy." She raises her head, lowering the shabby, tattered cloth from around her shoulders. He smiles as he recognizes the jacket she wears. He approaches the bench, placing the gifts by her side. She begins to sob as he begs, "Please don't cry. Today is Christmas."

She mutters in a teary voice, "Why do you care? Nobody else does. Not even my parents who bore me into this selfish world. The only true friend I ever had is lying in Water Creek Cemetery, where I should be."

He wipes a spot clean on the bench to sit beside her, placing a warm blanket around her. He says, "I still remember this beautiful young lady whom I had the pleasure of going to the prom with." He places the photo of the two of them in her lap, saying, "I thought you might like to have a new one since your old one is sort of worn-out." He turns his head to take a breath of fresh air, and then he says, "Candice, I truly understand your pain. A few months ago, I lost the love of my life by her own hands. She let the world dictate her life, and it ended in tragedy. I'm here pleading with you not to travel the same lonely highway Crystal did. In my mind, I still see you as that beautiful young lady I had the pleasure of spending a wonderful prom night with." He reaches into his coat pocket, pulling out his checkbook. "I want you to promise me you will take this money and get as far away from this place as you can. You still have a lot to live for, and I truly believe Vanessa would want you to be happy."

She looks at the check, saying, "Thank you, but I'm not looking for any charitable donations. This is my home now. This is where I belong." She gets up, giving the check back to him as he stands there with his hands behind his back. "Very well. I'll keep this money as a reminder of your generosity. I must go now. Thank you for your kindness, but please don't bother to come back out here to see me again. I don't want to be bothered."

He watches her shabby silhouette disappear into the dark tunnels of the sewer. She watches him in tears from a crevasse walking slowly back to his car. She weeps softly, looking at the picture of the two of them so happy together.

He reclines the seat back for a moment as the thought of despair weighs on his mind heavily. Leaving the park, he parks his jeep next to the curb, running through the snow to the entrance of the sewer, yelling down its pitch-black tunnels, "I believe in you, Candice! I will not accept you giving up on life because I care even if you don't, and I always will!"

CHAPTER 32

His family is gathered around the Christmas tree, laughing and talking as he enters the house. Clara says, "Honey, did you make someone's Christmas special?"

"Yes, I did, Mom. Now let's see what Santa Claus has for us."

Letha is sound asleep on the sofa, and Rusty is asleep, curled up next to her feet. They smile trying not to disturb them with their excitement and curiosity to see what gifts they have. At the end of the gift exchange, they move themselves to the entertainment room where James surprises them with some old videotapes of them from their first Christmas together. Clara cries happy tears, and Trevor and James laugh at each other's old-fashioned clothes and hairstyles. They look at each other, frowning, as Trevor says, "Dad, do you smell that, or is my mind playing tricks on me?"

"No, son, I smell it too." They get up scurrying to the kitchen.

Letha says, "Merry Christmas! I'm making you my famous chicken and fluffy golden-brown biscuits for breakfast."

They begin to dance around the table, chanting, "Chicken and biscuits, chicken and biscuits."

Clara says, "Mom, I thought you were asleep."

"I was pretending so you all would leave and I could prepare my famous breakfast," replies Letha.

Trevor and James are seated at the table, frothing at the mouth as she removes those golden-brown biscuits from the oven. This Christmas breakfast revives dormant taste buds as the fluffy biscuits seem to melt in their mouths. After breakfast, Trevor gets up from the table, saying,

"Thank you, Grandma, for a delicious breakfast. I think I better go lie down. My eyes are getting heavy from biscuit poisoning." Clara helps Letha tidy up the kitchen, while James returns to the living room, sprawling himself across the couch, listening to the crackle of wood burning in the fireplace.

CHAPTER 33

The holidays have come and gone. The airport is full of buzzing travelers. They give each other a group hug as his grandmother slips him one last present before he boards the plane. She says, "I think you will like this one. It's very special." He hugs her tightly, thanking her for such an exquisite Christmas breakfast.

First-class and business-class passengers begin to load the plane. Waving goodbye, he quickly disappears down the terminal. His last present is the old Bible his grandmother read to him when he was an infant in his crib. He smiles as the thrust of the twin jet engines lift them into the clouds above. Peering out of the small window, he waves goodbye to Alabama.

He steps off the plane, taking in a deep breath of California's salty ocean air as he walks toward the taxi booth. He laughs as he imagines his father driving around two hot sports cars feeling like he's young again.

The taxi driver asks, "What's your destination?"

He replies, "Mira Mesa University."

He's excited to be back in California to enjoy its warm climate and beautiful palm trees. The campus is quiet with a handful of new sports cars scattered in various parking spots. The smell of his room is like the garden of Eden. He drops his luggage in the middle of the floor and dives on his bed. He picks up the phone and calls an old friend.

A familiar voice says, "This is J. D. Hughes. How may I help you?"

He replies, "Happy New Year! I was wondering if you were interested in selling some valuable property to me?"

"Happy New Year! Everything has a price. The question is, are you willing to pay the price for what you want?" asks JD.

"I'm willing to pay the price for that beautiful piece of machinery you keep tucked away in your garage."

"Awww, someone must have had a very good Christmas," says JD.

"It was most enjoyable. Now how much do you want for that fine piece of machinery?"

"The voice of a true businessman. He knows what he wants, and he goes after it. It's going to cost you, but I'll make you a deal since I like you. I'll sell it to you for $100,000."

"Very well. I'll write you a check from World International."

"Did you say World International? Very impressive. All great minds do think alike. I'm on the board of trustees for that bank. I will deliver it to you right away, and congratulations on your second-best investment. I can see you're going to be a great asset in my corporation," replies JD.

The phone rings just as he puts it on the receiver. It's Tom, saying, "Happy Holidays, Trevor. I hope you enjoyed your family."

"Thank you, I had a wonderful time with my family. How was yours?"

"I was a little busier than I wanted to be trying to keep the books balanced. Crystal's videos, posters, lingerie, books, and everything else that has her name on it skyrocketed in sales this holiday season. There was also a record-breaking profit gain in all of your hotels, restaurants, and casinos. According to my books, you profited $400 million last year, and you have earned a cool half a million in the first three days of the New Year. You will also receive huge dividends from generous charitable contributions and investments when I file your taxes."

"Thank you, Tom. I'm expecting the arrival of the best Christmas present ever in just a few moments. I just purchased a rebuilt '69 Shelby GT 500 with all its original parts from Mr. J. D. Hughes. I left my Mustang and Ferrari at home with my father."

An anticipated knock on his door cuts his conversation short with Tom as he says, "Tom, Santa is at my door with the greatest Christmas present of all. I'll talk to you later on this week." He eagerly runs to the door, swinging it open to Naomi dressed as Mrs. Claus.

She says, "Merry Christmas, baby. I brought you a little something since we didn't get to celebrate Christmas together this year. I hope you like it."

He smiles, hugging her tightly, feeling a little disappointed because she wasn't whom he was expecting and he forgot to get her a Christmas present. A glimmering crystal panther emerges from the box. "Oh my gosh, this is great! I love it. I'm going to buy a pretty glass cabinet to place this in," he says. He quickly makes up a story of wanting to see her before he purchases her Christmas present to ensure she will like it.

A knock at the door makes his blood rush as he opens the door to JD's butler holding the keys to his dream car. He quickly takes the keys from his right hand, placing the check in his left hand as the butler says, "Thank you, sir. They're unloading your car off the truck for you."

Naomi looks baffled as they walk outside to see this astonishing piece of machinery. She says, "I thought you had a Mustang and a new Ferrari."

"I left the Ferrari and the Mustang at home with my dad," he replies. He runs to the passenger side, opening and closing the door for her, anxiously waiting to hear its powerful, supercharged engine come alive. He blindfolds Naomi, grips the steering wheel, and takes off down the highway. Naomi gets nervous as he pulls into an underground garage at Diamonds, an elegant palace of rare diamonds. He leads her up the escalator into the store where he removes her blindfold. She is dazzled by the large selection of beautiful diamond tennis bracelets.

A salesman comes over, saying, "Good evening, would you like to try on some of our bracelets?"

She looks at Trevor with a smile as wide as Texas. "Yes, we would like to see the three on the top shelf and the two in the middle on the bottom shelf," he says.

"What a nice selection, sir. I will give you a few minutes to choose the one you like," replies the salesman.

Naomi places each bracelet on her wrist one at a time, admiring its luster and unique design. "I can't choose. I like them all," she says.

The salesman comes back, asking, "Would you like a few more minutes, sir?"

"No, I think I like this one right here," replies Trevor.

"What a fine selection. That's our best-seller. This bracelet is 5.5 karats, and it looks astonishing on your wrist, ma'am."

"Naomi, it's your present. Do you like it?"

"I love it. We'll take this one."

The salesman asks, "Would you like to insure your purchase for a one-time payment of $1,000?"

"Yes, thank you."

"Your total is $6,000." He pays for the bracelet with his Platinum Plus Visa card.

Just as they are leaving, JD walks in, saying, "Hello, Trevor. I knew I recognized the beautiful machine in the parking garage. I see you have purchased a fine piece of jewelry for this beautiful young lady. The palace is vacant this week if you want to be alone."

He nudges JD's foot as she asks, "Trevor, what is he talking about?"

"My apologies, I thought she already knew about our secret hideaway. Please allow me to make dinner reservations for the two of you at Chateau de Plume. It's one of the finest restaurants in California," replies JD.

"Thank you for your hospitality. I will see you soon," says Trevor.

CHAPTER 34

Chateau de Plume's artistry and design reflect the Renaissance period with its elaborate paintings decorating the walls and ceilings. The host, well dressed in a tuxedo, asks, "Do you have reservations, sir?"

"O'Riely, party of two," he replies.

The host checks his book, saying, "Yes, sir, we have you seated in our romance section. Please follow me."

This section is very romantic with candlelit tables; soft, sensual music; and a perfect view of the ocean. Their waiter, dressed very elegantly, says, "Good evening, I will be your server tonight. This section comes with a bottle of wine of your choice on the house. Let me know when you are ready to order."

The menu seems endless with a variety of succulent meals, making it hard to choose. They view the wine list together, unable to decide. He has the waiter bring them the house favorite.

"How do you know Todd's dad?" asks Naomi.

"I was the guest of honor at his house a few months ago. He offered me a job in his company. He says I remind him a lot of himself when he was young and ambitious," he replies.

"Wow, that's very impressive and smart to have a person like J. D. Hughes admire you. Someone needs to give his spoiled brat son a few lessons on how not to be an idiot. I can't believe I almost went out with that creep. What a loser," she replies.

The waiter comes back with their entrées and wine. The chef decorated them in such a fashion that they're almost too pretty to eat. The waiter comes back around, saying, "Your check and tip have already been paid. Please stay as long as you like. I will check on you periodically to see if you need anything else." Dinner is superb. He takes the bottle of wine, and they quietly exit.

He reluctantly drives her to JD's secret getaway, cursing him in his head for being garrulous. There it stands, just as graceful as before. He smiles as his mind reflects back on the moments he spent with Crystal in this same setting.

She asks, "Why are you smiling so much? What are you thinking about?"

"Oh, nothing much," he replies.

"Let's get inside, mister, so we can continue our romantic evening," she says.

He looks at her abrasively behind her back as they enter the house. She dances around the hallways like Cinderella as he tries to move her away from the one room where he and Crystal lay together, inseparable from each other. She runs from room to room, gloating at its magnificence as they come to the one room he defies her to be in. She enters, enthralled by its contents and scenery. She says, "This is where I want to make love to you tonight."

The blood courses through his veins like hot water as he says in a gentle tone, "I would rather sleep in the other bedroom. It has so much more room."

"We don't need a lot of room for the things we're going to do tonight. I want you where I can reach you at any time," she replies. She looks at him in the same sensual way Crystal once did, creating an illusion of her in his mind. He falls into her passion, making love to her in the gentlest way he knows how.

The skylights automatically open as an early morning sea breeze blows through, arousing his motionless body to life. Yawning and stretching, he quietly gets out of bed, trying not to disturb Naomi. He walks to the other side of the bedroom glancing out of its enormous windows at two dolphins frantically playing tag with each other, diving in and out of the water. He sneers at them, disturbing Sleeping Beauty from her rest.

She rolls over, feeling blindly for his warm body, lifting her head, saying, "I dreamed I had countless orgasms last night. Come back to bed so I can enjoy countless more."

He turns and replies, "We better get back to campus. I need to prepare myself for class tomorrow."

"Don't be ridiculous. We have all day to prepare for class. Why don't I cook breakfast for us while you relax and enjoy this beautiful house?" she replies. She jumps out of bed and streaks to the bathroom to bathe in a unique shower where jets of water emerge from behind the ceramic tiles, spraying her simultaneously from head to toe.

A voice sailing on a breeze says, "Let me go. I'm free." He turns quickly, looking for a body to connect the spoken words to, but the room is empty, only containing himself. He asks, "Crystal, is that you?" Looking around frantically, the voice sails in again, repeating the same lines. He drops to his knees, weeping, complying with her request. He removes the diamond necklace from his neck, kissing its crystal clear diamonds. He dashes through the front door, stopping at the edge of the cliff with his arms stretched out, clenching the necklace tightly. He springs his arm back with all his strength, hurling the necklace as far as he can through the air. The sun seems to beam down on it, creating an unforeseen brilliance as it dances through the atmosphere, descending to its new home in the deep blue.

CHAPTER 35

Several months roll by like a whisper, and the thought of Crystal diminishes to only a few fond memories. His parents are doing exceedingly well as the profit margins continue to climb throughout his corporation. He fills his heart's desire with expensive toys and the pleasure of being with Naomi. His name is engraved in gold for academic excellence on a huge bronze plaque among several proud men and women dating back to the early eighteenth century. The greatest accomplishment in his mind is working directly for J. D. Hughes, one of the most powerful, influential businessmen in the world, as his intern.

Excited by the way his life is unfolding, he drops by Naomi's room to take her out for a little celebration on his lavish one-hundred-foot yacht he just purchased. Holding a dozen beautiful red roses before his face, he knocks on the door gently. Lauren comes to the door with a T-shirt on that barely covers her ass. "Mr. Sexy, how are you? Come in."

He slowly walks in, asking, "Where is Naomi?"

"She's at the library. She should be back soon." She walks over to the couch, bending over, exposing her lacy thong and firm ass. "Do you like it?" she asks.

"Do I like what?"

"My ass, silly. I know you're looking at it wondering how good it feels. Would you like to sample it?" She walks in a sexy, seductive way toward him with her nipples piercing through her thin T-shirt. Backing him against the door, she presses her firm body against his, saying, "Naomi told me…" She scurries to the bathroom as they hear Naomi singing, coming up the stairs.

He nervously sits on the couch, trying desperately to get himself together before she walks through the door. As she stumbles through the door with a hand full of books, he greets her with beautiful roses.

"Thank you. They're so pretty. What's the occasion?"

"You."

Blushing, she gives him a big hug and kiss. Lauren walks out of the bathroom fully dressed in flannel pajamas, saying, "All right, all right, that's enough."

"Lauren, don't you have a room with your name on it?" he asks.

"Yes, I do, but I stay here on Thursday and Friday nights after I finish teaching my aerobics classes. I don't like walking across campus by myself at night." She waves good night, walking into the bedroom, leaving the two romantics cuddling on the couch.

"I have so much studying to do I don't know where to begin," says Naomi.

"I have a little surprise for you, but it can wait until this weekend," he says.

"You can tell me now. My test isn't until Friday. I still have two full days to study."

"No, we have plenty of time to enjoy this. Right now, studying is more important. I better go so you can concentrate," he replies. She gives him the starry-eyed, pitiful look as he kisses her good night.

The campus is sparsely populated as he treks across campus to his dorm. Upon entering the building, he can hear his phone ringing. Hurrying up the stairs, he quickly opens the door, grabbing the phone. A familiar voice says, "Hello, brother, how are you?"

He yells, "Tyson, what's up man! When are you coming home?"

"I've been home for a week enjoying my parents and some other relatives. I was awarded the chance to come home a week earlier than everybody else for outstanding academic and physical excellence," replies Tyson.

"This is perfect timing. I will make sure you enjoy your visit. Your plane tickets will be waiting for you when you get to the airport tomorrow. I will schedule your departure for two o'clock, your time.

Don't worry about a cab because you're going to ride in style to campus," replies Trevor.

"Man, I've got so much to talk to you about. I can't wait to see you. My cousins just arrived. I'll see you tomorrow," replies Tyson. The excitement of Tyson's arrival won't allow him to sleep that night. He makes several phone calls through the night, planning trips for them.

CHAPTER 36

The hour seems to trudge by as he sits in class monitoring the clock instead of the lecture on ergonomical theory. Tyson's plane is due to arrive in less than half an hour. The anticipation is nauseating as he sits through this monotonous lecture. Time finally releases him from captivity, and he darts out of the classroom, running past Naomi and Lauren in the hall, telling them to be ready at six this afternoon. Scrambling to his dorm, he waits patiently outside for Tyson's arrival. A black limousine parks in front of his dorm. The chauffeur opens the door for Tyson, and he springs out with arms wide open. They embrace each other like brothers reunited.

"This is the best college campus I've ever seen. Is everybody on this campus rich? I saw at least five Lamborghinis as soon as we entered the gates. Some lucky, rich kid probably doesn't even realize how lucky he is to own one of America's finest machines, an original '69 Shelby GT 500," says Tyson.

"I'm sure the person who owns this beauty is very aware of his gift. Enough talk about cars, we have some partying to do, so let's get dressed," replies Trevor.

Time almost gets away as they bring each other up to date about various incidents that have occurred in their lives since they've been apart. "I'm calling Naomi and Lauren to see if they are ready," says Trevor.

"You got us dates for the night?" asks Tyson.

"No, I got us dates for the week," replies Trevor.

Tyson jumps up and down, screaming, "I'm going to get laid! I'm going to get laid!"

The chauffeur is waiting patiently by the car as they pile in. Naomi and Lauren are waiting outside their dorm as the chauffeur stops to pick them up. He introduces them to Tyson as Lauren whispers, "There is a god."

"I hope you ladies can dance in those high heels because we're going to Club Passion to see you shake what your mama gave ya," says Trevor.

Passion was jam-packed with hot, half-naked bodies as the DJ mixes it up with techno, rap, and booty-shaking music. The smell of cigarette smoke and alcohol perfumed the air as hot, sweaty bodies collide against one another, creating a decadent scene. They returned to their table for a break.

"Wow, Trevor, I didn't know you could dance like that. I'm ashamed to go back out there with you," says Naomi.

"He's always been good at dancing even when we were little. We used to have dance contests in the hallways at school before class began," says Tyson.

"A man who knows how to work it on the floor knows how to work it in bed," says Lauren.

"I'll vouch for that," replies Naomi.

They danced themselves to exhaustion, staggering out of the club at two in the morning. The chauffeur is asleep in the car as Trevor gently knocks on the window, startling him. He opens the door quickly, saying, "I'm sorry, sir."

Trevor instructs him to drive them to Bayside Yacht Club. Naomi and Lauren look confused as Trevor reclines back into the soft leather seat with a guilty smile on his face. Out of the blanket of darkness, the yacht club appears in colorful brilliance. Every yacht is unique in its design and size as they gaze upon a fleet of vessels aligned in perfect order.

"The captain is awaiting our arrival on one of these beautiful yachts. We will eat and spend the night in luxury fifty miles off the coast. Don't worry about anything. The Coast Guard is aware we'll be out here just in case something should go wrong. Please follow me. Our chariot awaits," says Trevor.

They walk to the end of the dock facing a huge, extravagant hundred-foot yacht.

"I would like to introduce you to the *Crystal Gale*, a floating palace," says Trevor.

"I know this isn't yours," says Tyson.

"My friend, it isn't what you know. It's who you know," replies Trevor.

"I'm starting to believe you're JD's long-lost son," says Naomi.

He smiles as the captain greets them, saying, "Good morning, I'm pleased to welcome you aboard the *Crystal Gale*. She is a three-story vessel equipped with powerful Stockholm engines that can propel us to more than twenty knots, six lavish master suites with full bathrooms, a game room, a full bar, an entertainment room equipped with twenty-five stadium-style seats, a pool, a Jacuzzi, a lavish dining room, a kitchen to prepare some of the most exquisite meals in the world, a two-million-dollar navigational system, a helicopter pad, and much more. Please enjoy the luxuries as my crew and I prepare to cast off."

They are amazed as their bodies are reenergized by all the excitement. Trevor gives them an elaborate tour of his floating palace from the captain's deck to the entertainment deck. The entourage camps out on the large plush sofas, listening to soft, crisp music from mounted cube speakers arranged on the ceiling. The laughing and joking lasts until five in the morning when they finally decide to go to bed.

The couples awaken to the captain's voice over the intercom, saying, "The time is 0900 hours. Breakfast will be served in thirty minutes. Please check your closets for your attire."

They roll out of bed, high on adrenaline, preparing themselves for today's festivities. The tables are neatly decorated, and they admire one another's semiformal attire and the smell of delicious pancakes. The party resumes as they sit at the table, enjoying one another's company, laughing and joking about their partner's sleep habits. The sound of thunderous clapping reaches their ears, and they rush to the captain's deck, investigating all the commotion. A black helicopter, with Crystal Palace embroidered on the doors, has landed aboard the *Crystal Gale*. The pilot ducks his head from the powerfully rotating blades, greeting them inside, saying, "Good afternoon, I will fly the four of you to our luxurious Crystal Palace, a five-star hotel and casino where you will enjoy a day of betting against the odds in our casino. You will also be pampered in our hotel's most prestigious penthouse suite for a night of peaceful sleep."

Trevor looks at them innocently, shrugging his shoulders as they load the helicopter. They feel like birds without wings as they tower above the huge metropolis of San Diego and Los Angeles, California. Tyson is exhilarated when the pilot invites him to be his copilot. Trevor stares out the window with a content heart as Naomi and Lauren gossip with each other about staying in a penthouse suite.

The hotel looks like a miracle of art as they land on the helicopter pad among several exclusively designed water fountains. Mr. Fisher, the general manager, greets them as they exit the helicopter, escorting them on a marble pathway to the entrance of this grand hotel. He types in a special code on this translucent elevator, and they zoom up fifty-five stories to their penthouse suite. A huge crystal chandelier hanging from the ceiling greets them as they enter the living room. They stand still in awe of the magnificence of the suite. This was like a dream they kept on dreaming. Mr. Fisher and Trevor step out for a moment to the privacy of his office.

"I'm pleased to see how well things are going. I've heard several great remarks from professors, friends, and several people around town talk about how nice our hotel is. That means it's genuine because no one knows I own all three Crystal Palaces. My parents were impressed by all the staff members' kindness and the cleanliness inside and outside the hotel. I'm also very impressed with the remarkable increase in profit. I'm going to show my generosity toward you and the entire staff by giving everyone a New Year's raise. My accountant, Mr. Tom Dunbar, will contact you Monday morning to discuss the percentages. I see a nice vacation and a bonus in your future," says Trevor.

"Thank you, sir, for your kindness and generosity. The entire staff will be pleased to hear the great news," replies Mr. Fisher. He takes a silver briefcase from his safe, giving it to Trevor as requested. The gentlemen shake hands and depart as if this meeting never occurred.

Everyone is lounging on the couches, chatting about what Trevor has up his sleeve as he enters the room.

"What are you up to?" asks Tyson.

"I had to go get our equipment," replies Trevor.

"Equipment? Are we having some wild, outrageous orgy or something?" asks Lauren.

He laughs, saying, "This briefcase contains the antidote to our freedom in the casino downstairs." They gather around him as he turns the combination, unlocking the secret contents of the briefcase. He opens the case, exposing four printed checks with their names on them in the amount of $10,000 apiece. They explode running out onto the balcony, screaming at the top of their lungs with exhilaration.

"This is your money to spend how you please, so let's go enjoy ourselves," says Trevor.

They spill into the elevator to the second floor where several people are betting their luck against the odds, hoping they will hit the jackpot. The ladies pair off to themselves, leaving Trevor and Tyson free to roam around the casino. They meet the ladies screaming while playing the slot machines as the sirens alarm, dispensing $2,000 in chips. Tyson and Trevor play the slot machines next to the ladies hoping they will get lucky enough to hear the sirens coming from their machines. They jump with excitement every time they hear sirens from other machines hoping they will be next. Their attention is turned for a moment to an older couple in the back who hit the jackpot on the slot machine for $200,000. Security rushes to their side, escorting them to the cash counter to exchange their chips for money. Trevor walks over to the same machine the previous couple just won $200,000 out of. He takes out a $100 dollar bill, puts it in the machine, crosses his fingers, closes his eyes, and pulls the handle. He opens his eyes to alarming flashing red lights as the audience claps for him. Tyson, Naomi, and Lauren rush to his side, jumping up and down, screaming as he looks up staring at $500,000 flashing above his slot machine. Five security guards crowd around them, escorting them to the cash counter.

The cashier asks, "Would you like this in cash or check?"

He replies, "Cash."

His friends stand there, buckeyed, as the cashier places stacks of $100 bills in a black briefcase. Two security guards escort them to the elevator and to their suite. They congratulate him on his winnings as he opens the briefcase, exposing his winnings. He takes a stack, counting out $10,000 in cash, giving each guard $5,000 apiece. They dance around the room, playing with their money, excited to see so many $100 bills at one time.

"Do you believe in fate?" asks Tyson.

"I do," replies Trevor. He opens the sliding glass doors to the balcony as a rush of wind blows past him, scattering money across the room. The skies are dark, with huge black clouds rolling across them. The wind blows furiously across the land, creating swirls of dustlike tornadoes. They stand against the rails, waving their hands as they resist the forces of nature pushing against their bodies. Their clothes beat against their bodies as they enjoy the rush of the warm winds blowing fiercely, creating the sound of a wild coyote howling. He takes five $100 bills from his pockets, yelling, "May fate find you a new home in someone's life!" The $100 bills race away in separate directions to a new destiny as the day becomes night and haphazard displays of lightning flash across the black sky. Heavy plops of rain begin to sporadically fall from the heavens, creating a thud-like sound against the surfaces.

Lauren looks at Tyson, saying, "I love to make love when it rains." He walks over to her, kissing her passionately as the rain begins to shower them. The couples retire to their bedrooms, encountering a fierce battle of lust and passion on their soft oversize beds.

A few hours pass by as Trevor wanders aimlessly in the dark toward the kitchen for a glass of water to quench his thirst. Feeling refreshed, he stumbles onto the couch right on top of Tyson. They both scream like little horrified girls as Trevor turns on a small lamp, asking, "What in the hell are you doing sleeping out here on the couch when you have a sexy, hot, naked chick lying in bed?"

"We were in the heat of the moment, and I thought I was ready to do this. But I started to think about Maria and I just couldn't do it. She got pissed off and kicked me out of the bedroom, so I found some blankets in the closet and made the couch my bed," replies Tyson.

"Maria must mean a lot to you."

"She means the world to me. Someday, I will marry her, and I would love for you to be my best man," says Tyson.

"You have a deal. Please allow me to give you and Maria an early wedding present. I want you to gather all the loose money on the floor and in the suitcase for yourself. It's all yours." Tyson sits up with a look of astonishment in his eyes, not knowing what to say or do. He smiles, patting Tyson on the head, returning to his queen. Their pleasures continued in several exotic places until the last minute of time as they shuffle through the airport before Tyson misses his plane. He waves goodbye to them, running through the terminal minutes before the stewardess closes the gates.

CHAPTER 37

A few months pass by, and Trevor finds himself in junior-class status with the highest GPA on campus. He receives a letter in his mailbox from J. D. Hughes, congratulating him both on his success and becoming the newest intern in his company. He decides to visit an old spot where his friends once took him when he first arrived at Mira Mesa. The thought of them saddens his heart as he wonders where they are and how they're doing. He faintly hears Chris's voice, saying, "Hey, let's go see Lana." Sunset Beach is still just as beautiful as it was before. He strolls down the beach, enjoying the cool feeling of small waves crashing on his feet. He stops for a moment in front of Lovers Cave, thinking about Crystal and her beautiful blue eyes.

A gentleman walking past stops and says, "You're the guy I've been looking for." Trevor looks at him strangely as the gentleman says, "Please forgive me. My name is Luke, and I'm the dance choreographer/manager for Men of Desire. I saw you at Players a couple of months ago, and I was very impressed by the way you move on the dance floor. You move very sinuously like it's second nature to you. Are you a dance choreographer?"

"No, I just do it. It's the only thing I was good at other than being a nerd when I was in grade school," replies Trevor.

"How would you like to become a member of Men of Desire? I believe with your skills, you could become a very important asset to the group," replies Luke.

"No, I don't think I want to become a stripper. I'm in college right now at Mira Mesa studying business. Thank you, but I don't think this is for me," replies Trevor.

"Here, take my card, and if you ever feel like getting wild and loose on stage, give me a call anytime," says Luke.

He waves goodbye to the gentleman, shoving the card in his pocket, laughing at the thought of himself becoming a stripper.

CHAPTER 38

A few weeks pass by, and he has not complied with JD about becoming his intern. He scrambles his brains trying to figure out how he would tell JD he's not going to accept the position. He decides to confide in Naomi, telling her everything about the inheritance. He knocks on her door as a sexy voice from behind says, "She's not home. I saw her at night study, and I think she's going to be there a little while."

He turns slowly, saying, "Lauren, why don't you move in with her? You're always here."

"Hey, what are friends for? Besides, I told you once before. I stay here when I have aerobics class, or did you forget? Why don't you come inside and wait for her? I'm going to take a shower, and I'll keep you company until she arrives," she replies.

He turns the stereo on, plugs in the headphones, and reclines back on the couch, listening to soft jazz music. Drops of cool water roll down his forehead, startling him from the sounds of relaxing vibes. He opens his eyes to Lauren standing above him, dripping water from her long blond hair.

"Do you mind if I listen?" she asks.

He takes the headphones off, giving them to her as she sashays around the room with a short towel wrapped around her hourglass body. Her movements begin to intrigue him as he watches her half-naked body frolic around the room. He sits up on the couch, stuffing his hands in his pockets, trying to hide the evidence of an erection, but that only escalates the problem. She plops down across his lap, exposing her heart-shaped ass as the rush of blood from his brain to his head begins to possess his thoughts.

"I know you want it, so why don't we stop playing childish games and go for it?" she says. She straddles him, taking his hands from his pockets. The moment becomes so intense his vocal cords become paralyzed as he sits there helplessly staring into her eyes. "Relax and let Mama show you how it's done," she says. She unzips his pants, undressing him piece by piece. She grabs his erect dick aggressively, squeezing it, stroking it, and teasingly licking it, sending his mind and body into unbearable passion. "I see you're genetically endowed where it counts the most," she says. She stands up gripping a handful of the soft black leather as she slowly descends onto his throbbing dick. He lays his head back on the sofa, rolling his eyes into the back of his head as sensual pleasure course through his body. Harmonious melodies spew out, filling the room as she climaxes.

The blood begins to rush back to his brain, sending out panic alarms all over his body as he picks her up, tossing her naked body on the couch. He frantically puts his clothes back on, quickly disappearing without a word. Running in full stride back to his room, he collapses on the steps out of breath, nervously trembling, asking himself, "Why did I do it?" He runs upstairs to his room, stripping himself of his clothing and showering in cold water. He steps out of the shower, shivering, with chattering teeth from the hypothermic water. Wrapping himself in his towel, he walks to his bedroom trying to make sense of this ordeal. He sees Luke's card lying on his nightstand beside his bed. He picks up the phone, frantically calling him for advice.

"Hello, this is Luke."

He says in a shaky, nervous voice, "Hey, Luke, this is Trevor. I'm sort of in trouble right now, and I don't exactly know what to do."

"Calm down, take a deep breath, and tell me what the problem is," replies Luke.

"In short version, I just banged my girlfriend's best friend, and I don't know what to do," replies Trevor.

Luke laughs for a moment, saying, "I have the perfect job for you to get this off your mind. Why don't you meet me at the Black Rose on the corner of Twenty-Fourth Avenue across the street from Bungalow's Bar and Grill at seven o'clock?"

CHAPTER 39

The parking lot is full as a few late arrivals hurry to the door, hoping they will get in. He slowly walks across the street, approaching two giants dressed in black guarding the entrance. One of them asks, "What can I help you with tonight?"

"Luke is expecting me," Trevor replies.

They look at each other as one of them walks into the club to get Luke. He comes out greeting Trevor, saying, "I have the perfect job for you. Come on in and let me introduce you to the guys." The club is packed with sexy, screaming women as the DJ hypes the crowd with a variety of music. "Guys, calm down for a minute. We have a guest and possibly the sixth member of this group. Trevor, I would like to introduce you to Mike, aka Sexy Chocolate; Patrick, aka Spicy; Rico, aka Latin Lover; Tim, aka Brown Sugar; and Tony, aka Delicious. Trevor is going to be our bar runner tonight, delivering drinks to all the hot, thirsty women we have in the house tonight," says Luke.

"If he's going to be our bar runner, then he has to dress like one," says Pat. He passes him a pair of his black tuxedo pants with a black bow tie, saying, "Try it on and let's see how you look. Oh yeah, this is a no underwear facility."

Trevor changes clothes in the bathroom, looking at himself, wondering how the hell he got himself into this as he adjusts his bow tie. The guys say awesome as he walks out of the bathroom shirtless, displaying his well-developed upper torso.

"Rocco, our bartender, is going to mix the drinks, and you will take the orders and deliver them. He's waiting on you, so I'll see you later," says Luke.

They throw glitter on him, making him sparkle as he leaves the dressing room. The ladies scream at the top of their lungs as he walks out to the bar. The DJ plays their anthem as he introduces the gentlemen one by one to the dance floor. Green money seems to hover in the air as the sultry females wave their hands for drinks. He takes a deep breath, entering the lioness' den of horny women. They grope him mercilessly as he makes his way through a crowd of pantyless, flashing women, serving them drinks. Twenties, fifties, and one-hundred-dollar bills are stuffed down his pants as he mingles among the crowd. At the end of the night, all the glitter has been rubbed off, his pants are full of money, and he has smeared lipstick all over him. The guys sit around laughing at him as he talks about his adventurous night.

"Well, how did you enjoy your first night on the job?" asks Luke. He looks at Luke smiling, pulling money out of his pants. "Well, I guess this means we will see you next weekend?" asks Luke.

"Yes, I'll be back," replies Trevor.

Rico comes out of the dressing room counting several $100 bills, saying, "I'll check you guys later. I have a bed full of whores fighting over who's going to swallow my cum."

CHAPTER 40

His mind is clear; he feels exhilarated sitting in class thinking how outlandish this experience was and, at the same time, how free it makes him feel from his life of the straight and narrow. His attention diverts for a moment as the professor is interrupted by the dean, summoning his presence outside. The professor returns with his head held low as he summons Trevor to step outside for a moment. Trevor senses something is wrong by his mother's solemn appearance.

James says, "Son, I have some terrible news. Your grandmother passed away peacefully yesterday afternoon while entertaining family and friends."

He stands there for a moment completely silent, trying to cope with the loss of another great woman who has been taken away from him. The pain inside suppresses him emotionally, not allowing him to grieve for this magnificent woman who loved him dearly and helped in teaching him the essence of life. The professor gives his belongings to his parents, offering his condolences to the family. Trevor walks slowly outside the building, staring into the heavens, trying to understand why God has blessed him and cursed him at the same time. Falling to his knees with a broken spirit, he begins to cry relentlessly as the pain seems to crush him with every heartbeat. His parents kneel by his side, trying to hold back the tears as they console their son.

His grandmother lies there so peaceful and calm in eternal sleep as he stands above her lifeless body dressed in her Sunday's best. Decorative flowers from family and friends adorn her casket as they view this lady of grace for the last time. He reflects on the good times they shared together, slightly smiling during this tumultuous moment. He stands with dignity, pride, and respect as the preacher calls forth the pallbearers to carry her body to its resting place to be guarded by the angels and Mother Earth until the end of time.

CHAPTER 41

It has been a month since his exciting encounter with the Black Rose and its six decadent dancers. Standing across the street, he stares at its empty parking lot, contemplating the idea of returning to its audience. A group of loud motorcycles park in front of the building, followed by an entourage of howling women. They quickly get inside as the crazed women beat on the door, trying to get in. He's amused by the women screaming, leaving their panties with their phone numbers written on them on the seats and handlebars of their motorcycles. He walks across the street as the last of the caravan of women finally give up and leave. Knocking once and then three times in sequence brings Luke to the door. He immediately opens the door to greet Trevor, inviting him in to join them.

"Where have you been? I haven't heard from you in one month," asks Luke.

"My grandmother passed away, and I needed some time to think," he says.

"I'm sorry. Well, it's good to have you back. We're rehearsing a new routine that's going to blow the ladies' minds and pockets. Come in and join us," replies Luke.

The offer is irrefutable as he walks inside, happy to be among them again. The music begins as he watches Luke teach them a newer, sexier combination that makes him want to join in.

"Okay, guys, take five. We still have a few loose ends to tie up," says Luke.

Most of them scatter outside looking for the loose, hot women who followed them to the club. Trevor stares at the stage, rehearsing the dance steps in his head. He turns the music down low enough for him to hear as he places a black mask across his face. He begins to imitate the routine better than Luke. The song ends as they emerge from behind the curtains, impressed by his powerful performance. They give him a standing ovation as he seems to have put his soul into the routine, making it look much more appealing and sexier.

"You have to perform with us tonight with your costume. It was perfect. I've never seen such a graceful performance as I've seen now. Guys, say aye if you think Trevor should dance with us tonight," says Luke. They yell aye, confirming him a member of Men of Desire.

Rico walks in with his sunglasses on, wearing a wifebeater and tight black leather pants. He arrogantly says, "I'm here. Let's go through this new routine. I have bitches to get back to."

"Rehearsal's over. We have a new lead man," says Luke.

"Show me this new stud," asks Rico. Trevor steps out of the crowd without saying a word. Rico says, "You mean our timid little barmaid who disappears without a trace for one month? I admit, he's a beauty, but he's no Rico. I feel sorry for you guys because without me, this group is finished. I'm fed up with you losers anyway. I'm going to start my own group, and maybe I'll hire some of you when your pockets are empty."

"If you walk out that door, you're no longer a member of Men of Desire," says Luke. Rico laughs at them as he puts his shades back on, slamming the door behind him. "Let's go through it once more. I have a few surprises I want to add to tonight's show," says Luke.

The house is packed with sex-crazed women, screaming, "We want Rico! We want Rico!"

Luke walks backstage to the dressing room as they prepare for the night's show.

"Guys, I think we made a mistake letting Rico go. I mean, we're all one group, but we all know the ladies are here to see Rico. Listen to them chanting his name. What's going to happen to us when they find out Rico is no longer a member of our group?" asks Mike.

"Guys, I have a strange feeling that Trevor is going to take us to the next level, and in a few months, no one will even remember Rico," replies Patrick.

"Okay, guys, this is it. Let's go make some panties wet," says Luke.

The DJ stops the music as the ladies rev up for a hot performance. "Hello, ladies, are you ready for Men of Desire?" asks Luke. The Black Rose explodes with screaming women falling all over one another, fighting to see sexy flesh grind on stage. The club goes black as smoke machines billow out clouds of hazy smoke onto the stage. A thunderous growl like a lion in the jungle snaps the attention of the house as Trevor comes out by himself disguised behind a cloud of smoke. The ladies begin to clamor after him as he seductively moves his body on stage. The lights come up as the rest of them join him on stage, adding to the fire of desire. The security guards have to restrain a few overzealous women from climbing on stage while the other guards catch flying panties and bras all night.

The show is a hit as Luke walks backstage to celebrate success with his group. The men are very impressed with Trevor, hoisting him in the air, chanting his name as Luke says, "Gentlemen, we made more money tonight than we ever have before. Congratulations on a terrific show, and let's give it up to a young man who made all of this possible, Mr. Trevor O'Riely."

He steps in the middle of the group, saying, "Tonight's success wasn't by my efforts alone. I think each and every one of you contributed to tonight's success, and I believe it's only going to get better from here."

"If it does, I'm going to have to buy a safe to hold the money because we profited $65,000 tonight," says Luke.

CHAPTER 42

The campus is deathly quiet as he jumps on his bed at 3:45 a.m. His body does not feel tired as he hops around his room, high on tonight's performance. His answering machine displays six messages. He ignores them, responding to a soft knock on his door. Lauren is standing there, draped in a big yellow raincoat. He invites her in, asking, "How the hell did you know I was home, and what the hell are you doing up so late?"

"I want to play this little game called naughty nurse," she replies. She drops the raincoat, uncovering a sexy nurse uniform with fishnet stockings. "You're my patient, and you must do as I say, or you won't get better," she says. She escorts him to his bedroom, making him sit upright quietly on his bed while she performs a little striptease for him. "We're going to try something a little different tonight," she says.

He smiles as she takes a bottle of something out of her first aid kit, massaging it all over his dick. He lies back on his bed, waiting to feel the pleasure of her hot, tight pussy. He raises his head, saying, "Damn, Lauren, why does it feel so much tighter this time."

"I told you, we're doing something different tonight. Don't worry. My boyfriend was a little concerned at first, but now he loves it, and so do I. It drives me wild. Now lay back and let me do what I know best." He obeys her command, lying back enjoying the sensation of a tighter fit that seems to feel a little bit better to him and a lot better to her.

He pushes her away as she tries to cuddle up next to him.

"Do you treat all women this way after you fuck them?" she asks.

"This is wrong. I can't do this. I'm sorry, but you have to leave now. I need some time to think," he replies.

"We just had great sex, and now you're acting like a little bitch," she replies.

"Lauren, I'm sorry, but you really need to leave now."

"Fine! I'll see you when you get off your period." The air shocks prevent her from slamming the door as she abruptly exits.

CHAPTER 43

Naomi sees him stuffed in a corner in the cafeteria. She walks over, sitting in front of him, saying, "I'm sorry to hear about your grandmother. Are you okay? I tried to call you all day yesterday, but the only thing I got was your answering machine."

"We need to talk," he replies. Those words send chills down her spine as they walk silently back to her room. He paces back and forth around her room, silent for a moment, as she sits on her bed with a pillow on her lap. "Naomi, I have a lot of things on my mind right now that's preventing our relationship from flourishing like it should. I know things between us seem to be going well, but deep inside, I'm tormenting myself trying to make something happen that just isn't there. Naomi, I don't love you, and no matter how hard I try, it's still the same. I think it would be better for the both of us if we go our separate ways."

She feels like a thousand daggers are stabbing her heart all at once. She wipes the tears from her eyes, saying, "You will never stop loving her, will you? I hear you call her name in your sleep, and I know in your mind you're making love to her, not me. I knew this day would come soon, and I have been trying to prepare myself for it all along. Needless to say, it still hurts because I love you." She kisses him on his cheek, opening the door as he slowly walks out down the hall, never to return again.

CHAPTER 44

The Black Rose is silent as he jumps on stage, pops in a CD, blasts the volume up, strips his shirt off, and dances vigorously all across the stage. Sweat pours from his body as he continues to drive himself harder and harder across the stage, dancing his frustrations away. The battle ends at the end of the stage on his knees, with his arms spread out and his head hanging in between.

Luke yells, "Bravo! Bravo! That was magnificent. I want you to do that Thursday night. It will drive the ladies mad."

"You mean Saturday," replies Trevor.

"No, I mean Thursday. Come, let me show you something," replies Luke. Letters flood his desk and the whole floor as he picks several of them up. "This is fan mail from hundreds of women requesting us to do more shows. The ladies want to see more of the hunk behind the black mask. I'm going to inform the rest of the guys at tomorrow's rehearsal. I thought red roses were beautiful until one of your fans sent you a dozen black roses. I've never seen a black rose until now. They're gorgeous," says Luke.

"Let's give them what they want," replies Trevor. They sit reading letter after letter of wild sexual fantasies and requests for more performances from the Men of Desire.

CHAPTER 45

He feels a degree of liberation as he parks in front of JD's house.

Elizabeth comes to the door dressed very elegantly, with a smile that would brighten the coldest man's heart. "Trevor, what a surprise. How are you?" she asks.

"I'm fine. Is JD here?"

"Yes, he's in his office doing the business thing as usual. I'll escort you."

JD is comfortably reading his newspaper in his recliner with a cigar in his mouth as they enter the room. "Trevor, what a pleasant surprise. I've been expecting you. Thank you, darling. Would you leave us alone for a moment. We have a bit of business to discuss," says JD.

"JD, thank you for giving me the opportunity to become an intern in your company, but I'm going to have to turn the offer down. I've been given the opportunity to work for the Crystal Corporation, a fairly new organization that is making remarkable gains every quarter. I hope this doesn't jeopardize our friendship," says Trevor.

"I must admit, it's disappointing to lose such an intelligent young mind, but I respect your decision. I would not be where I am today if I hadn't ventured out on my own. I think that's a very wise business decision. That company's investors have done a hell of a job in securing its future since Lana passed away. It's funny how things happen. Lana and I go way back. I loaned her a million dollars to buy Jack Pot's Casino from its previous owner who was addicted to every drug created. The place was going to shams. All its profits were being spent on women, parties, and drugs. The place had been burglarized so many times the insurance companies dropped him. Lana and I made a deal, and she bought the place and completely turned it around. In fact, she was so business-minded she purchased two more that are still doing very well. She could've lived a lavish lifestyle among the rich and famous with offers of marriage from the most elite entrepreneurs in the world, but she continued to choose the life of a hooker even after she elevated herself out of the gutter. I guess the old saying is true, once a hooker, always a hooker," replies JD.

He sits there crumbling inside as he looks at JD and asks the question that will open Pandora's box, "How did you meet Lana?"

JD gets up cracking the door, peeking out to see if the halls are clear. "I'll tell you the story. I trust you will keep it between these walls." He nods. JD fires up the old cigar again and reclines back in a comfortable position as if he were about to read a story to a group of kids. "I was introduced to her through one of my business partners. He found her hooking on the streets of Los Angeles and fell in love with her beauty. We would have what we called business parties, inviting several young ladies over for business entertainment. The more money and alcohol we gave them, the more clothes came off until we were all engaged in one big orgy. I remember Crystal, which was her real name, coming over to me, standing above me buck naked, pouring a glass of vodka all over me. She licked every crevice of my body and then fucked the hell out of me. I never experienced sexual pleasure to that degree. It was like she was a pro. Elizabeth is a gorgeous woman, but she does not arouse me like Crystal did. I found myself wanting more and more of her, so I invited her to my little getaway every weekend to explore my sexual fantasies. She didn't care what I did to her. I used to ram my dick up her tight ass, and she would scream for more. I never understood why she became a porn star because the casinos were doing so well at that time. Money was not what she was after, and I never asked her why she continued this type of lifestyle. I would sometimes sense that she was unhappy, but she would always mask it with sex. I hate that she's dead because no other woman has ever been able to sexually satisfy me the way she did. This world is so funny, because I financed her to buy that casino, and now the investors of the Crystal Corporation won't even accept my phone calls. Tell me, what is the secret to getting into this corporation?"

He looks at JD with a straight face, holding back the tears and pain, saying, "You should know the answer to that. We learned that in class and from corporate America. It's not what you know. It's who you know." He gets up and shakes JD's hand, saying, "Thank you for making the picture clearer." He walks down the hall trembling with rage against a man he admires so much. He sits in his car for a moment, drowning in tears, blaming himself for not listening to her heart cry out to him. He blames himself for being selfish and not paying enough attention to her when she tried to tell him about her horrible life. His mind begins to play tricks on him, making him think he's partly responsible for her death.

He drives himself to the Black Rose, parking in the back. The building is desolate as he turns the heat up to ninety degrees. Walking on stage, turning the music up as high as it will go, he begins to dance vigorously for hours until he pukes in a garbage can on the side of the stage. He lies on the stage floor as streams of sweat flow from his body like a small water fountain. Exhaustion mixed with a hundred-degree climate on the outside and a ninety-degree climate on the inside contributes to him passing out on a pitch-black stage.

Patrick arrives early the next morning, opening the doors to sweltering heat. Turning the lights on, he shuts off the heat and turns the air conditioner on high. He panics when he sees Trevor lying on the stage motionless. He shakes him, yelling his name as he begins to show signs of life. "What the hell are you doing, trying to start a fire? If you want a sauna, we can purchase one with all the money we're making," says Patrick.

Trevor looks at him obliviously, asking, "What time is it, and why is it so damn hot in here?"

"It's six in the morning. Did you sleep here last night?"

"Oh, shit! I must have passed out last night sometime after I finished a few dance routines. I remember dancing pretty hard. I had some things on my mind," replies Trevor.

"I appreciate you practicing, but why don't you try to practice in cooler temperatures next time?" They laugh as Patrick helps him to his feet, asking, "Are you going to be okay? We have a big show tomorrow night."

"I'm fine. I'm going to get out of here for a breath of fresh air. I'll see you tonight for rehearsal," replies Trevor.

CHAPTER 46

The fragrance of his room fills the hallway, appeasing his mind as he enters the Panther's Den. He gulps down two glasses of cold California water, quenching his deprived body of thirst. He sheds himself of his foul, sweaty-smelling clothing to enjoy the gratification of a cool shower. Feeling refreshed, he answers his phone to an anonymous caller, asking, "Does it taste as good as it looks?" The caller hangs up as he smirks, throwing the cordless receiver on the couch, thinking it's one of his friends playing a trick on him. A white envelope glides across the floor to his feet. He bends down picking the letter up. He laughs out loud as it contains the same question as the anonymous caller. He glimpses a shadowy figure moving around from a crack underneath his door. Rushing to the door, he swings it open to a beautiful woman dressed seductively in shorts and a tiny T-shirt, exposing her breasts. She pushes him back into his room as he scuffles with his towel, trying to keep it on his waist.

"Do I know you from somewhere?" he asks.

She places one hand on her curvy hips, throwing her long brunette hair out of her face, exposing her full, glossy lips. "No, you don't know me, but I know you, Mr. O'Riely," she replies. He tries to hide an oncoming erection by placing his hands in front of him as she says, "There's one thing I don't know." She pauses for a moment, kneeling down on her knees in front of him, snatching his towel off his waist, exposing his erect dick. She looks up at him, asking, "Does it taste as good as it looks?" His dick disappears into her mouth as she aggressively takes more and more of it down her throat. He stands in the middle of his living room with his head back as far as it will go, balancing himself on the edge of his couch, with his eyes rolled into the back of his head. He fights to stand erect as his knees begin to buckle from a tingling sensation that's spreading from his core like a wildfire. He begins to tremble, uttering broken English as she continues to suck his dick like it's never been sucked before. Finally, he braces himself against the back of the couch as he erupts, collapsing slowly to the floor as she maintains her position until his cock is empty and limp. She grabs his towel and wipes her mouth like she just finished a three-course meal. He remains on the floor, slumped against the couch, unable to move as she says "Thank you" and walks out the door.

Rejuvenated, he jumps to his feet, dresses himself quickly, and runs to Lauren's room, banging on the door. She opens it quickly, yelling, "What the hell is going on—"

He grabs her by her throat, stifling her from completing her sentence. He asks, "Who's the chick you just sent to my room?"

"I don't know what you're talking about. Let me go. I'm late for my tennis match." He spins her around, bending her over her desk, swatting both of her pantyless cheeks. The sensation turns her on as she says, "Mmmm, I like it rough. Do it again, and I might tell you who she is."

The mood between them begins to intensify as he continues to smack her soft ass, leaving his handprint on both cheeks. He leans over her, pressing his dick against her red ass, asking, "Have you had enough? Are you going to tell me who she is?"

She looks at him with glazy, lustful eyes, saying, "No."

He grabs her long blond ponytail, twisting it around his hand, snapping her head back as he unzips his pants, thrusting himself deep inside her hot, wet pussy. She gasps with passion as he continues to pound her harder and harder with every stroke. This climactic scene is short-lived, and he soon lies limply cradled over her on the desk. Breathing heavily with beads of sweat rolling off their foreheads, they stumble around the room on a sexual high, trying to rearrange their clothing. "Have a great tennis match," he says. Walking out the door, he laughs as she struggles trying to untangle her hair.

CHAPTER 47

They arrive at the Black Rose at the same time. "I see someone looks well rested and an hour ahead of schedule," says Patrick.

"My friend, it isn't sleep that has me perky. It was the pleasure of two women. This babe whom I never saw before shows up at my door, asking me this crazy question, and then gives me incredible head. It was the best I've ever had! I went to visit this chick I know on campus because I thought she sent this babe to my room, and I ended up banging the hell out of her. I tell you, this day has been awesome," replies Trevor.

"With all that excitement, are you going to be able to do our routine tonight?"

"Man, are you kidding me? I feel like a million bucks."

"It's good to see you so revved up about some pussy instead of a pair of hairy balls. We had one of those in our group, and it's damn good he's gone," says Patrick.

"You mean Rico was gay."

"Rico was homosexual, bisexual, trisexual, and any other kind of sexual if the price was right. I remember he invited me to one of his social gatherings that consisted of a house full of filthy rich, fat gay men. Needless to say, I left before the party started, and I never went to any of his other social events again," says Patrick. Some of the other members begin to arrive, and they end their conversation to prepare for rehearsal.

Thursday night starts off with a bang as the parking lots and the curbs are packed with cars. Hundreds of screaming, lively women fill the sidewalks to see the lusty Men of Desire. Luke parks two bodyguards at the front doors to control the mob of women from flooding the building. The doors open, and women of different ethnicities, shapes, and sizes pour into the Black Rose, quickly filling it to capacity. He instructs the gentlemen to close the line, turning away several disgruntled women. The air conditioner circulates the Black Rose with a hundred different kinds of perfume as they eagerly await the arrival of desirable hunks of flesh.

The night begins with the cracking of a loud whip, followed by streams of colorful, misty smoke. The hungry women snap their attention to the stage as Trevor speaks into the microphone from backstage, arousing them to the edge of their seats. The sound of a crackling whip snaps again, driving the passion meter to its boiling point. Their sexual cravings make them squirm in their seats, yearning to release their frustrations on one or several of the men behind stage. Two beautiful Black Panthers emerge from the smoke, belting out a loud roar, startling the crowd as they gracefully walk across the stage, taking their positions at each corner. Five of the gentlemen appear onstage dressed in white, diagonally from one another, as Trevor walks out dressed in all black, centering himself in the front of the group. Raising his hand, the lights go out as a single beam from a spotlight shines down on him. He walks off stage, pointing at several women in the audience. They scream as the gentlemen join him bringing the action out into the audience. They select women from the crowd to help undress them piece by piece down to their shiny black G-strings. Running back to the stage, the gentlemen put on an electrifying performance of sultry dance styles, driving the ladies wild. Trevor runs off stage, tantalizing the crowd, disguised behind a black mask as several women stuff $100 bills in his G-string. The house is rocking as the ladies scramble to their feet, trying to caress their hard bodies as they come off stage, teasing the crowd.

The after-party spills into the parking lot as several ladies linger around, getting their boobs and asses signed by the Men of Desire. Trevor is inside with Luke, celebrating a victorious early Friday morning, drinking a cold glass of Sprite on the rocks. Luke turns up a bottle of Vodka, drinking half of it before he slams the bottle down on the table.

Mike comes inside, saying, "Trevor, there are some hot young ladies waiting for you outside in a limousine."

He waves good night to his brothers as Luke tosses him a roll of money wrapped in a rubber band. He sees Patrick outside getting smothered to death by the breasts of two voluptuous blondes. He walks over, dropping the roll of money into Patrick's hands, saying, "Enjoy yourself, brother."

The chauffeur opens the door to three sexy women as a familiar voice says, "Get in. We won't bite you until we get you in bed." The dim lighting disguises their identity, making it hard for him to recognize the face behind the voice. "You don't have to hide from me, Trevor. Your secret is safe with us." She leans forward, exposing herself beneath the interior lighting.

"Tara, how did you know?"

"I have something you don't have," she replies. He looks at her strangely as she spreads her legs, exposing her shaven pussy, saying, "Don't blame Rico. He couldn't help himself after I promised him a piece of pie."

A second voice from the shadows says, "Great performance, Mr. O'Riely, but I have one more question. Does it feel as good as it looks and tastes?" He sits straight up in his seat, snatching his mask off as she reveals herself, twirling her tongue around a cherry lollipop.

"Trevor, please allow me to formally introduce you to Cherry, a beautiful vixen you informally acquainted yourself with in your dorm room, and Mrs. Fleming, my personal assistant," says Tara. Cherry puts a piece of ice in her mouth, kissing Tara passionately on her neck. Mrs. Fleming encircles her nipples with a piece of ice, making them erect as Tara reaches over between her thighs, fingering her, making her quiver with excitement.

He reclines back against the soft leather seats, enjoying the sight of three beautiful women copulating. The chauffeur pulls into the driveway, opening the door as the ladies gracefully exit wearing nothing but their high heels. He follows behind them, smiling, as they enter Tara's mansion, walking straight to her oversize bedroom, sprawling themselves across her oversize bed. They subdue themselves into a swathe of fiery sex that lasts until their bodies are drained of vitality.

The vibrating alarm on his wristwatch awakens him trapped between two soft asses. He looks at his watch realizing he has an hour before class starts. Quietly maneuvering himself from such a comfortable position, he puts on his clothes, running to the car, beckoning the chauffeur to drive him back to campus quickly. A hot shower mixed with the rush of adrenaline rejuvenates his lethargic body as he runs across campus to class. Naomi is standing outside with some friends as he arrives panting like a dog, displaying black bags under his eyes from lack of sleep.

"Hello, Trevor. How are you? I haven't seen you in a while," says Naomi.

"I'm fine, but I could use a little more sleep. Well, I'll see you later. I'm almost late for class," he replies.

Two young ladies are talking about the performance from the Men of Desire as he walks into the classroom. One of them stops him, saying, "Trevor, you have a panther on your arm just like the lead dancer of Men of Desire, and you sort of remind me of him. We saw them perform last night at the Black Rose. They were fantastic." She whispers to her friends, "I wonder if that was a sock in his thong or if it was really that big."

He asks, "Who?"

"Never mind," they reply.

He sits in his seat smiling as the ladies rave about him and the group not realizing they're sitting two desks away from the Black Panther.

The courtyard is buzzing with groups of young ladies showing off their autographed asses and breasts as they excitedly talk among one another, attracting the curiosity of other females on campus. He hears himself described by several as the one to fulfill all their sexual desires as he changes classes. The hype drives him to join a crowd of females, saying, "Hello, ladies, what's all this hype about the Desire of Men?"

They laugh for a moment as one of them reply, "It's the Men of Desire, and they happen to be the hottest male strippers in all of San Diego."

"What makes these guys so much better than any of the other male strippers in California?" he asks.

One of the young ladies in the crowd says, "Their shows are so much different and much more exciting. Last night, they opened the show by unleashing two beautiful Black Panthers on stage. The lead dancer traps your mind and body in a sexual trance as you watch him move across stage like nothing you could ever imagine. You and the lead dancer share a love for Black Panthers because he has one tattooed on his arm just like yours."

He looks at his arm, saying, "It was nice to meet all of you. Have a great day."

Class after class is filled with groups of young ladies huddling together, whispering about the Men of Desire. His emotions are high as he struts across campus, ecstatic after receiving rave reviews of their performance from some of the hottest babes on campus.

Throwing his book bag on his bed, he calls Luke to tell him of their success. Luke answers, yelling, "We're going to Vegas, baby!"

"Luke, why are you so excited about going to Las Vegas when we're only a few hours away?"

"We're not just going to Las Vegas. We're going to perform in Las Vegas at the exclusive Diamond Palace. The guys are here waiting for you. I'll explain everything to you when you get here, so hurry your ass up. It's time to celebrate," says Luke.

He could hear the blaring music from outside as he approaches the Black Rose. He opens the door to a shower of champagne as the guys hoist him in the air, chanting his name.

"Congratulations, Trevor! You just opened the doors wide open for all of us. It appears you moistened the panties of Sonia Blake with your performance the other night. She personally called me this morning, inviting us to perform in her club. She also sent you a pretty little gift wrapped with a pretty little bow," says Luke.

The guys yell, "Open it! Open it!"

He tears into it, opening the box to a 14-karat gold Rolex embedded with diamonds. He snaps the watch on his wrist, waving his arm around in the air as the guys gawk at this stunning gift.

Patrick steps on stage, saying, "Gentlemen, I told you this man would lead us to the top. Let's give him a round of applause for improving our performance and making our pockets fatter."

"All right, all right, the party's over. We have the biggest performance of our lives this Saturday at the Diamond Palace, so let's go through this new routine Trevor and I put together," says Luke. They attentively watch the performance and then practice half the night away, trying to synchronize the routine. "That's a wrap. We're done for the night. I'll see you here tomorrow at 7:00 p.m. sharp, ready to rehearse this routine over and over until we are in sync with one another," says Luke. The midnight hour is alive with people partying and socializing at the local restaurants, clubs, and bars as Trevor drives through the downtown San Diego, enjoying the weather and scenery.

CHAPTER 48

The gentlemen drink vodka and juice to the beats of Q106.7 in the luxury of the limousine sent by Sonia. The days before were grueling as the six of them practiced for hours preparing for this day. They were confident and ready to perform in front of a sellout crowd at the Diamond Palace. DJ Mix from Q106.7 advertises their expected arrival at the radio station within a few hours. They listen as several women from San Diego and Las Vegas call into the radio station trying to win backstage passes. DJ Mix hypes the female audience, advertising a guaranteed get-your-panties-wet party at the Diamond Palace featuring the sexy male strippers of Men of Desire. The phones ring off the hook with several women inquiring about this spectacular event.

"Gentlemen, tonight is ours. We will leave our names forever written in the city of lights. I don't have to remind any of you how important this is for all of us. Let's go in there tonight and send these ladies home hot, wet, and bothered. Gentlemen, tonight's performance will set the standards for all to follow," says Trevor. They cheer, toasting their glasses.

The female receptionists and interns at the radio station gather around the six of them, smiling, hugging, and kissing them as they arrive. DJ Mix welcomes them and leads them to the studio for a quick interview and a few phone calls from some of their anticipating fans. Two thunderous growls of a Black Panther fill the airwaves as DJ Mix says in a low, deep voice over the microphone, "Yes, ladies, that sound can mean only one thing. The Men of Desire are here in the studio ready to tuck you into bed. Caller, you're on the line.

What's your name, and what would you like to know about the Men of Desire?"

"My name is Isabelle, and I was at their show last Thursday. My question is for the one who wears the black mask all the time. I want to know if you can move in bed as well as you do on stage?"

DJ Mix says, "Woooo! It's getting hot in here."

Trevor replies in a sexy, deep voice, "Isabelle, if you're lucky, you may get the chance to see how well I can move in bed."

They could hear her and her friends scream before they click over to the next caller. DJ Mix says, "Ladies, I want to make it clear. Only the grown and sexy will be allowed to enter tonight's show. Your driver's license will be checked at the door. You must be twenty-one to get in. Next caller, what's your name and question?" Caller after caller added more steam to every question, and the Men of Desire answered each caller, sending their audience over the top. "Ladies, that's all the time we have. These gentlemen have to get to the Diamond Palace to get ready to entertain you tonight on stage. For some of you lucky ladies, the party could continue in the bedroom. Don't forget, you must be twenty-one to get in, and bring an extra tampon to keep the seats dry," says DJ Mix.

The six of them stand backstage silent and nervous. They rehearse every dance step with mental precision as they prepare to feast on the passion of a sold-out club of sexually ravenous women. The music begins, and they seductively dance their way to the stage, multiplying themselves across the stage. An array of fire and smoke mystifies the audience as the gentlemen feed their sexually explicit bodies to their depraved audience. The ladies are chomping at the bit, trying to reach the stage to fondle the hunks of flesh who have driven their minds into sexual overload. The Men of Desire electrify the stage for two hours, pounding the audience mercilessly with their lusty, half-naked bodies. They exit the stage in a hail of smoke and blazing flames. The ladies are in a frenzy, screaming and chanting for the Men of Desire to return to the stage.

Luke runs to the stage with a microphone, introducing each of them by their stage names. "Ladies, I have a special request from the sixth member of our group," says Luke. The house is in instant silence as he continues, "The lead dancer and co-choreographer wants to deliver a message to one of you lovely ladies tonight."

Trevor walks out on stage enhanced with baby oil, wearing a white thong with a black rose imprinted on the front. He's carrying a crystal vase with a single black rose inside it. He raises the vase and rose high above his head as the lights capture its magnificent beauty. "Ladies, this rose is a gift to a very special woman in the audience who will get the opportunity to spend the night with me, to do whatever she wants," he says. They burst into an uproar, waving their hands in the air, hoping they'll be the lucky one to be chosen. He jumps off stage as the club bouncers surround him, protecting him from the clamoring women. He stands still in front of Sonia, placing the vase in her trembling hands. She screams holding the vase high above her head as he leads her back to the stage.

"On behalf of the Men of Desire, we would like to thank you for coming out tonight. I hope you ladies enjoyed the show. Have a good night," says Luke. The house lights come up as the Men of Desire entertain a few lucky ladies who won backstage passes.

An hour later, the packed house has diminished to a few cleanup crews shoveling paper and empty beer bottles into the trash cans. Several members of the group found themselves hot women in the audience and left with them. A few others went to spend some or all their money at the Crystal Palace, but Trevor sits in Sonia's office, gossiping about how proud he is of their performance and how well the audience reacted to them. Sonia sits back in her chair, admiring the beauty of the black rose.

"You sure know how to put on a good show. I've never seen so many women go berserk like they did tonight. The black rose deal was the icing on the cake. I mean, you had every woman in the house on her feet, clamoring for the lustrous black rose," says Sonia. He looks at her from the corner of his eye, smiling. "You really had those poor fools believing you," she says.

He walks over to her, kneeling before her, placing his chin in her lap, saying, "I meant every word of it."

She looks at him, asking, "Are you serious?" He arches his eyebrows, looking at her with a straight face. "I'm probably twenty years your senior," she says.

He pulls her out of the chair, onto her knees, leaning toward her until his lips are only inches away from her glossy red lips. He whispers, "I'm not afraid. Are you afraid?"

She inches a little closer to him, slightly touching his lips, saying, "I'm not one of those little college girls you're used to fucking. It's going to take a lot more to satisfy me."

He stands to his feet, unzips his pants, and pulls out his dick, asking, "Is this enough to get started?"

"I'm impressed, but just because you have a big dick doesn't mean you know how to properly use it," she replies.

"I've always been a good student. Why don't you teach me the proper way?" he replies.

She stands up, seductively caressing her lips with her tongue, gently stroking his hard dick, saying, "Remember, you asked for this. My place or yours?"

Stepping out of the shower soaking wet, he enters her bedroom, crawling between her thighs, teasingly kissing her lips. She lies back on the soft pillow mattress as he climbs on top of her, positioning himself between her warm, supple thighs. She arches her back to the sensation of his hard dick against her wet vagina. She moans with passion as he caresses her D-sized breasts, gently biting her erect nipples. Their tongues intertwine as he places his hand between her legs, fingering her warm, wet clitoris. Ecstasy jolts through her body like a sharp bolt of lightning. She gouges his flesh as he slowly climbs deep inside her. She breathes heavily with passion as he completely fills her, satisfying her deepest yearning with every stroke.

An hour later, she says, "Wow! I have to apologize for underestimating you. This is the best sex I've had in a long time. You're far beyond your age when it comes to making love. I can't believe it. I didn't have to fake an orgasm, and it felt so good."

"I'm happy to be of service. Let's get started on round 2," he replies.

"Let's take a five-minute break so I can catch my breath," she replies. He smiles looking into her sleepy eyes as she snuggles up close to him, sound asleep within a few minutes. He quietly eases out of bed, takes a piece of paper from her dresser, and shapes it into a rose. He places it next to her on the pillow and sneaks away like a thief in the night.

The Crystal Palace is quiet as he takes the elevator to the top floor. He opens the door to an orgy as three of his partners have their faces pressed between the cheeks of three lovely young ladies on his couch. He shakes his head, walking over to his table, wondering why Patrick and Mike have their heads down on the table, beating it with their fist.

"They have bets on who will cum first," says Tim. He looks through the glass table at four ladies taking turns giving them head.

"I hope you guys don't get any jizz on my table," he says.

"Your table...this isn't your table. How was it with Grandma?" asks Tim.

He replies on his way to the shower, "It was the best I've ever had." He opens the door to the master bedroom where three young ladies are lying naked, cuddled up next to each other in the bed. He walks into his bathroom discovering two other young ladies passed out in his shower with vodka bottles in their hands. He ignores them as he turns the water on to take a shower. He leaves them in the shower wet, drunk, and undisturbed as he climbs into bed between three young ladies. He's awakened to the pleasure of an early morning ride from one of the young ladies who was sleeping next to him.

She says in a sensual voice, "I hope you don't mind, but I couldn't let that hard dick go to waste."

"Stop, stop! Get off for a minute!" he screams.

"Just a few more seconds. I'm about to cum," she replies.

"In a few more seconds, you're going to have a pussy full of piss."

She quickly jumps off as he dashes to the bathroom, stumbling over the two ladies that he shared the shower with. They lie on the cold floor half naked in a puddle of each other's vomit inches away from the toilet. Returning to the bedroom, she says, "Damn, what happened to that long, hard dick I was riding a few minutes ago?"

"Open your mouth, and it will rise like the sun," he replies. The other two ladies remain asleep as they continue their morning fiesta.

CHAPTER 49

Monday morning welcomes him with strange stares and whispering among the ladies on campus. Entering the classroom, he finds a black mask on his desk with a white envelope. He pretends to be confused as he quickly scans the seductive faces of the females surrounding him. He sits down opening the envelope to a letter that reads, "I enjoyed this weekend's events. I would love to do it again real soon." Once again, he looks confused around the room for the culprit who blew his cover.

Class ends, and he walks to the student center for an hour of relaxation before his next class. He's disturbed by the recording of a fierce panther growling. He quickly turns his attention to the back of the lounge as a sexy figure struts down the aisle dressed in a black cat suit disguised in a black mask. She throws a painted black rose in his lap. Several ladies crowd the lounge, and she unmasks herself, pointing him out as the lead dancer of the Men of Desire. He recognizes her as the lovely lady who gave him a pleasant early morning ride in his penthouse suite. He smiles, snatching her close to him, spanking her ass, saying, "You naughty little girl, you blew my cover." He turns to the crowd, saying, "Yes, ladies, it's true. I'm the Black Panther and lead dancer of the Men of Desire." The ladies scream, pulling their shirts up, exposing their breasts of different size, shape, and color for him to sign.

The next three months were grueling for Trevor as the group performed at several different clubs in several different states. Every Friday, they pack up to travel to places as far away as Texas. This makes class and entertainment very demanding for him. Nevertheless, he still maintains the highest GPA on campus. They purchased two buses, converting them into luxurious suites on wheels to make life on the road a little easier. Money soon becomes second nature to these gentlemen as every show sold out. Thousands of screaming women jam the clubs for a chance to see them perform and to be the lucky one to receive the infamous black rose. Sex and alcohol are the driving forces behind them as they travel back and forth through the hot summer deserts, fulfilling dreams and desires. Their end-of-summer gig is hosted at the beautiful Diamond Palace. They're excited to perform here once again in front of a crowd full of the sexiest, hottest women they could imagine.

"This is our final show. Let's send them home hot and horny," says Trevor.

The crowd explodes, and the Men of Desire take the stage, driving the ladies crazy with their electrifying performance. By the end of the night, they are exhausted and ready to go home. Sonia walks backstage, congratulating them on another great performance and on record-breaking profits. Several screaming ladies can be heard outside as the gentlemen are escorted out of the building under heavy security.

Once again, the Crystal Palace is their home of rest before their journey home in the morning. Women filled every square inch of the hotel's plaza, lobby, and halls for a chance to spend a seductive night with the sizzling Men of Desire. Sonia and five other women wave goodbye to the crowd as the elevator zooms them to his penthouse suite. They sit around chatting about some of their wild adventures before Trevor says, "Gentlemen, it's been a wild crazy ride, but we made it. Thank you for believing in me and yourselves. We've successfully raised the bar to another level."

"I think it's fair to say you're the cause of our success. I mean, I never believed we would make it this far. A year ago, we were just another group of exotic dancers just like every other group in California, and now we're the number 1 group in California," says Patrick.

Mike takes two rolls of $100 bills from his pockets, saying, "From one brother to another, I'd like to thank you for extending my bank account way beyond my imagination. I knew you were the one when I saw you dancing that night at the club. You have exceeded my expectations of you, and I'm proud to have you as a member of the Men of Desire."

The ladies and gentlemen raise a toast to him, honoring their success, as Sonia says, "I'd like to thank you guys for performing in my club and for bringing me this fine specimen who knows how to satisfy a woman's needs."

"Thank you so much, but I couldn't have done it without you. With that being said, I bid you good night, sleep tight, and don't let the ladies bite," replies Trevor.

"Trevor, I almost forgot to give you this. It's another gift from one of your fans. Open it. Let's see what you received this time," says Luke.

"Not tonight. I have a bigger, better present to unwrap. I'll see you in the morning," replies Trevor.

CHAPTER 50

The ride home is invigorating for him as he relaxes in his comfortable bunk, watching last night's performance on his mounted twenty-inch flat screen. He opens the present that Luke gave him last night from one of his fans. It's a beautiful crystal coffin that plays a harmonious melody when he opens the lid. He ponders for a moment, unsure of the meaning of this gift. Placing it aside, he continues to critique their performance. Finally, they arrive. The drivers carefully park in the garage behind the Black Rose as they welcome the sight of where it all began.

He trudges over several letters scattered on his dorm room floor from females longing for his affection. In the months following his discovery on campus, his door became a swinging pendulum of ass. His phone rings as he's sifting through some of his fan mail.

A sweet familiar voice says, "Stop what you're doing, and meet me at Sunset Cliffs in half an hour." He grabs his keys, dashing out of his room, eager to meet his assailant. The cliffs are quiet and beautiful as the sun casts a sparkling brilliance across the ocean beneath. The winds are calm as seagulls fly above, looking for their next meal. His mind wonders back in time when Chris, Mike, and Joe introduced him to this paradise. He smiles thinking of the good times they had together sneaking into the girls' dorm, getting chased by security, and having the all-night campfires on the beach playing truth or dare with the ladies. His concentration is broken by the sound of a dying car horn blowing. He turns as a lady beckons him to get in the car. He walks reluctantly toward the old hunker, trying to recognize the face behind the dark sunglasses.

"Hurry up before somebody notices me," she says.

She takes her sunglasses off, revealing her identity, as he says, "Elizabeth, why are you driving this old heap? What's wrong?"

"I'll be happy to explain everything later. Hurry up and get in. This is my disguise. We're going to take a little trip to my private beach house, and I don't want JD or any of his goons following me," she replies.

The scent of her body arouses him as he lay his head back on the tattered seat, closing his eyes, wondering what she has planned. A jolt from a small pothole opens his eyes. He looks at her smiling as she sings along with the radio. His eyes drift down to her beautiful thighs as her dress inches further and further up her legs. Intense sexual thoughts begin to swell in his head and pants as he scans her soft body, taking mental pictures.

"Here we are, my little hideaway. It's not as big or as lavish as my husband's, but I like it," she says.

He admires its architecture, tucked away in a cove facing the ocean. The atmosphere surrounding the house seems so serene as she leads him hand in hand into her den.

"I found out a secret of yours from a close friend of mine," she says.

His mind is trapped by her exquisite silhouette as the sun shines through her thin sun dress, vividly exposing her well-shaped body. She turns as he quickly asks, "I'm curious to know this friend of yours who knows me so well."

"Her name is Sonia. We graduated from high school together. She told me you're better in bed than you are on the dance floor," she replies. She crawls on top of the bed, pulling her dress up, exposing her tanned round cheeks. "Come and feed me. I'm starving," she says. He looks for a moment, dazzled by the shape of her ass before he serves her a full-course meal. She screams, ripping the sheets off the mattress, yelling, "Harder, harder, fuck me harder!" The excitement level is so intense he pounds her for forty-five minutes nonstop before he collapses to the half sheetless mattress drenched in sweat.

"Revenge is so sweet," he mumbles.

"What did you say?" she asks.

"I said that was great. I hope I wasn't too aggressive."

"I loved every inch of it. The last time my ass was pounded that good, I had to schedule a private procedure with my doctor to have it surgically removed," she replies.

"I don't understand how JD could overlook such beauty," he says.

"Trevor, JD and I loved each other when he was a poor, struggling businessman right after he graduated. His love is power, money, and every other woman in the world except me. I stay because of my financial status. My love for him disappeared a lifetime ago. I believe he loves you more than he loves me or his own son. He probably would pat you on the back if I told him you pounded me with about nine inches of hard dick. Anyway, enough talk about the boring things in life. We have the whole night together. JD thinks I'm in Las Vegas visiting Sonia."

The next morning, they're awakened to the sound of crashing waves against the rocks.

"Sonia was right. You do know how to satisfy a woman's needs. What are you doing this afternoon?" she asks.

"I have to get back to campus to preregister for next semester, and I need to catch up on some sleep."

"Do you want me to make breakfast?" she asks.

"No, I really need to get back to campus." She rolls over, opens the drawer beside the bed, and takes out two stacks of $100 bills. "I know you might not need this, but I want you to have it. It's my early graduation present to you." He accepts the money without question as she gets out of bed to take a shower.

He leans over kissing her pretty red lips, saying, "Thank you for the early graduation present."

"It was a pleasure. I hope we can do it again soon," she replies.

He waves goodbye as the old hunker disappears down the hill, leaving a faint trail of smoke behind. His attention is diverted to a homeless gentleman rumbling through the trash can, mumbling to himself.

He walks over, saying, "Sir, I can provide you with a nice, hot meal, clean clothes, and a nice, soft bed to sleep on if you like." The man turns, lowering his hood. They stand locked eye to eye, shocked to see each other. "Rico, why the hell are you out here living like a degenerate human being?"

"You should know the answer to that. You're the reason why I'm out here."

"I didn't kick you out of the group. You left on your own."

"That's right. I did leave because you stole my group and my life. Tell me, how does it feel to be me?"

"I'll let you back into the group. The guys will be happy to see you."

"Are you fucking kidding me? Do I look like one of your fucking bitches? Thanks for your charitable contribution, but I'd rather rot out here with the rats before I come back to a group full of weak fags."

"I see you still have that ignorant ass attitude. That's what put you out here, not me. Look at you, the great Rico, a man who put himself above all others, is now a rotting piece of flesh digging through the garbage for his next meal. If I were in your shoes right now, I would be begging for the chance to once again live a life of luxury instead of eating scraps out of a garbage can."

"You and that fucking group can go to hell. I don't want any of your support. Now why don't you hop in your little car and take your pansy ass back over there with the rest of your no-talent buddies."

"Ignorance is excusable, but not acceptable!" yells Trevor.

Rico turns as he's walking away, yelling, "Fuck you and the group!" Trevor gets in his car, shaking his head as he glances at Rico stumbling up the hill, picking out of the garbage cans.

He hopes no one recognizes him as he arrives on campus disguised behind a baseball cap pulled down tightly on his head and a pair of dark sunglasses. He parks his car looking around to see if anyone is in the parking lot before he gets out. The coast seems clear as he dashes from his car, sprinting to his dorm and up the stairs before anyone sees him. He smiles, thinking he's escaped Alcatraz when a gentle knock followed by a feminine voice says, "Open the door, Trevor. I saw you run in from the parking lot." He opens the door to Naomi standing in his doorway with her arms folded and angry. She barges in, yelling, "Trevor, you need help!"

He repeats her, saying, "I need help? I don't think so. Take a look around you. The world is mine. This is my last year of school, I'm filthy rich, I'm the lead dancer of Men of Desire, which is the hottest male group on the West Coast, and I'm getting so much ass I can barely keep up. Now tell me again who needs help?"

"You're the smartest dumbass I've ever seen in my life. Do you realize everything has consequences? Nothing in life is free. The wild life you're living right now is going to catch up with you eventually. Why don't we leave together after you graduate? I can transfer to another law school to finish my degree, and we can put all of this behind us," she replies.

"Ohhhh, now I see what your point is. You think we still have a future together—"

Before he could finish, a knock followed by a familiar voice says, "I'm horny, and I need some satisfaction."

Naomi jerks the door open to Lauren, saying, "I never thought my best friend would sleep with my ex-boyfriend behind my back, but I should have known. Once a whore, always a whore!"

Lauren retaliates, saying, "Someone had to teach him how to fuck because you sure didn't know how."

"So how long have you two been fucking each other?" asked Naomi.

"Long enough to know that I'm better in bed than you are," replies Lauren.

"How could you do this to me? I was your best friend," replies Naomi. She runs out of his room, slamming the door, heartbroken and betrayed.

"You really shouldn't have done that. Do you feel better now?" asks Trevor.

"No, I'm still horny, and I'm tired of vibrators. I need a real, hot, hard dick like yours inside me to quench my thirst."

"There are lots of hard dicks floating around campus itching to get a piece of that ass. Why didn't you choose one or several of them to satisfy you?"

"Do you think that's all I'm good for? Do you think I just let anybody get between my legs?"

"Hey, I call it like I see it. It was pretty easy for me and the football team. Why are you getting mad? Everybody has some special skill they're good at, and yours is sucking and fucking. Now if you don't mind, I would like to get on with the show because I have more important things to do this evening," he replies. She briskly puts her panties back on, stomping out of his room like a bratty little kid.

CHAPTER 51

A persistent cough makes Trevor clench his chest in pain. He stumbles to the bathroom, hacking up blood-tinged sputum into the toilet. The answering machine is beeping as he walks back into his bedroom, feeling a little faint. Patrick has left him a message, asking him to call back immediately. The phone rings once as Patrick says, "What's up, brother! I haven't seen or heard from you in a couple of days. Do you still love me?"

He laughs at Patrick, replying in a hoarse voice, "Don't worry, you're still my favorite bitch. What's going on?"

"Dude, what's up with your voice? You sound like an old man."

"It's nothing. It'll clear up in a few minutes. What's up?"

"If you're not too sick, I want you to go with me to the grocery store and vitamin shop. I've started a workout program in the gym, and I want to eat a little healthier so I can get buff like you and get more ass," replies Patrick.

He laughs, saying, "Sure, I'll go with you."

Another violent coughing spell drops him to his knees as he hangs up the phone curled up in pain. He takes a teaspoon of cough suppressant, hoping this will cure him of this dreadful cough.

The grocery store is packed full of hot women. They go down each aisle pretending to shop for food, but they're really shopping for females with the best asses.

"Damn, look at that ass bent over in the fruit section. Hold my glasses. I need to go introduce myself," says Trevor. He walks up behind her, saying, "Excuse me."

She turns around smiling with heavily stained teeth, dark bags under her eyes, and dark splotches all over her face. She asks, "Hey, aren't you—"

He quickly answers, "No."

Patrick is leaning over in tears, laughing at Trevor as he returns with a scorched look on his face. "Oh, come on, Trevor. She has the ass of a queen. Put a paper bag over her head, turn her around, and hocus-pocus, you have beauty."

"That's it, let's get what we came here for and get out of here," replies Trevor. Patrick continues to enjoy the moment as Trevor hurries from aisle to aisle. In the parking lot, Trevor notices Patrick staring off into the distance instead of helping him put his food in the car. "It would be nice if you would give me a hand. I want to get out of here before that swamp monkey comes out of the store," says Trevor.

"Trevor, look at this goddess coming out of that tanning salon."

"I'll wait here while you go introduce yourself," replies Trevor.

"Trevor, you really need to take a look at this one. She's so hot the pavement is melting," says Patrick.

He raises his head for a moment to see this angel of beauty. Patrick points him in her direction as she makes her way to her car on the other side of the parking lot. "Wow, I think we struck it rich. Let's go introduce ourselves," says Trevor. They catch up to her as she's getting into her car. "Hello, how are you today?" asks Trevor.

She sweeps her long, curly hair out of her face. "I'm fine. How are you?"

He stumbles back a couple of inches with excitement in his eyes. "I'm looking for a sexy science teacher to tutor me. I think you're perfect for the job."

She looks at him strangely, saying, "I'm sorry. You have mistaken me for someone else. I'm not a science teacher anymore."

"You'll always be my science teacher," he replies.

She gets out of her car, curious to know who the handsome gentleman is behind the dark sunglasses. "What do you mean, and how did you know I was a science teacher?"

He lowers his head, slowly removing his sunglasses. "Your lips are as sweet as honeysuckles."

She raises his head, screaming, leaping into his arms. "Trevor! Oh my gosh! How are you?"

Patrick nudges his arm discretely. "This is my friend Patrick. He actually brought you to my attention. Thanks, Patrick, you're always looking out for your fellow man."

"So what are you doing later on this afternoon?" she asks.

"Nothing much. I'll probably sit around watching TV," he replies.

"I have a better idea. Why don't I give you my address and we can do a little catching up?" she says.

"Great, what time?" he asks.

"I'll see you around seven tonight. Here's my address," she replies.

They wave goodbye as Patrick says, "Thanks a lot!"

"Dude, she was my science teacher in high school. Trust me when I say we've already formed a chemical bond," says Trevor.

CHAPTER 52

A security guard stops him at the gate, asking, "Who are you here to see, sir?"

"Melissa Sherman," replies Trevor.

The guard steps into his shack, confirming his arrival with Ms. Sherman before he opens the gate, allowing him to proceed. He's impressed by this community of well-designed condominiums tucked away quietly in a valley of blossoming trees. Her door silently opens to his knock. A voice yells from the back, "Come on in and make yourself at home!" The smell of a sweet fragrance grasps his attention as he enters along with the unique murals painted on her walls. She greets him in the living room as he admires her taste for art. "Are you impressed by your surroundings?" she asks.

He turns enthralled by her beauty, saying, "In the presence of magnificence, how could you not be?"

She smiles, saying, "I hope you like the dish I've prepared for us tonight. It's a new recipe."

"Thank you so very much, but you didn't have to do this."

"It's no problem. Cooking is one of my favorite pastimes." The sound of chimes permeates her home. She answers the door to a friend chattering about how a different style of curtains would bring out her walls. She introduces her companion to Trevor, saying, "This is Jeana, the world-renowned interior decorator who's responsible for the art you admire." Jeana stares at him as if he were a true god. "Damn, I know he's handsome, but do you have to look at him like you want to eat him?" says Melissa.

Jeana mutters, "Oh my gosh, it's you. It's really you. I can't believe I'm standing in your presence."

"Do you know him?" asks Melissa.

"Melissa, you don't know who this is? Remember I told you about the Men of Desire, the hottest male strippers in California? Well, you're standing in the presence of the lead dancer, aka the Black Panther."

Melissa looks surprised as Trevor bows to the ladies, taking a black rose from behind his back, giving it to Jeana. "It's a pleasure to meet you, Jeana. I'm very impressed with your work."

Jeana pleads, "Melissa, can I please take him home with me? I promise I'll bring him back in the morning."

"Jeana, your time is up. Say good night to Trevor. It seems we have more catching up to do than I expected," Melissa says. "I'll savor this Men of Desire ordeal for dessert. Right now, please have a seat at the table. Dinner is served."

She sits with her feet tucked beneath her like an eager kid at story time. He tells her his journey of becoming a member and lead dancer of the group. Her ears seem to stick out, filtering every little detail through her brain. A couple of hours dwindle away as they discuss his adventurous lifestyle.

"You're a very popular man. I've heard hundreds of women speak of you at work, in the gym, at the grocery store, in my own home, and everywhere else you can possibly imagine. I've also heard several women speak of how good you are in bed. That's funny, because I remember a little boy who was 100 percent curious and 100 percent virgin at the same time," says Melissa.

"You knew I was a virgin even after I was brave enough to lift you off your desk and kiss you?"

"It was obvious. You were trembling like a wet dog, even when you kissed me. I must admit, it was innocent and sweet, but I knew you weren't ready." He lies back on the sofa, laughing at himself. She walks toward her bedroom, pulling her skirt up halfway, saying, "I still don't wear them. They still irritate my skin."

Flames of passion begin to roar inside him as he leans against her bedroom door, eager to dance between her tanned thighs. She elevates herself on her elbows with her legs spread, barely exposing her pantyless world. He steps in her direction. She quickly closes her legs, saying, "There's no one to interrupt us this time. Are you sure you want to come inside?" The fires of lust breach their boundaries as he takes charge of her bed, kissing her sweet lips and caressing her firm ass. To feel her beautiful body again intensifies every moment as they make love in several positions all over her bed. A ravenous passion for each other fuel them through the night into the early morning hours. Raindrops dancing on the surface creates a soporific melody that suspends their minds and dampens the flames of passion.

She awakens to the repeated melody of chimes. She opens the door to Jeana slinging cold rainwater all over her from her umbrella. "Oh my gosh, you look like you got your brains fucked out last night. Okay, come on, give it to me. I want the whole scoop, detail after detail of how it was to sleep with one of America's most wanted," says Jeana.

"Shhhh, you'll wake him! I'll talk to you later," whispers Melissa. She returns to the comforts of his arms as he opens his eyes, smiling, lying motionless, pretending to be asleep. He feels invigorated lying beside her, listening to the tranquil sound of the rain. Flashes of lightning illuminate the room, creating an eerie scene as they lie still, comforted by each other's rapture.

He startles her, saying, "That was worth waiting for. Thank you for such a pleasant night and morning."

"I should be the one who's doing the thanking. I expected it to be good, but not that damn good. The sensation still has my body tingling. Your name fits you perfectly. You're definitely a man of desire."

"I'm happy we got the chance to become reacquainted with one another after so many years. This meeting between us was long past due," says Trevor.

"I hope our next encounter will be soon," she replies.

His alarm on his watch vibrates, startling him as he looks into the indigo-lit screen reminding him of a scheduled appointment he has with the group in an hour. "I hate to break up this moment, but I have to get back to my room and change. We have a meeting tonight at the Black Rose," he says.

"This weather is too bad to travel in. I think you should stay here with me and protect me from the storm."

"We'll have this moment again, I promise," he says. He rolls out of bed, dressing himself, as she tugs on his arm, whining, trying to get him to reconsider. He opens the door to forceful winds carrying cool rain. He quickly kisses her goodbye and raises his shirt over his head running to his car.

CHAPTER 53

He opens the door stumbling over a large brown envelope in the center of his floor. He quickly opens the package once he sees it's from Tyson. His heart is filled with joy as he reads Tyson's acceptance letter to begin training as a top gun pilot. Reaching further inside the package, he finds an elaborately designed letter announcing his engagement to Maria. He quickly runs to the phone to call his longtime friend to congratulate him on a job well done, but he disappointingly gets the answering machine. He quickly types up a letter on his computer and grabs his checkbook and a blank envelope. He makes a check out in the amount of $1 million dollars and places it in the envelope with the letter. He takes a quick shower and rushes out of the house with the envelope flopping in his hand. The rain has become a light drizzle as he dodges in and out of traffic, trying to get to the meeting on time. He gives a sigh of relief as he arrives at the Black Rose at the same time Luke shows up. The guys are happy to be together, laughing and talking about how much fun they're going to have fascinating the ladies again.

"Hey, guys, pull up a seat. I have some bad news and some good news to share with you. I was informed last night that Rico was found dead in Lovers Cave on Sunset Beach early Saturday morning. The police reported his death a drug overdose because he was found with a syringe sticking out of his arm. The coroner, who is a very good friend of mine, said an autopsy report showed that he had contracted HIV/AIDS and could have died of complications from the virus. The authorities have this information, but they're not releasing it to the public. They feel it may cause a big panic in the community. I would encourage all of you to go to the health department to have yourselves tested. I know some of you have very promiscuous lifestyles, and it's better to know than not to know," says Luke.

"I would prefer not to know because that will put a serious deficiency on how much pussy I get. I need my daily dose of ass to keep me calm. If I knew I had AIDS, I wouldn't be able to enjoy the pleasures of this world," says Mike.

"Trevor should be the first one in line to get tested. Just the other day, I saw a gorgeous babe in the parking lot, and Mr. Lover Boy came along and swooped my piece of ass right out from under me," says Patrick.

"I don't think Trevor has to worry about having any kind of virus. He always picks those high-profile, high-class bitches that act like their shit don't stink," says Tim.

"You're a smart man, my friend. You're damn right. I pick the best of the best, not just some rundown piece of trailer trash. I have several black books in my room with the names of a few high-society women I like to keep in touch with. If some of you would watch whom you stick your dicks in, maybe you would be just like me, worry-free. Enough talk about AIDS. What's the good news?" asks Trevor.

"The good news is I'm bombarded every day by women asking when we're going to perform again. The most exciting letter I've read comes from a big club owner in Muscogee County, Georgia. He invited us to perform in his club, and he's willing to pay us twice as much as we made at the Diamond Palace," replies Luke.

"I was born there. Call him back and tell him we will have our first performance since our three-and-a-half-month layoff in his club on my twenty-first birthday on October 1," says Trevor.

CHAPTER 54

He jumps in his car feeling elated as he speeds back to campus. His answering machine illuminates the dark room, displaying one message. A beautiful voice says, "Hello, Trevor, this is Elaine Fincher. I would love to see you to discuss a business proposition that's been on my mind for a very long time. If your schedule allows you to, I would love for you to drop by the office tomorrow afternoon." He quickly erases the message and calls Tyson, talking to him for an hour and a half about how proud he is for fulfilling his dream of becoming a top gun pilot and his engagement to Maria. He reminds Tyson, before they hang up, to check his mailbox for a special package he should be receiving in a couple of days.

He sits on his couch, turning his TV on to some shocking news. A reporter reports, "The adult entertainment industry has come to a halt again. Tara, top-producing female adult star, was found dead along with six other female stars that worked for her. Authorities say the young ladies committed suicide by gunshot wounds to the head when they discovered they had contracted the HIV/AIDS virus. Suicide letters were written by the young ladies to their families, explaining their inability to live with such a fatal disease. In closing, the seven ladies asked their families to forgive them for their mistakes. This is the second time the adult entertainment industry has suffered a great loss. It's only been a year and a half since Lana, top female adult star, tragically took her life at her California home. This is Jay Howard reporting to you live from Tara's estate in Crofton, Texas."

He turns off the TV with a sickening feeling in his stomach. He grasps his throat, gasping for air as he falls to the floor, coughing up big clots of blood onto his carpet. Every breath is a battle as he continuously coughs up more clots. His vision begins to blur, and he becomes light-headed as he crashes to the carpeted floor, unconscious.

The next morning, he awakens in a pool of blood to a faint voice calling his name. He deliriously looks around his room, searching for the person who woke him up. He sees no one in his dimly lit room as he shuffles to his feet, turning the lights on. He panics looking at the amount of blood on his carpet. Stumbling into his bathroom, he turns the lights on looking into the mirror at his bloody face. He quickly fills the sink with water, washing his face of all the dried blood. He opens his mouth, sticking his tongue out looking for signs of continuous bleeding. He begins to feel the strength returning to his body as he looks at the clock, discovering his first class begins in an hour. He covers his carpet with a blanket and prepares himself for class.

His appetite for sex increases tremendously on and off campus. He sets higher standards for himself by targeting elite, overworked, sexually frustrated businesswomen, lawyers, and doctors. He begins to fill page after page in his black book with the names of some of California's most powerful women. He revels in his abilities to sexually satisfy any woman of desire who crosses his path. A storm is brewing in the distance as he pulls into the parking deck of Fincher and Fincher, one of the most powerful real estate companies in the world. Mrs. Fincher is a real estate tycoon who grew up in the business under the leadership of her father. She inherited the business when she was twenty years old after her father and mother were killed in a car accident. He has had a few business deals with her in the past and was very intrigued by her astuteness in turning her father's million-dollar dream into a billion-dollar dream in just ten years.

Her executive secretary buzzes her office. "I have a Mr. O'Riely here to see you, ma'am."

"Please send him in." She quickly gets up from her desk, straightening her collar and making sure her hair is in place.

He steps into her office with a charming smile, twirling a beautiful red rose in his hand. "A beautiful rose for a beautiful lady." She blushes as he gives her the rose, staring into her beautiful green eyes. In the distance, he can clearly see the storm quickly approaching while standing on the fifty-fifth floor surrounded by stained plate glass windows. "Do you mind if I go out onto your patio? I love the smell and sound of rain," he says.

She gets up from her desk wearing a tight-fitting black skirt with a split in the back. He watches her ass move gracefully in her skirt as she walks out onto her patio. The sky above is turning grayer and grayer by the minute as they sit together enjoying the cool breezes blowing in from the storm. He's captured by the moment as she flings her blowing hair out of her face, exposing the wonders of a push-up bra.

"I called you here for a personal matter, not a business matter. I hope I haven't wasted your time," says Elaine.

"You're a beautiful woman. How could any time spent with you be wasted?"

"Thank you, I needed to hear that someone still thinks I'm sexy. I work out in the gym everyday just like you, but I feel so unattractive when I look at myself in the mirror."

"Stand up and walk back and forth for a minute. Trust me, your feelings of sexual insecurities are a figment of your imagination," he says. The sky is totally black, causing the streetlights to come on. A few raindrops splash against his forehead as they sit together in darkness. "Take my hand. I will alleviate you of your insecurity. Don't be afraid. I will only bring you pleasure, not pain. Take hold of the rail and don't let go under any circumstance," he says. He steps up behind her, spreading her feet apart, gently massaging her tight calves. Working his way up her leg, he soothes every tense muscle with a gentle touch. He places his hands under her skirt, massaging her firm ass with his strong hands. She rolls her head around, moaning with pleasure to his every touch. From her ass to her back to her breasts, he continues to enchant her mind with ecstasy. Standing closely behind her, he whispers, "Are you feeling relaxed?"

"Yes, yes," she says in a passionate voice. He could feel her heart pounding in her chest as he unsnaps her bra, caressing her erect nipples. "Someone might see us! We're going to get wet!" she says.

"Shhhh, don't say a word. Just let me relieve your mind and body of its stress," he replies. He reaches down, pulling her skirt up, ripping her panties off as he unzips his pants, pulling his erect dick out, inserting it carefully between her throbbing lips. Her knees buckle to the sensation of his hot dick gently sliding deep inside her, easing her mind with sexual pleasure. She grips the rail tightly as the passion inside her begins to spill out high above the city. The rain begins to fall heavier and heavier, pasting their clothes and hair against their bodies. He continues to drive his dick deep inside her, smacking against her wet ass, creating a unique sound that takes control of his mind. She reaches behind him, grabbing his ass, forcing him deeper and harder inside of her. She screams with satisfaction as they slither to the wet cement floor, trying to catch their breath as the rain washes their sins away. She awakens in her penthouse suite to another beautiful red rose and the fragrance of his cologne sprayed on a letter on a pillow next to her. She reads, "I hope our business encounter has left you feeling vibrant about how beautiful and sexy you truly are. Until we meet again. Yours truly, Trevor."

CHAPTER 55

The next few months are filled with excitement as the Men of Desire rehearse night after night in preparation for their first big performance after a three-and-a-half-month layoff. They're out-of-control maniacs fueling themselves with sex, sex, and more sex. Women of all races pour themselves out to them like water falling from a waterfall. They take life for granted, running through it like a bat out of hell, not giving a damn about the consequences. Fame, fortune, and a thirst for desire makes Trevor feel invincible as he races through time doing as he pleases, whenever he pleases. Talks of graduation mixed with his upcoming twenty-first birthday send him spiraling deeper into the abyss of darkness as he loses all consciousness of reality.

The day finally arrives as the seven of them stand inside the airport, sheltering themselves from the sweltering heat. The pilots stop in front of the building as they excitedly board the private jet. The soft leather seats, gold seat buckles, and separate eighteen-inch flat screen TVs spoil them as they nestle themselves down in luxury. The pilots taxi the runway, preparing to takeoff. The tower gives them the okay as the powerful twin jet engines pin them to their seats, lifting them into the air toward their destination.

They celebrate Trevor's arrival to manhood by drinking Cassava, the finest, most expensive wine in the world. They all sing a poor rendition of "Happy Birthday" to him, pouring him more wine, laughing at him as he clutches his chest, coughing.

The phone rings. "Answer the phone, Trevor. It's for you," says Luke.

He answers the phone, "Hello, this is Trevor." Tears form in his eyes as his mother, father, Tyson, and Maria all sing "Happy Birthday" to him twenty-five thousand feet in the air.

"I hope you have a wonderful time in Cozumel, Mexico. I wish we were there celebrating your birthday with you. Have a great time, honey," says Clara.

"Son, I wish you a wonderful twenty-first birthday. I hope you have a wonderful time with your friends," says James.

"Maria and I thank you so much for such a wonderful early wedding present. Your parents explained everything to me. Don't worry, your secret is safe with your brother. Maria and I decided to name our son after you. I wish I was there to celebrate with you. Happy birthday from the three of us. We'll see you when you get back," says Tyson.

Tears of joy roll down his face as he thanks them for this surprise before he hangs up the phone.

"Surprise, surprise, I contacted your parents last night. I hope you didn't mind me telling them we're going to Mexico to celebrate your birthday. I thought they might take that a little better," says Luke.

A celebration in the clouds and chaos on the ground as hundreds of news reporters stand outside the blockades of prestigious Mira Mesa University. News anchors report, "The CDC has shut this prestigious campus down, forbidding anyone from leaving or entering. Reports from the CDC say a modern-day Black Plague has erupted on campus, infecting more than one hundred students and faculty. It's reported a new strand of the HIV/AIDS virus has been discovered. Reports from the CDC say the virus has mutated, destroying the body's immune system one hundred times faster than the original virus discovered twenty years ago. The ritzy upper-class community surrounding this campus is outraged, finding it hard to believe something like this has tainted their community. Several members of this community have crowded the local hospitals and clinics to get tested for this deadly virus. This is a major setback for the HIV/AIDS Research Center, which recently introduced a new drug that could possibly eradicate this virus in patients that acquired it within a three-year period. I've just received the latest confirmation stating the president of this university has tested positive for this new strand of HIV/AIDS. He has locked himself in the president's mansion, refusing to deliver a statement at this time."

Police rush to the president's mansion after hearing a gun discharge. Upon entering, they find the president slumped over in his chair from a fatal gunshot wound to the head.

CHAPTER 56

The frigid Georgia wind greets the gentlemen as they step off the plane, underdressed for this climate. They curl up running to the two limousines waiting for them on the flight deck. Hundreds of women stand at the gates screaming and waving signs as they roll down the windows, sticking their heads out, waving to the crowd. Airport security, with the help of the police department, restrains the fanatical women as they pass through the gates. Trevor throws black roses out of the window to several females who expose their breast as they pass. Huge billboards display them as they enter the city limits. Hundreds of beautiful women are standing in the cold, waving to them as they drive by, throwing red roses in the street. The police escort them to Le Bella, a five-star hotel. Women crowd the entrance as several police officers clear a path, escorting them into the building. The president meets them in the lobby, escorting them to the top floor. A hand-selected staff has been chosen by the hotel's president to serve these gentlemen during their stay. They were given separate rooms elaborately designed and decorated with Jacuzzis on the balcony. Trevor enters his room feeling faint as he directs the attendant to place his luggage on the bed. He takes a few pills to ease the pain as he lies down on the pillow mattress for a couple of hours of sleep.

Patrick knocks on his door, entering his suite. "Get up, Sleeping Beauty. It's time to get dressed for the biggest night of our lives. You should be downstairs celebrating your birthday with all the lovely ladies, not sleeping your life away."

"I feel so damn dizzy, and my chest is on fire," replies Trevor.

"You cheap drunk, you only drank half a glass of wine, and you're buzzing. That's embarrassing," says Patrick.

"Get the hell out of here so I can get dressed. I'll see you in a minute." He stumbles to the bathroom, clutching his chest, gasping for air like he's choking. The symptoms begin to subside, and he prepares himself for tonight's event. The lobby is crammed with staff and several elegant women as they walk downstairs, dressed in tuxedos, to their limousines. Trevor takes a black rose from his pocket, kisses one of the lovely young ladies standing at the door, and gives her the rose. She screams, running behind the gentlemen as they get into their limos. One of the security guards restrains her from jumping in the limo with Trevor as he taunts her with kisses.

The Dice Club is packed with women standing outside awaiting the arrival of the Men of Desire. They pull into an underground garage greeted by Mr. Chris Peoples, owner of the Dice Club. He escorts them to their dressing rooms, giving Luke a check in the amount of $180,000.

"Mr. Peoples, thank you for being so generous. Tonight, you're going to see a performance like you've never seen on your stage," says Luke.

Chris takes the stage, introducing the fabulous Men of Desire. Screams fill every corner of this sold-out performance as he exits the stage. The lights go out as the sound of rustling bushes and heavy breathing gets louder and louder. The growl of a ferocious panther fills the building as the Men of Desire appear on stage under the spotlights clouded by smoke. Trevor snaps the black whip, and the action begins. He steps out across the stage, collapsing facedown on the floor, convulsing as blood spews from his mouth. The ladies scream louder and louder thinking it's part of the show.

Patrick runs over to Trevor, turning him over. "Somebody get a doctor! Somebody get a doctor!" yells Patrick.

The music shuts down, and the lights come up as his friends and the audience watch him cough up blood. The sirens of the ambulance could be heard approaching as the bouncers clear a path for them to get through. The paramedics start IVs in his arms, secure him to the stretcher, and race him to Mercer Medical Center. They jump into their limousines, following the ambulance to the hospital.

Clara and James are at home, horrified, watching the latest breaking news about the events going on at Mira Mesa University. James tries frantically to get in touch with his son, but the phone just rings, collecting messages. Frustrated, he hangs the phone up, calling the airport, telling the attendant to fuel the jet for California. Another breaking news report comes in from Georgia as James is instructing his pilots to be ready when he gets to the airport.

"The lead dancer of a popular exotic male group, the Men of Desire, collapsed on stage while giving a performance here at the Dice Club. Sources say the gentleman is a student at Mira Mesa University. The authorities along with the local CDC have quarantined part of the emergency room until they do further testing to see if he is infected with this new strand of HIV/AIDS. The owner of this club says the gentleman's name is Trevor O'Riely, and he was celebrating his twenty-first birthday today."

Clara collapses to the floor, screaming with grief. James responds to a loud, continuous knock at the front door. He opens the door quickly as two gentlemen dressed in black suits and a police officer asks, "Sir, is this the residence of Trevor O'Riely?"

"Yes, it is. I'm his father."

One of the gentlemen dressed in a suit flashes his ID badge, saying, "Sir, we're from the CDC. Your son is at Mercer Medical Center in Muscogee County, Georgia. We have reason to believe he is infected with the same virus a hundred other students have contracted at Mira Mesa University. Sir, we have a plane ready to fly to Mercer Medical as we speak."

"My jet is fueled and ready to go. You gentlemen can go with us if you like," says James.

CHAPTER 57

James rushes to the desk. "I'm Mr. O'Riely. What room is my son Trevor O'Riely in?"

"Sir, we had to take him to surgery. The doctor will be out to see you as soon as possible," she replies. James comforts Clara as they both try to rationalize what's going on with their son. An hour and a half later, the attending surgeon comes to the waiting room where Clara and James are waiting desperately to hear something about their son. "Mr. and Mrs. O'Riely, hello, I'm Dr. John Brown, the attending surgeon on your son's case. I'm not going to beat around the bush and tell you your son is okay. The truth is, he has contracted a new form of HIV/AIDS that has completely destroyed his immune system. His lungs have deteriorated beyond any surgical procedure that can be performed. It appears he formed an infection in his lungs from a simple cold, and his body didn't have an immune system to fight it. The infection continued to spread until it completely consumed both his lungs, preventing them from functioning. It's amazing your son has survived this long in this condition. I'm sorry to have to say this, but your son has maybe three or four days to live. My staff and I will do our very best to make sure you are comfortable. Once again, I'm truly sorry."

Clara sobs heavily as James struggles to suppress his emotions. "Where did we fail? Our lives were so perfect. we have the best things life has to offer. Why is this happening to us? Why is God taking our baby away from us?" asks Clara.

"Clara, we didn't do anything wrong. We provided, loved, and cared for our son just like we should have. It's hard for me to say, but our son did this to himself by making poor decisions in his life. God never left him. He left God," replies James.

A nurse comes out, consoling them in their time of grief. "Your son is recovering from surgery just fine. You may see him if you like."

James takes Clara's hand, and they follow the nurse to their son's room. Trevor lies there with his eyes barely open. Tears begin to trickle down his face when he sees his parents standing in the doorway.

"Mom, Dad, what's wrong with me?" he asks.

Clara rushes to his bedside, comforting him as the lingering effects of anesthesia put him back to sleep.

The next morning, he awakens to his mother and father uncomfortably sleeping in two foldout chairs. He looks around for a moment, frightened by all the lines and tubes connected to his body. "Mom, where am I? What's going on?"

Startled by his voice, they both jump up standing by his side.

"You're in the hospital, honey," she says.

He looks at his dad, "What's going on Dad? Why are all these lines connected to me?"

James steps out of the room for a moment. He wipes his eyes, taking a deep breath as his hands tremble uncontrollably. Gathering himself, he steps back into the room. "Son, the doctors and the CDC have informed us that you, along with a hundred other students at Mira Mesa, have contracted a mutated strand of HIV/AIDS that destroys the immune system at a much faster rate than the regular virus. Because of this virus, your lungs are shutting down due to an infection you acquired from a simple cold. Your mother and I were told you only have a few days before your lungs completely shut down."

He looks at both of his parents with tears in his eyes. "I'm sorry, Mom and Dad. I'm so sorry for being stupid." They comfort their son, hugging him and crying at the same time. He sits up in bed, drying his eyes. "Dad, I once told a friend that ignorance is excusable, but not acceptable. I guess I should have listened to my own advice. Now it's too late."

Clara dries her eyes. "Honey, I almost forgot to give this package to you from a beautiful young lady that stopped by earlier this morning. She was so beautiful and sweet. She told me to tell you thanks for giving her life back to her. I invited her to stay for a while, but she said she couldn't do this all over again." He opens the package, smiling as he looks at the same prom picture he gave her in the park. He lays his head back with his fist in the air.

"Clara, I told you that looked like the girl he took to the prom," says James.

A note was taped to the back of the picture. It read, "You'll always be in my heart." He places the picture on his nightstand, speaking in a wheezy, muffled tone, "Mom, Dad, I want to tell you this before my time runs out. I'm leaving my entire empire to you. Both of you have done a tremendous job doubling our profits and improving customer and employee satisfaction. I'm proud to know our company can stand in the same ranks as Mr. J. D. Hughes. One more thing, promise me you will do everything in your power to educate and prevent the spread of this deadly virus. I don't want any more families to suffer a loss like this." He clinches his chest, struggling to breathe. The monitors begin to alarm as several nurses and doctors rush into the room, quickly ushering his parents out. These episodes continued through the night as his parents pray and prepare themselves in their private guest room.

An early morning knock on their door sank their restless hearts beneath their feet. James slowly opens the door to a nurse. "There's a young man by the name of Tyson saying he wants to see his brother. I wouldn't allow him to come any further until I spoke with you."

"It's okay. He can come up. He's like my son. They grew up together. How's my son doing? Is he awake?" James asks.

"Sir, he is very weak. I don't know if he'll survive another night like last night," she replies.

James and Clara walk down to get Tyson and his fiancée. Tyson is pacing the floor, crying and pleading to them to let him see his brother.

"Tyson, it's okay. Don't cry. You need to be strong for him now," says James.

He dries his eyes. "How is he? I got here as fast as I could. Please tell me he's not dying, please," begs Tyson.

James looks at him. "I'm sorry, but what you heard on TV is true. He has the mutated strand of the HIV/AIDS virus, and yes, he's dying."

Maria stands in the corner, crying, as Tyson walks up to the bed. "Hey, brother, it's me. I brought my family with me. Our son wants to say hello."

Trevor barely opens his eyes, trembling as he smiles at Tyson. He reaches his hand out, speaking in a low, raspy voice, "Don't cry over me, brother. This isn't your fault. I want you to remember all the good times we had together and tell your son about it when he gets old enough. I'm sorry I won't be in your wedding, but I wish you and your family the best. I'm happy I get the chance to tell you in person how proud I am of you for getting into top gun pilot training school. It's all you used to talk about when we were kids. I want you to know I've always loved you and considered you to be my brother. I guess that makes me an uncle."

Tyson calls Maria over to his bedside as Clara and James stand around Trevor, holding his hand. He points to the ceiling as he hears a peaceful voice say, "Peace, be still, my child." His hand slowly descends down by his side as he eases away into eternity, surrounded by family and friends, on a cold October morning in Muscogee County, Georgia.

The End

About the Author

Terence Ramone Gills grew up the oldest of two boys in Tuscaloosa, Alabama. He has a loving mother, a great brother, two outstanding children (Aaliyah and Tevin), stepson (Trent), and granddaughter (Evelynn).